ELLORA'S CAVEMEN

JEWELS OF THE NILE

VOLUME IV

ELLORA'S CAVE
ROMANTICA PUBLISHING

Enlightening Lucinda
M.A. Ellis

Lucinda is scarcely the quintessential Victorian widow. She paints male nudes, ignores society's dictates and is on a quest to regain a sexually explicit journal confiscated by her late husband's partner, Gideon. It contains information she plans to explore. With Gideon.

Gideon admires Lucinda's unconventionality and has never refused her requests—until now. But if Gideon won't enlighten her, Lucinda threatens to find someone who will. Abiding loyalty goes only so far when the woman you adore leaves you little choice. Lucinda will learn her lessons well and her proficiency will be thoroughly tested. By Gideon.

Mating Run
Tielle St. Clare

When Cat loses a bet, she has to participate in her Pack's Mating Run—an archaic tradition to match strong males with clever females. It's nothing more than a Pack-sponsored orgy in Cat's opinion but there's no getting out of it. If all goes well, she'll get a night of sex.

She isn't prepared when two males chase—and catch—her. Devon and Trejean have haunted her fantasies for months and now they tell her she doesn't have to choose between them. They want to share her.

Reader Advisory: Contains scenes of male/male sexual interaction and ménage a trois.

Midnight Seduction
Dawn Halliday

Lacey is terrible in bed. A fact confirmed by her ex when she caught him in bed with another woman. After that, whatever confidence Lacey had was ground to dust.

Now Lacey's dating her boss, the scrumptiously sexy Kyle Turner. But every time Kyle touches her, she panics, pushing him away rather than risk exposing her lack of bedroom finesse. Lacey is about to lose the man she loves. She needs help, and she's about to get it from an unlikely source—Kyle—who's not even aware of his ability to seduce her in her dreams.

Moon Magic
N.J. Walters

Under the light of the full moon, Meghan Flynn stands before an ancient stone well and wishes for a lover. The magic of the hot summer night surrounds her and she gives in to her sensual needs, pleasuring herself beneath the moonlight.

Watching from the shadows, Rory Shaunnessey is entranced. When she returns the following night, he steps forward, offering himself as her lover. But a hot summer fling can only last so long and when Rory pushes for more, Meghan must face the demons of her past if they are to have a future.

Practically Perfect
Allyson James

Between bounty-hunting jobs, Walker stops at Station 358 for some R&R—and perhaps a chance to scorch the sheets with the gorgeous woman assigned as his guide.

Guides are forbidden to fraternize with guests, but Tierre is captivated by the handsome hunter. She willingly explores the strange sensations he invokes...until her secrets betray her. Tierre isn't what she appears—but she can still teach Walker lessons in life, love and sacrifice that will change him forever.

Third Course
Alexa & Patrick Silver

Lesley's marriage is in a rut. Her husband is wonderful, but the spark has gone. She stops at an exclusive restaurant every day and flirts with the bartender, but she knows nothing will come of it. Or at least she *thinks* nothing will come of it!

Lesley's fortieth birthday brings a surprise that promises to shake up her world. Her husband and a mystery man have arranged a night of surprises, both in and out of the bedroom. Lesley is the main course in a string of sensual delights to fill the body and soul.

An Ellora's Cave Romantica Publication

www.ellorascave.com

Ellora's Cavemen: Jewels of the Nile IV

ISBN 9781419958168
ALL RIGHTS RESERVED.
Enlightening Lucinda © 2008 M.A. Ellis
Mating Run © 2008 Tielle St. Clare
Midnight Seduction © 2008 Dawn Halliday
Moon Magic © 2008 N.J. Walters
Practically Perfect © 2008 Allyson James
Third Course © 2008 Alexa & Patrick Silver
Editorial Team: Raelene Gorlinsky, Pamela Campbell, Shannon Combs, Sue-Ellen Gower, Briana St. James, Kelli Kwiatkowski, Denise Powers.
Cover design by Darrell King.

This book printed in the U.S.A. by Jasmine–Jade Enterprises, LLC.

Electronic book Publication December 2008
Trade paperback Publication December 2008

ELLORA'S CAVEMEN: JEWELS OF THE NILE 4

ഇ

ENLIGHTENING LUCINDA

M.A. Ellis

Chapter One
London, 1879

୨୦

"Barnaby, darling. Bring your hand a smidge farther down the barrel."

"Like this, milady?"

"Perfect." Lucinda smiled, rolling the bristles of the thinly tapered brush into the dollop of white paint at the bottom of her palette. She glanced from her canvas to Barnaby and back once more before highlighting a bulge of rippling muscle with a quick stroke.

The drawn-out creak of the heavy oak door echoed through the sunny room and she silently prayed for patience. Her predominantly female staff had spent the last week inventing reason upon reason for entering her studio. Truly, she could hardly blame them. Her model was a decidedly delicious specimen.

"No time for tea, Mrs. Darsley. I'm at a rather major apex at the moment."

Footsteps, muffled by the somewhat worn rug, continued to advance. A rush of warm breath tickled the back of Lucinda's neck, offering a second's warning before a large, strong hand came to rest upon her waist.

"That couldn't possibly be considered this side of *major*, my lady," a familiar deep tone whispered near her ear, the buttery voice sending a shiver through Lucinda's body. One she craftily covered by a dramatic shrug of her shoulders but not before the sexy timbre had all but curled her toes.

"I've only your word as proof, Gideon," she replied with an exaggerated sigh.

His thumb rubbed teasingly against her lowest rib, causing a gradation of heat to roll through her suddenly tense form. His touches had become more frequent within the last month, bolder than what society would deem acceptable. His hand stole away, but not before his fingers trailed over her lower back and Lucinda turned her head to hide her smile. Ah, yes. Unacceptability. It was a trait they mutually admired.

Gideon was a bit improper and as such, he never once questioned what the tittering society matrons and their equally unamused spouses considered Lucinda's lack of decorum. He championed her taking an interest in what were now her vast land holdings. He stood by her side when she told her late husband's male family members that she needed not a single one of them to take their place as head of her household. He hadn't even raised a brow when she took the daring step of cropping her long auburn tresses and throwing the strands into the wind.

Most importantly, in her quest for independence, he had not dissuaded her when she made her intentions known to him and her most trustworthy staff that she was through painting insipid still lifes, choosing to embrace subjects a bit more controversial than bowls of fruit and strategically arranged flora. The only time he had balked at her unconventional choices was when he viewed the inaugural painting. Gideon had covered his shock quite well. But then, men of his restrained demeanor generally did.

"Do you think I have the angle of the pheasant correct?" she asked with feigned innocence.

"I do fancy myself a worldly fellow, Lucinda." His lips hovered near her cheek, his heated whisper a soft caress that caused her breasts to swell beneath the fabric of her gown. He boldly brushed an unruly curl behind the shell of her ear with the tip of his nose and she closed her eyes as her nipples hardened. She waited, hoping that he might rise above his deep-seated sense of honorability and touch her — as a worldly man might touch a young, desirable woman.

"In this case," he said, taking a step back. "I have no earthly idea if I should say 'yea' or 'nay'."

Lucinda exhaled the breath she had been holding. Free of the permeating distraction of his body heat, she reined in her libidinous thoughts.

"So you've never been pleasured by a cock?"

A gasp echoed from her model's lips and she jerked her attention his way.

"Gently, Barnaby," she quickly ordered. The man was clutching the feather-covered stocking full of corn tightly to his crotch with such force she feared it might burst. "We need our faux bird to look recently alive and not something the dogs had a go at."

"Really, Lucinda," Gideon scolded, a trace of humor in his voice. She hadn't shocked *him* at all.

He strolled around her left side and stood before her, his handsomely attired frame effectively blocking her view of the all-but-naked Barnaby. Gideon brushed an errant lock of jet-black hair from his forehead and arched one equally dark brow.

"How is it you know of such things, my lady? Which of your maids has been spinning tales best left silent?"

Lucinda's gaze roamed across his broad shoulders and then over the front of his pristine white shirt. Somewhere betwixt the front door and her studio he had shed his sack coat and she gave a little sigh, pleased he rebelled against the formality of a waistcoat unless one was stringently required. It made him all the more enticing.

He crossed his arms over his chest, the starched fabric covering his biceps straining in a manner one rarely saw from a man of his station. She fantasized about those arms, having once been privy to their naked splendor when Thurmond had dragged her along to the West London Boxing Club, ordering her to remain in the carriage like a dutiful child while he went inside to make good on a wager. Her inquisitiveness would not permit her to obey. She had slipped inside behind his lordship and spied Gideon in all his half-naked glory, his chiseled torso glistening with sweat as he climbed down from the ring. It was that evening when her lurid dreams concerning his arms—and a great deal more—had begun.

"Allow poor Barnaby his leave. Your work is clearly finished for the day," Gideon said in a somewhat amused voice and she forced her gaze to his face. The strong angles were more than alluring but it was the wry quirk of his full mouth that caused a jolt of liquid heat to roll through her abdomen and settle in her cleft.

He gave her a slow, wicked grin—one that suggested he discerned her exact thoughts. "Your audacity has shocked the poor boy into flaccidness, my dear."

Lucinda blinked, peering around Gideon's large frame. She watched Barnaby's grimace as he peeked under the fake pheasant.

Lucinda sighed heavily and set her palette and brush aside. "You may go, Barnaby. Tomorrow at ten?"

"Ten, milady," he said in an obviously relieved tone. He wrapped a sheet around his waist, inclining his head in their direction before walking behind the screen at the far end of the room where he would change and leave through the side entrance.

Lucinda went about cleaning her brushes, knowing all the while Gideon's soft gray-green gaze followed her every move. It was quite unnerving at times and a great deal similar to the exotic snow leopard she had once seen at the zoo—a beautiful and patient beast, yet one prone to pouncing without warning. She continued to wait for Gideon to leap, to roll her beneath the weight of his powerful body.

She felt her cheeks heat and attempted to focus on something other than the man who had haunted her dreams both day and night, month upon month. Dreams that had left her skin damp with sweat and the juncture of her thighs slick and throbbing. Dreams that, it appeared with each passing day, would not be fulfilled, at least not by Gideon. While she owed not one whit of loyalty to Thurmond's memory, it was evident that Gideon did not feel the same.

She gave the brush a final tap, undid her paint-stained frock and tossed it aside. She turned, taken aback by the fierce look on Gideon's face.

"One day more of those lackluster threads," he said gruffly as his gaze roamed over her ensemble.

"Yes. I'm so looking forward to the daring leap to crepe-trimmed black silk," she said sardonically.

"Equally depressing," he agreed, his eyes softening as they met hers. "But not quite as dull."

She snorted, unable to agree. She longed for the brilliant hues and sumptuous fabrics of the gowns being stored until the prescribed length of mourning was at an end.

"And what would you see me in when I drop my widow's wear?" she asked, arms outstretched, secretly hoping his request would be to see her in nothing at all.

"I'm sure you and your conspiratorial staff have given that a great deal of thought. It's certain you do not need my input," he said, offering her a suddenly benign smile.

He is truly too much! The man could deflect a flirtation like none other. It rankled and she doubled her efforts.

"Frankly, I'm anxious to concentrate on what I shall not be wearing...with whom I'll not be wearing it." She gave a slow smile, pleased at the way his jaw clenched before he pulled forth his ever-present calm and cleared his throat.

"Will you require my assistance in arranging transport of the painting?" His voice was suddenly quite businesslike as he diverted her comment.

Lucinda chuckled. Two could play at the art of deflection. "You're quite transparent, Gideon."

"Am I?" he asked, his voice dropping.

"Indeed. This is the first time I have not shared the name of my patron and while you've garnered high marks for showing restraint and not asking who it might be, I know you're most curious to discover the commissioner. Do not deny it, Gideon."

"I'm far from interested in who finds the notion of running the feathers of a dead bird against his burgeoning prick so erotic that the image need be immortalized in oil," he said matter-of-factly.

She paid his coarse language little heed. "I believe I once read feathers brushed against one's skin can be highly stimulating."

The lines around his mouth tightened and Lucinda gave herself a mental ovation for deftly turning their conversation exactly where she needed it to be.

She closed the distance between them and smiled sweetly. "I want the journal, Gideon." She smoothed the fabric covering his shoulders, drawing her fingers down the crisp points of his collar before boldly sweeping her fingers across his chest, raising her eyes to his when she felt his muscles twitch.

"Do you think that best?" His query was barely audible. It was clear he found her demand unwise.

"You know I do. I've asked repeatedly and you've held me at bay with the greatest aplomb. My full mourning ends tomorrow and any misguided sentiment that my constitution can not survive the contents, due to my grave upset over Thurmond's passing, will be put to rest. We both know it was a pitiful excuse on your part from the start, Gideon, but I allowed it because I had no wish to upset you. But I now desire to read each and every page, to see what delights I might have experienced had Thurmond had the inclination— which we both know he did not.

"And while I'll continue to outwardly adhere to society's dictate of another twelve months of bereavement for a man who would have had not a single soul questioning him for seeking companionship had it been my body lowered under the sod, I have no intention of denying myself the fullest of life's pleasures any longer."

He opened his mouth, undoubtedly to object, and she soldiered on.

"I have mastered secreting my profession from the ever-watchful eyes of the ton these past twelve months and were it not for love of my family and the desire to uphold the pristine reputation of their name I would tell each and every one of those bombazine-bound biddies to go bugger themselves. I am utterly sick of their archaic rules!"

"So you believe you can lead a dual life?" he interjected. "Continue the appearance of the sequestered, grieving widow while covertly quenching your passions."

"I am quite stealthy," she said, catching her breath. "As my dearest friend, you know that better than any other."

Had she not been intently watching his green gaze she would have missed the unperceivable narrowing of his eyes. "Can you bring it 'round tomorrow?"

"You find your quest for knowledge that imperative?" he asked, his voice strained.

Lucinda purposely shifted her gaze to the painting. "Indeed, I do."

She was unprepared when his strong fingers circled her upper arms, his hands all but scorching her skin. She attempted to place some distance between them but he held her firm.

"You think your young groomsman seasoned enough, my lady?" Gideon's heated gaze roamed over her face and she swallowed against the sudden dryness in her throat. His voice was low and harsh and she faltered in her response.

"I-I think him kind and eager…and certainly loyal."

"Dear god! You've all but described your prized setter." He laughed without a bit of mirth and pulled her closer, loosening his hold to lightly run the tips of his fingers up the back of her arms, and her breath hitched. She would have willingly stepped into his embrace had his lips not curved into a purely arrogant smile that was so unlike the Gideon she had come to adore.

"Barnaby and I can learn together," she said, defiantly straightening her shoulders. "The few pages I read before you snatched it away seemed quite in depth. It shouldn't be difficult to follow some crude drawings and straightforward text."

He stared at her long and hard, uttering a vivid curse as he set her from him. "As always, your ladyship, it will be as you command."

Lucinda felt a blanket of coldness cover her heart. *Your ladyship?* He was angry. She had meant to tease him to the point of action, not incur his wrath.

"Gideon, do not call me that."

She had thought, in that moment when Gideon realized Barnaby was to be her chosen tutor, that he would overlook his pledge and offer himself. She had spent one season in London before her marriage and knew well the look of an interested male. Gideon was most definitely interested. Damn his eyes! His desire apparently took a rear perch to his abiding loyalty.

"I'll be certain your property reaches you by tomorrow midmorning. Will that be acceptable?" he asked curtly.

Lucinda didn't appreciate his cool manner—not one whit. There was absolutely no reason for his ire. She spun around and walked briskly to the small low desk where she drafted her correspondence.

"While you're carrying out my *wishes*," she huffed, bending over to take pen to parchment. "Please have this amount delivered in funds. I shall be traveling to the lake at week's end and anticipate incurring any number of expenses."

When she turned around he was an arm's length away, his eyes dark and disturbingly unreadable. She handed him the paper, raising her head regally. He whisked the note free, not taking the opportunity to temptingly brush her fingers as he had done numerous times in the past. Nor did he take her hand and raise it slowly to his lips to linger over her knuckles for what was considered an objectionable length of time. He simply stared at her a moment longer, his gaze turning glacial as he turned on his heel and stalked out the door.

* * * * *

Gideon halted at the bottom of the steps and straightened his coat. He ground his molars, attempting not to loose a stream of obscenities that would most definitely send the female passersby into fits of the vapors.

"By Christ and all that is holy," he muttered, setting foot toward home. Lucinda—his *friend*—drove him to an extent of madness which became worse with each passing minute. The woman was insufferable. Hardheaded. Determined. Completely unconventional...and too beautiful to be ignored.

When she had bent over her desk, the curves of her lush ass faintly outlined by the drab garb she was compelled to wear, his cock had all but begged him to take her then and there—silencing her obstinate raving with one deep thrust. How easily he could have flipped up her skirts and teased his way into her softness. A softness that had been untouched for over a year and before that, if Thurmond's drunken ramblings were fact, a pussy that had merely received a dutiful and quick fuck now and again in a pitiful attempt to produce an heir.

Gideon walked briskly across the street, memories of the blindsiding moment when his partner had told him he would seek a bride rushing through his mind. His shock had doubled when he'd learned Thurmond's intended was an unknown cousin from some familial estate far to the west.

His disbelief had increased—on a very sunny morning months later, a thoroughly disheveled and undeniably still-drunken Thurmond had staggered into Gideon's study and begged him to meet his betrothed at the train station in his stead—as he had watched Lucinda step down from the railcar. Her beauty and innocent grin had knocked the breath from him. Her lilting laugh had made him, a man prone to stoicism, smile in return.

He had been prepared to find objection with her at first sight. In fact, he had convinced himself she was quite possibly an opportunistic relative intent on nothing more than enhancing her family's meager coffers at the expense of his friend's freedom. But before he had deposited Lucinda, and the young maid who accompanied her, on the doorstep of her dowager aunt's home, he'd recognized his misconception. Lucinda had not one ounce of subterfuge in her entire being.

If truth be told, he had become enamored with her that very day. Memories of how her deep blue eyes had widened when he had taken her gloved hand and brought her knuckles to his lips remained quite vivid. He had waited with her on the stoop, her hand trembling as she pulled it free of his grasp. Just before the door opened he had promised her his assistance. A man whose word was never brought into question, he had aided Lucinda in every way possible. All but the one every heated fiber of his being urged him to offer. The one that would have him breaching his personal code of allegiance.

Gideon took his front steps two at a time and wiggled his key into the lock. He would not linger on what bit of providence had him giving his staff a much-deserved week off, but he was pleased there would be no one there to cringe from his utterly foul mood. With the exception of Haynes who, if Gideon knew anything about his driver's habits, and he knew them well, was probably in the courtyard diverting the duties of the buxom widow who arrived twice weekly to tidy up. Gideon could bellow to the heavens and Haynes would care naught.

Gideon stalked into his study, shrugging out of his jacket and dropping it carelessly over the arm of a wing chair. With jerking movements he undid the buttons at his neck before wrenching the links at his wrists free. He was hot. The fire kindling in his balls beginning to spread as it always did when he failed to push thoughts of Lucinda from his mind.

He yanked the bottom drawer of his desk open and pulled the journal forth, placing its spine flat against the leather desktop, allowing the covers to fall open as they would. He leaned forward, palms flat as he studied the intricate drawing and neatly printed text, knowing with deep certainty that Lucinda had never viewed the pages that had randomly opened to his perusal.

He recalled the day shortly after Thurmond's demise when he and Lucinda had been in the library going through the man's business effects. He alerted at her intake of breath and turned sharply, immediately recognizing what had caused her shock. He'd whisked the volume from her hands but not before she'd grasped what it contained. She had first demanded. Then, intelligent woman that she was, her tone had turned to a request. She'd done everything but beg. To no avail. The slim volume had never been meant for her eyes and he had told her such.

He looked down at the ink renderings and shifted against his growing erection. The drawings were finely detailed, right down to each curly, glistening pubic hair. It was far too easy to imagine it was his fingers pulling back the little cape of skin hidden below the curls, that the soft, slick folds of womanly flesh beneath the tiny exposed kernel belonged to Lucinda. The mere thought made his cock unbearably hard and he closed his eyes.

The lady would not relent. She rarely did when she truly desired something. Her nature did not warrant ignorance in any measure. She would never be satisfied until she learned all. He admired each and every one of those qualities…when properly placed. But the way his logical, albeit lust-filled mind reckoned, he was presented with absolutely no choice. As it were, he was destined to burn in Hades for coveting his friend's wife. What harm in sealing his eternal fate?

He flipped the slender volume shut, splaying his fingers over the cover. Her ladyship would soon find out every bit of knowledge the journal had to impart. But not by studying its pages in the soft evening light at her lakeside estate with young Barnaby as her devoted instructor. She would learn her lessons well. And her proficiency would be tested. By Gideon. And none other.

Chapter Two

ഇ

Lucinda jostled within the confines of her carriage, incensed over the audacity of the male species. First, Barnaby had begged off sitting for her and then Gideon's missive had arrived. The message had been unexpected and boldly succinct.

Suggest visiting solicitor yourself to obtain funds for bacchanalia. I shall be otherwise engaged this morning.

Gideon

Honestly! Did he think she'd simply hie herself off without an explanation on his part? The carriage rolled to a halt and she opened the door before Hastings had descended from his perch. She accepted his hand, her perturbed gaze focusing on the dark green door a few dozen feet away.

"Milady, wait!"

"Stay seated, Ann," Lucinda ordered over her shoulder. "Your presence is not required at the moment." She adored the woman who had been by her side from the moment she had left her father's home but in her current state, Lucinda did not need anyone within earshot. She highly doubted Gideon would appreciate an audience when she issued a setdown for his ungentlemanly behavior.

Marching up Gideon's steps, Lucinda set the knocker in motion, the sound of brass on brass echoing loudly. She waited, counted slowly to twenty as she made a surreptitious inspection of the blessedly empty street and then knocked once more. Gideon would find it far from amusing if one of his neighbors were to see her alone on his doorstep. And despite her stance on the antiquated views of society, she would not flaunt her independent nature to the point that it hurt others.

"I know you're in there, Gideon." *Why did the man obstinately refuse to properly staff his home?* Surely his elderly butler, Roswell, couldn't be that far from his post.

"I went directly to your office. Your clerk informed me as to your whereabouts. You cannot hide. Open this door, you coward," she goaded.

Minutes stretched and her indignation churned into worry. Perhaps he'd taken ill, racked with the fever so many were contracting of late. It would explain his uncharacteristically terse note. Without further thought she turned the brass knob, tension mounting when she found it unlocked.

"Gideon?" she called, stepping into the eerily silent foyer. She raised the veil of her bonnet and walked cautiously around the staircase. "Roswell? Haynes?"

Lucinda hesitated and then mentally chastised her lack of courage. Hastings was just outside, should she need him, and Ann, despite her petite appearance, was quite possibly more formidable than her burly driver. She turned the corner and saw the open door to Gideon's study.

"Gideon?"

"Yes?"

The reply was faint and Lucinda rushed into the room. She was halfway across the carpet when the door thudded shut behind her, the lock clicking into place with echoing finality.

"Welcome, my lady," he said softly, pausing by the fireplace to set the key on the edge of the mantel.

"Dear *lord*, Gideon. You gave me a start," she admitted, hand over her heart. He pinned her with a heated gaze and the beating under her fingers increased. "Where is your staff? No one was present to permit me entrance."

"Gone," he simply stated. "I'm pleased you've arrived. I wasn't certain you would come."

He strode slowly toward her, his gait so predatorily catlike her heart began to hammer. She stood rooted to the floor as he advanced, her head tilting back to hold his gaze when he halted a few feet before her.

He plucked her bag from her hand and her peripheral vision caught the path it traveled as he tossed it onto a chair. The silk bands of her bonnet's bow brushed the undersides of her jaw as he slid the binding free and a moment later it joined the purse.

Hunger, raw and intense, shot through his eyes as one large hand snaked its way through her wavy auburn hair, his fingertips leaving a tingling path against her scalp.

"Gideon?" she asked breathlessly, body cinching with a blend of alarm and desire as her mouth went dry.

"Yes?" he replied, the sensuality of his voice welcome, yet confusing.

"What are you doing?" she whispered.

"Doing?" he asked, lowering his head as he studied her lips. "That which you've been silently begging me do for quite some time. The studies you've yearned for are about to commence, my dear. Prepared to be enlightened."

Gideon relished her momentary bewilderment. It had been an eternity since he had commandeered an advantage. It was a position he had every intention of keeping.

In direct contrast to his desire to plunder her lips until they ached, he brushed his mouth against hers in a soft caress, watching until her confusion cleared and her eyelids fluttered shut. He allowed her visual retreat. Soon he would ensure that her need to see all overrode the temporary safety she found behind closed lids.

He set his palm against the column of her neck, running his thumb around the large jet bauble attached to her earlobe, over and over, until her muffled purr vibrated against his hand. Time and again he had dreamed of tasting her sweetness. His blood warmed with the knowledge that his wait was near an end. He slanted his mouth, catching the ridge of her upper lip between his lips, giving it a tiny nip, his effort rewarded by her snaking her gloved hands around his neck and stepping into his body.

He leaned back, covering her trembling fingertips with his own, bringing each one to his lips for a quick caress before maneuvering her petite body backward. She made a startled sound when the globes of her ass hit his desk.

"Are you ready to begin, Lucinda?" He guided her palms to the desktop and positioned them to his liking.

"I-I thought we had," she said breathily, eyes suddenly alert.

"Hardly," he chuckled. "Keep your hands just as they are."

"Gideon—"

"I'm aware you care little for my demanding tone." He leaned forward, bringing his lower body flush against hers and her blue eyes widened. "To be taught, one must surely obey. Don't you agree?"

He rolled his hips, the torture more his own when his erection brushed against the V of her legs. She gasped and he smiled at the sound, pressing a bit harder as he waited for an answer.

"If I must," she eventually said.

Gideon framed her flushed face with his hands and grinned challengingly. "Such a falsely martyred tone. Who's being transparent now, Lucy?"

He melded their lips before her combative nature had time to rise, running his tongue along the crease of her mouth, teasing softly until she relaxed and his tongue was permitted freedom to explore. He stroked the smooth skin inside her lower lip, ran the tip of his tongue against her teeth before dipping again. She tasted delightfully sweet—a blend of her favorite black tea and a touch of honey. Reluctantly, he relinquished the treat.

"Tell me you'll do as I ask—for once. Without query." He had been certain that once he tasted her he would be lost. It was that fear that reinforced his resolve when it had threatened to cave over the past year. His suppositions paled in comparison to the extent to which he suddenly realized, deep in the pit of his very core, that he needed her. "It doesn't mean ceding control, Lucinda. You're not blind to the effect you have on me. I'm certain you haven't been for quite some time."

"I've wanted you for so terribly long," she confessed.

"This is to be more than simply assuaging mutual desire," he said, his pride swelling at her admittance. "We could do that this very instant." Her brows furrowed and she looked down between their clad bodies and he smiled, tipping her chin up with one finger.

"This is to be your illumination of all the tantalizing ways your body deserves to be worshiped. Trust me, darling. Surrendering to my demands will be nothing like what you were forced to acquiesce to in the past. Let me show you how a man makes love to the woman he desires."

Lucinda's lips were throbbing from Gideon's seductive assault. He could, in all likelihood, feel every portion of her quivering form. Her legs, her arms, the mass of warm, damp flesh nestling his erection.

She looked into his penetrating stare and simply said, "Yes."

"You are so very special," he whispered, leaning forward to place a feathery kiss against her temple.

Lucinda prepared to tell him exactly what he meant to her as well when his words froze her.

"Unbutton your dress, Lucinda."

His tone was firm—the sort that brooked no argument. Shockingly, his demand had forced a gush of moisture from between her folds.

He turned and she watched him tug a large armchair close before hooking his thumbs beneath his suspenders and pulling them down his arms. *Dear lord!* How had she failed to notice his casual attire—that the uppermost buttons of his shirt were undone, the sleeves rolled up over his hardened forearms? Her gaze swept down his tall, lean form, hesitated at the bulge behind the band of his trousers and then continued on until she met with the shocking sight of his bare feet.

"Lucinda," he said in a surprisingly indulgent tone. "Must I help you?"

She blinked as he came closer. "I dreamed you would," she dazedly blurted.

The corners of his eyes crinkled as he moved forward, his knuckles grazing the underside of her chin as he worked the top buttons of her gown free. Warm fingers danced against the hollow of her throat before moving to the soft swell just above the material of her chemise and she sucked in a breath. She shivered from the contact, needles of excitement dancing over her skin until it tingled. He reached the button at her breasts and her heart tumbled against the inside of her chest as, with excruciating slowness, he pushed the button free.

Warm hands drifted outward, caressing her through the light cloth, the tips of his fingers dancing unerringly over her nipples until they became granite hard. He took each aching nub between thumb and forefinger and gently rolled the taut flesh, the sensation nearly levitating her from the carpet as a jolt of pure pleasure arrowed to her core. She gripped his wrists, torn between stopping him and begging him to repeat the torture.

"Gideon! I felt that all the way to my—"

"Pussy," he whispered, quickly undoing the remaining buttons and the cool air washed over her heated skin. "We'll call it what it is, Lucinda. There has never been anything but the straightforward truth between us, that shan't change at this point. Stand up, darling."

She obeyed and a second later he whisked her gown down her legs, taking her petticoat with it before tossing both aside. She was left standing before him, nipples straining against the fine lawn of her chemise, pussy throbbing.

"I'm so very pleased with your unconformity," he admitted, the wicked gleam in his eyes scorching her from head to toe. "I would have hated to wrestle with the closures of a corset."

Lucinda leaned back against the desk for support, closing her eyes. She truly needed to get her wildly beating heart and the thrumming between her thighs under enough control that her mind might properly function. She felt a tug at the tiny satin strings at her bosom and peered through shuttered lashes at Gideon loosening the silken bow. He eased her chemise down the slope of her breasts until it rested against the top of each distended nipple, temptingly hesitating before dragging the soft fabric over the puckered flesh in a manner that had her nails curling into the palms of her trembling hands.

"More beautiful than even my dreams," he said huskily as he looked up and caught her peeking. She closed her eyes tightly and heard him chuckle. "Do not become suddenly coy, my lady."

She felt the tip of his long, straight nose brush the furthest edge of one areola, the skin contracting before he slid into the valley between her breasts. With feathery kisses he worked his way up the expanse of smooth skin, the top of his silky head forcing her chin backward to allow him access to her collarbone. And then his teeth began to drive her wild. Tiny nips at her shoulder, along the sensitive crease between her breast and upper arm, down to the inside of her elbow. He nibbled a little harder and Lucinda squirmed.

He grasped her hips and lifted her onto the desktop. She reached backward for balance but he chose that moment to rotate his head and capture her nipple with lip-covered teeth. Handhold forgotten, she grasped his head, electricity rocketing from breast to belly to dew-slicked core.

He insinuated his hips between her legs, his palm slapping against the desktop as he wrapped a supporting arm around her, forcing her upper body backward. His other hand cupped her breast, weighing the soft pale globe as he raised it to meet his lips. Slowly, with infinitesimal licks he bathed her nipple, never fully touching the hardened center.

"Please," she groaned, burying her gloved fingers in his hair. "I'm ready."

He pulled his head from her grip and gave her a sinful smile. "Indeed?" he asked skeptically, running his hand down her arm and then across the top of her exposed thigh. His palm covered her kneecap, his thumb tracing tiny serpentine patterns on the sensitive skin of her lower inner thigh. So focused on that delight, she barely felt his other hand move until his finger stroked the delicate skin that separated her thigh from her abdomen—short, soft caresses that made her clitoris pulsate.

"Are you wet?"

She gasped as he jerked her leg wide. She was aware the opening of her drawers was gaping, that if he looked down he'd see the answer to his question. His hand shifted, hovering over the split fabric, heat torturously radiating from his palm.

"Are you wet?" he asked again, stroking her damp pubic hair, twisting it into a curl around his finger. He tugged gently and she cried out.

"Yes!"

"I had thought as much. You essence surrounds me." His nail raked the tiny cord of muscle above her clit and she nearly sobbed. "Do you ache?"

"Gideon." Her voice was raw with emotion. For him, she'd plead. "Touch me...please."

"Show me how," he said.

"I-I do not comprehend," Lucinda lied, her face flushing at what he suggested.

"My lady," he countered, untwining his finger before lowering himself into the chair. "Your sexuality has grown to the point that it all but radiates." He encased her ankles with his fingers and Lucinda's heartbeat echoed through her head. Ever-so slowly he brought first one foot and then the other to rest upon his widespread knees.

"I'm convinced you've not been completely chaste these last twelve months. In fact, I'd wager I know near the moment you learned your present conception of womanly pleasure."

Lucinda watched his eyes drift to her exposed pussy and she felt the wetness roll from her folds.

"It was August, was it not?"

"How—"

"You were creating the portrait of the two sisters sharing the paisley chaise. But they really weren't sisters, were they? The underlying theme was far from lost on me, Lucinda. It was extremely erotic. Not at all sisterly...positively Sapphic."

Her face flamed at memories of her subjects. Of the women's boredom growing into silliness. The giggles quieting as they began kissing, stroking each other, bodies writhing. Lucinda had tried to look away but could not. The mingled cries that had echoed through her studio that day would not soon be forgotten.

"I'd wager they taught you much," Gideon stated, sliding her forward until her pussy was hovering at the edge of his desk. "Did you join them?"

"No!" she said, his suggestion nearly too shocking to comprehend.

"That pleases me," he admitted, removing her slippers. He placed the soles of her feet higher up his legs and she felt his muscles flex beneath her feet.

"The ladies showed you how easy and natural it is to bring about pleasure. Now show me."

"Gideon! I cannot."

His thumbs dipped inside her drawers, rubbing little caresses against the pillowy flesh of her outer labia and she arched her spine. "Touch yourself, Lucinda. For me."

For Gideon. The man who had secretly held every aspect of her world together since the moment she'd set foot in London. Her stalwart friend. Her confidante. And now, as she had dared to eternally hope, her lover! All she need do—

"Lean back and bring yourself to the precipice, Lucy." His voice had taken on a reverent tone and she met his simmering gaze and knew, in that instant, she would do whatever he asked if only he would touch her. As if discerning her thoughts he said, "I'll help you to shatter, darling. I promise. Into a million blinding pieces you never dreamed possible."

Lucinda took a deep breath and leaned back on one hand. She exhaled and slowly closed her eyes just as she did when she was beneath her coverlet in the darkness of her bedchamber. Her hands trembled as she removed her gloves and reached between her thighs to touch her drenched thatch of hair and tentatively caress her mound. A sharp intake of breath sounded—Gideon's, not hers—her own breath hitching a moment later as she brushed against the very top of her clit.

"God, yes," he urged in a husky whisper and her fingers dipped, bonding against the aching bit of flesh. Rhythmically, she circled the hidden nub, lightly at first and then with an increasing pressure until it popped from beneath its protective veil.

"Your folds are crying for attention, Lucinda."

She felt the whisper of his words against her knee, his closeness spurring her forward as much as the recognizable heat blossoming low in her belly.

"Do you not touch yourself between them?" he whispered.

"No," she said on a pant of breath.

"Never?" he questioned and she jumped when his fingers ran along the backs of her stocking-clad calves.

The beautiful tightness was beginning. That first time it had frightened her but now...now Lucinda knew exactly what it heralded.

"Lucinda?" He placed a hot kiss on her upper thigh and her legs began to tremble. "Have you never buried your fingers deep inside?"

"No," she said on a shaky moan, dropping her head backward. Tension drew her feminine core into an aching bundle of electrified nerve endings as her desire climbed. She was nearing the peak, mere strokes away, when his fingers curled around her wrist and tugged her hand toward him. She whimpered, a curse forming on the tip of her tongue as she struggled against his cruelty. He brought her desire-slicked fingers to his mouth, shocking her motionless. He rubbed her digits against his lips before sucking them deep into the warm wetness of his mouth, curling his tongue around them.

Despite being wrapped in a pre-orgasmic haze, she caught her breath at his audacious caress.

"Delicious," he said, smiling devilishly, looking up at her through sinfully long lashes. "But certainly just an *amuse-bouche* of what's to follow."

He trailed one solitary finger up her wet folds and down again and the desire that had momentarily ebbed suddenly flamed.

"Forgive me, love."

"Forgive you?" Lucinda asked on a moan as he stretched the gaping linen of her undergarment and ran the knuckle of each index finger against her engorged sex. He grabbed the material and rent it in one smooth move.

"I cannot wait another minute to see you."

His eyes roamed over her throbbing flesh and her breathing faltered. "How I've dreamed of touching you here," he said, catching one of her swollen pussy lips between thumb and forefinger and rubbing lightly. Lucinda could do naught but groan and lower herself onto her elbows.

"Gideon, please. Put an end to this."

"We're focusing on prolonging your pleasure, darling."

"It's not pleasure," she cried. "It's pain."

He raised a hand to cup one breast. "At times they're one and the same." He ran his thumbnail across the center of her hardened nipple to prove his point.

"No," she gasped, grabbing his hand to prevent him drawing it away.

"Oh, yes," he said, rotating his hand until Lucinda's breast was in her own grasp, her fingers resting against the puckered center.

"You'll learn there are times when desire requires appeasement furiously fast." The fingers teasing between her thighs slid lower and began stroking, never quite pressing into her hot flesh. "And other times—exceedingly special first times—when fulfillment should be held at bay until the last possible moment."

His fingers stroked upward along the inside of her folds. Soaked in her essence, they slid one by one, hovering over her clit before he touched her with an indirect pressure to the swollen little nub. It was nothing like the unswerving assault she had been applying moments before. It was a hundred times more torturous.

"There is no need to wait. I'm no untried virgin." She flexed her ass to press harder against his caress. "Thurmond–"

Gideon rocketed out of the chair with a speed that startled her. He grabbed the back of her head, bringing his lips to hers with a force that left her wide-eyed and well aware she should not have mentioned her husband's name. He bore down and she grabbed his shoulders and pushed, dug her nails into the firm muscle and a moment later felt a shudder ripple through him. The pressure of his lips lessened and he ran his tongue over her teeth, along the soft underside of her bottom lip, until Lucinda gave just a bit. He slid the tip of his tongue between her teeth and she gently nipped.

His groan was a delightful vibration between their mouths. Slowly, he pulled away and Lucinda caught her breath. His eyes were glazed. His breathing far from steady as little bursts of air drifted across her nose.

"Open your mouth." Had she not felt the tension bunch the muscle beneath her fingers she would have surely known by the mere tone of his voice how affected he was. Something had snapped his resolve. Clearly, he wanted her as desperately as she needed him. Pure, unadulterated feminine satisfaction stole through her and she shook her head in the negative.

His slow, wolfish grin made Lucinda wonder if she might have erred in thinking she held some power. The fingers at the base of her skull flexed and he manipulated her head to the side, whispering in her ear. "I can be persuasive."

His lips grazed the soft skin beneath her earlobe and Lucinda shivered with delight. She had never given his skills at seduction a single thought. She should have. His featherlight touch left a trail of pure heat in its lingering path.

"Perhaps a very wet kiss here," he said, offering her only the simplest of pursed kisses on the sensitive area at the side of her throat. Lucinda felt the heat seep slowly down her body, coming to rest in the pulsing flesh between her thighs that his tormenting fingers barely touched.

"Or maybe open-mouthed adoration somewhere even softer?" he suggested, shifting his hand, boldly cupping her aching sex.

"No!" *He could not mean –*

"I will taste you everywhere. From those full lips you refuse to open straight down your gorgeous body. Over your pert breasts and lower still until I reach the font of your desire."

His gaze darkened and Lucinda let the breath she'd been holding escape through her nose. The sound was harsh in the quiet room.

"And I will drink until I get my fill. I'll lick everywhere your fingers have been. Where mine are poised at present." He circled lightly against her opening and Lucinda's eyebrows rose.

"How priceless your surprise would be if my cock wasn't on the verge of exploding. I desperately need to fuck you, Lucy."

Lucinda's mind had nearly grasped his words when he slid one finger into her pussy. Her inner muscles had only a second to embrace the intruding digit before it was gone.

"All but untried," he said, easing his finger and another back into her warmth with a little twist of his wrist. "You are so very, very snug. It's torturous, Lucinda. Knowing my cock will be stretching you to the fullest. So very, very soon."

She felt him withdraw almost completely and knew the little grunt of disappointment that echoed through the room belonged to her alone. The sound turned into something completely different when his fingers filled her once more and began to tease. In and out, never filling her fully, the motion drawing more and more wetness from her core. Each little plunge took him closer to some inner spot Lucinda had been completely ignorant of. She sensed something out of the ordinary awaited. It grew in its fullness...blossoming from her very depths. Impatient to draw it forth, her hips began rocking on their own accord.

She looked into Gideon's stare. The raw desire was still evident but it mingled with a look of total determination. "I'll have my taste now, if you please."

He buried his fingers in her pussy at a depth that had Lucinda crying out. His firm lips captured hers, his tongue taking advantage of the open access of her mouth and he alternated the thrusts of his tongue with those of his fingers until she was shaking.

Her mind blanked as every nerve in her body came alive. His tongue swirled around hers as his fingers circled within her channel and she thought her heart might actually explode. Their tongues dueled, 'round and 'round in perfect unison with his fingers brushing against the front of her vagina. Lucinda hung on as long as possible before tearing her mouth from his and gulping for air.

"Gideon…please…it's…agonizing."

He dragged his hand around her neck and straight down her body, burying his fingers in her wet curls.

"Help me, darling. Bring your hands to your breasts. Take your nipples between your fingertips. Drive me to madness as I drive you over the edge." He captured her clit between two fingers and her thighs tightened against the exquisite sensation.

Lucinda cupped her breasts and did as he asked, running her thumbs over her nipples as he watched. She tugged the elongated tips and he squeezed her in return, the action surging her desire. And then his thumb was upon her, brushing against her captured pearl, causing the familiar roiling to build, more intense than ever before. Her body heated, the blood flowing through her veins seeming to boil.

The fingers buried in her pussy pressed higher and harder and Lucinda's hands automatically clenched. She rolled her nipples and heard Gideon's soft curse. And then she heard nothing else. She merely felt. Felt the tempo of his fingers on her clit and in her pussy synchronize. Felt the rush that flowed from her extremities directly to her throbbing pussy. Felt his fingers push upward and his thumb press harder. Felt it all until she was forced to answer his ministration with a keening wail as wave upon wave rocked her body into a blinding orgasm that took her beyond the barriers of all that existed.

Chapter Three

ಶೋ

Gideon prayed the image before him might somehow emblazon itself in his mind forever. Lucinda was sprawled flat against his desk, her body still quivering from the extent of her climax. One black-gloved hand rested against the paleness of her breast, the other had drifted downward to cover his where it lay against her mound. But it was the sight of his fingers still entrenched in her cunt, tiny contractions still gripping them, which had him to the point of nearly shooting his release against the front of his desk.

He had truly never wanted a woman more, nor had he been dishonest. He wanted to fuck her, hard and quick until the desire he had held in check for so long was purged. Then he would take her again. Slowly. Thoroughly.

She all but purred his name, her voice low and unmistakably satiated and his cock demanded freedom and a reward for its patience. He eased his hand from her pussy, her clinging essence making it difficult to work the closures of his trousers free. He wiped her wetness against his leg and freed his cock before reaching for the placket of his shirt and quickly divesting himself of that article of clothing.

"You are truly the most beautiful woman in all creation, Lucy." He turned the palm at her groin over and gripped her hand. "As breathtaking as that pose is, I need you up, darling. Our first time shall not be amidst papers and pen well."

He pulled her gently to a seated position and heard her gasp.

"Heavens!" she whispered, staring directly at his cock. "And I thought Barnaby graced by the gods."

"Woman," he said gruffly, trying to disguise his smile. "I thought it clear that I have no tolerance for hearing another man's name spoken from your lips." He guided her legs over his hips, lifted her off the desk and carried her to the low satinwood daybed. He held her close, staring into her eyes. "There shall always be a penalty to pay for such offense."

She threaded her fingers through his hair and leveled a look of unmasked expectation, one he found surprisingly clear for a woman in a state of post-arousal, and his already turgid cock lengthened. Her well-kissed lips turned up at the corners. "I can't promise the threat of punishment will make me behave. It rarely has before."

He felt her breath along his jaw as she nipped her way up to his ear, his balls pulsing in response to each tiny bite. *Dear god!* There was no doubt she should have always been his.

"Nonetheless, a penalty must be meted out," he said, giving her firm ass a little squeeze for the sheer joy the action brought.

She ran her tongue against the bottom of his lobe and whispered. "Should I expect another bruising oral assault from your talented mouth? My lips are still tingling, you know."

"Lucinda," he groaned, every remaining ounce of blood in his body seeming to heat at her innocuous words and rush strait to his groin. He stretched his fingers over the smooth globes of her ass, dipping into her cleft and passing quickly over her puckered rim until he was stroking her wetness.

"I did not mean *those* lips," she gasped.

"So you believe," he said, lowering her to the floor. He grabbed the edges of her chemise and drew it over her head and up her arms. The sight of her thus, breasts drawn upward, tight nipples silently pleading for the caress of his tongue, made him growl. Her brows furrowed. He twisted the fabric around her wrists and she glanced upward, unintentionally offering the column of her neck to his hungry lips.

He nibbled the pulsing vein along her throat, moaning when she leaned into him, her damp curls teasing his balls.

"I can picture you with a length of silk binding your wrists to the post of my bed, unable to stop me as I discover every succulent inch of your body, squirming as I lick every hill and valley with you able to do naught but cry out my name and beg me to stop."

"I wouldn't care to be bound," she said, but her hips shifted against him. He pulled her chemise free and tossed it aside before swiftly bending and yanking her tattered drawers down her legs.

"I believe you'd care for it a great deal, Lucy." He leaned forward and inhaled, barely resisting the urge to bury his face in her damp curls and stroke her pussy with his tongue. He pulled away from temptation and rose.

"My stockings?"

"They shall stay. Allow me to undo you."

"You already have," she said softly, eyes gleaming as she offered her wrist.

Gideon held her gaze and then went quickly to work. He had longed for her touch for what seemed like an eternity and within seconds the tiny pearl buttons were loosed.

"Thank you," she said, placing her middle finger between her teeth and tugging in a most unladylike fashion—one that had his balls tightening yet again.

And then her hands were bare and grazing a hot path across his chest. She went slowly, studying each pad of hardened muscle as if it were a rarity, moving her palms over his ribs, trailing a finger down his sternum until she stopped just above his navel. She pushed her thumb into the indentation and gave the skin a little pinch that sent a jolt straight to his already-straining cock. It gave a twitch and her surprised gaze shot to his. Then she smiled. The sultry little smile he had come to both love and fear. That smile was generally a precursor to her taking complete and utter control of whatever was at hand.

Gideon looked down his body and trapped her fingers. He could handle a great deal where Lucinda was concerned. Her wrapping her delicate fingers around his cock was not one of them. The woman had no clue as to the force he was desperately fighting to keep leashed until they were joined deep and her lush form was writhing beneath him.

"Your efforts to distract me are in vain, my lady," he said, taking a few paces backward. He pushed his trousers off his hips and stepped out of them. "No man with even a shred of his mental faculties intact could be dissuaded from your unknowing suggestion to 'orally assault' so fine a pussy."

Gideon stood before her, a gloriously naked mass of defined muscle, his thick cock hugging the flat planes of his abdomen. He was utterly breathtaking and he was staring at her with such a singularly desirous look that she could scarcely breathe.

He pulled her into his arms and instantaneously her skin was ablaze, the warmth of his body seeping into her very soul. He maneuvered her backward until her calves hit the edge of the daybed and then eased her down.

"I wish I had the control to carry you upstairs and make love to you properly," he declared, arranging a few small pillows behind her back and head.

"But you cannot," she said, brushing a strand of silky dark hair from his eyes. "Because you must fuck me first."

"Dear god! Your audacity drives me wild," he whispered, trapping her wrist against his mouth. He kissed his way down her arm and over the smooth skin at the corner of her breast. "I will never, ever be able to get my fill of you," he vowed, his lips drifting over her collarbone to the soft hollow at the base of her neck. Lucinda tipped her head to the side, giving him full access as he nibbled an upward path, his warm breath drifting over the shell of her ear when he spoke.

"Spread your legs, Lucinda. I wish to lick my way to your very core." He punctuated his command with two open-mouthed kisses that brought him to the point where her neck and shoulder met.

He sucked her skin deep into his mouth and bit down gently, the pressure of his clamping teeth sending a frisson of desire rocketing to her pussy. Her thighs fell open as her back arched.

"You are so very responsive, Lucy. I barely touch you and your body begs for more." Lucinda let out a ragged breath as he trailed his fingertips up her arms and over her breasts. He circled her tight nipples and then opened his hands and brought them close enough that she could feel the heat radiating from his palms.

Like a shameless wanton she shifted her shoulders and pressed her aching breasts into his hands, rubbing against him. He spread his fingers and captured her breasts fully, her distended nipples resting in the little valley between his thumbs and forefingers.

"You like this, do you not?" he asked, slowing closing his fingers. He licked a little circle against her neck with the tip of his tongue and Lucinda nodded. She liked it all. Very much.

"Say it, darling, and I shall tweak harder. You know that's what you crave."

"Yes, Gideon," she groaned, hips rising from the cushion when he caught her nipples between his fingertips and squeezed. A gush of moisture seeped from her folds and she shifted against the seat.

"There is no sweeter sound than you calling my name," he said.

Lucinda watched through half-closed lids as he lowered his head and nuzzled first one breast and then the other. He hummed when he tasted each nipple and she thought she would go mad from the erotic vibrations against her flesh. He worked his way down her belly in little licks and nips at a pace that had her squirming. When he reached the top of her pubic curls he pushed himself backward and then slid to a kneeling position on the floor.

He laid his head against her thigh, the juxtaposition of light and dark enthralling. The steeliness of his biceps teased her skin as he threaded his arm under her thigh and hooked her knee over his shoulder. He brushed his knuckles up the inside her other thigh with the smallest amount of pressure until she opened fully and dangled her leg over the edge of the daybed.

"It's all I can do to not devour you," he said huskily.

Lucinda trapped her lower lip between her teeth. Her pussy felt beyond full. While she found the sight of him staring intently at her most intimate of places the pinnacle of eroticism, she would be utterly dishonest with herself in refusing to admit a certain level of trepidation. Her opinion changed a moment later when his thumbs dipped inside her pussy lips and opened her slick folds. He held her thus, stretched open for heartbeat upon heartbeat, until she nearly screamed with anticipation.

"What a delicious shade of pink you are. Rather like the color of a raspberry ice," he said.

Her breath caught shockingly in her throat as the flat of his tongue wound back and forth across her opening, the pressure so slight it was complete torment. She clutched the cushion and closed her eyes, breathing deeply through her nose for fear she might actually faint.

"Mmmm. And just as sweet a treat," he said when he had worked his way to the top of her sex. The little vibration had her shifting her hips. "Shall I consume you just as leisurely, your ladyship?"

He licked two slow, broad swipes up each side of her labia and Lucinda felt as if her limbs were about to ignite. He did indeed take his time—kissing and nibbling and sucking every pulsating inch of skin until her breath came in short little bursts. "Faster, Gideon. Please."

"Faster?" he asked, pulling his mouth away and Lucinda grabbed his head between her hands, intent on forcing him back toward her aching flesh and into a motion that would satisfy her. His thumbs slid lower, caressing her swollen flesh as if it were some rare gem in need of a good polishing. "It's not so far a stretch to pretend I must pick up my pace because you're melting. Your pussy is glistening with wetness, darling."

"Then stop this bloody torture and lick it dry," she yelled, mortified by her words but praying he would do naught but obey.

Mercifully, he brought his lips against her flesh, lapping steadily at her folds, never breaking rhythm, not even when her hips moved on their own and rocked against him. She had climbed once again nearly to the peak when he slid his hands under her ass and tilted her hips upward.

His nose bumped against the bottom of her clit and her low moan echoed through the room. His tongue hardened, penetrating her pussy over and over as he used his hands to slide her back and forth. She dug her heel into the taut muscles of his back and Gideon quickly pulled his tongue free.

"Come for me," he whispered against her flesh, his mouth grasping her clit with a degree of firm suction that had Lucinda crying out. With the barest of caresses he rolled his velvety tongue around her button, increasing the pressure and tempo as her responses became louder, each pass tightening the links of the chain of yearning that wound its way through her body and into her very soul. She cursed him one moment and then pleaded with him the next, until the shattering climax claimed her and she merely sobbed his name over and over and over again.

Gideon would have treasured the chance to continue his assault, would have basked in the glory of bringing her to the brink again but the creamy taste that coated his tongue and chin, the musky essences that hung in the air between them drove him past the point of rationale.

He stood and took his cock in hand, gave his shaft one long stroke until his fist was tight against his balls and watched Lucinda's hips continue to shift against the cushion, knowing her tight pussy was clenching still. He could no longer wait. Kneeling between her legs, he ran his cock head against her pouty folds, the little noises whooshing from her parted lips encouragement of the sweetest variety.

She was hotter than his engorged flesh and he spread her pussy lips wide, gritting his teeth as he slid his hard length into her slickness, pausing when his cock head was engulfed in her warmth. He watched her eyes shoot open and held her gaze, pressing slowly upward until he was well and truly seated.

"Gideon," she gasped, a look of near panic clouding her eyes. "I feel as if I can scarcely breathe."

He clenched his jaw, fighting not to surrender to the tiny pulses that were milking his cock. It felt so bloody good he was afraid to move. He brushed loose wisps of her hair back from her forehead and gave her a strained smile. "Your pussy's just like you, darling. Very accommodating. It will adjust, I swear. Trust me."

"I-I do trust you," she said as he pulled his hips back. Her eyebrows rose when he carefully thrust forward again.

"See," he said, rolling his hips to stretch her further. "Already it's given me leave."

"You've set my entire being on fire," Lucinda said, wrapping her hand around his hip. "I've wanted this for so desperately long. Teach me, Gideon...show me what I have missed."

Her words, coupled with the enticing little movements inside her body, were enough to force Gideon to overlook his gentlemanly intentions of loving her slowly. He groaned, thrusting into her in steady, even strokes. He could feel the tickle of sweat breaking out along his upper lip as his balls started to clench.

"Dear lord! I feel as if…surely it can not happen again?" she asked, her voice filled with wonder as she innately began to meet his hard thrusts.

"It can, love." He grabbed on to the arm of the daybed and rocked into her harder, watching the increasing bounce of her breasts. He bent his head and captured one nipple between his teeth, the rocking of their bodies forcing it to be tugged and released as she arched her hips upward and clutched his ass. Her nails dug into his skin and he leaned forward and rocked in earnest.

Flesh against flesh — the sensation of his balls slapping the tight puckered skin of her rim — heralded the end of his self-control. She didn't utter a word or sound but snaked her other leg around him and fully met his thrusts. Orgasmic contractions rippled around his cock as he buried his face against the side of her neck, closing his eyes against his own impending release. He called her name as he let loose his control and came, his hips continuing to move against her softness long after his balls had quit pulsing and he had pumped every drop of his seed inside her.

They lay entwined, listening to the sound of their breathing until, fearing his weight too heavy for her delicate frame, he rolled them onto their sides, bodies still joined. She continued to clutch his back and he basked in the feel of her embrace, lovingly stroking the fullness of her ass until their harsh erratic tones had returned to an easy rhythm.

"Gideon. That was truly wonderful," she said softly against his chest.

Dear *god*, how he loved the sound of his name on her lips. He pushed himself onto an elbow, not wanting to pull his softening cock from her delicious warmth, but knowing he must. He looked into her beautiful, completely satiated face and fought the urge to stay right where he was and kiss her until he again became as hard as marble.

"Indeed it was, your ladyship," he said teasingly, waiting for her usual admonishment in addressing her as such. She remained silent, but smiled, and he dared to hope his lovemaking had spun her into a delighted daze from which she might be willing to never return. Regretfully, he eased from her body, her pussy clinging to his shaft until it released him with a little wet pop.

"Goodness," she snorted, closing her eyes as she rolled away from him and onto her back, wiggling into the warmth of the cushion.

"Unparalleled goodness," Gideon replied, smiling. He bent down and ran a palm across her hipbone before moving higher to caress the smoothness of her belly. He placed a kiss on her temple and said, "Under peril of torture, you are *not* to fall asleep, Lucy."

"Mmm-hmmm," she mumbled.

"I'm serious, Lucinda," he said, rolling off the daybed and reaching for his trousers. He pulled them on, buttoning them quickly.

"But you've completely exhausted me."

He watched her thighs press tightly together, her hips wiggle, and his cock let him know it was far from fatigued. He scooped his shirt off the floor and yanked it on. Their play would have to end...for now. If he did not leave this very instant, he quite possibly never would.

"I need to have a word with Hastings—"

Lucinda squealed, sitting up with astonishing speed. Her look of abject horror caught him momentarily off guard.

"Do not worry, love. I shall send him on his way and then scrounge up something for luncheon."

Her huge blue eyes looked up at him. "I left the man—
and Ann...oh dear heaven—sitting on the street for—" She
looked at the small clock resting atop the mantel. "Oh dear
god," she groaned, covering her face with her hands. "I have
never been so inconsiderate...so rude...so—"

"Completely lost in a pure, mind-addling sensation that
forces everything surrounding you to seem inconsequential?"
He hooked two fingers under her chin and raised her face then
leaned down slowly, his amused gaze never leaving hers as he
kissed her softly. "Accustom yourself to the phenomenon,
darling. We shall be experiencing it for the remainder of our
days."

He recognized his presumptuousness and refused to give
it a whit of contemplation. He walked around the desk and
removed the journal from the middle drawer.

"Some light reading...while you await my return." He
tossed it into her lap.

Lucinda picked up the slim volume, stared at the
nondescript cover and then back at him.

He offered her a wide grin and started toward the door.

"Begin with page twenty-four, Lucy. It's where we shall
be losing ourselves next."

Chapter Four

ℬ

Lucinda stared at the wooden panel long after Gideon had pulled it firmly shut. In point of fact, he had finally succeeded in rendering her speechless. From the moment she had received his dismissive note, to his declaration minutes before that alluded to the fact that their relationship would be much more permanent than that of passing lovers.

She clutched the journal to her chest and felt her heartbeat drum against the smooth cover as she recalled the wonder of what had transpired. She had been startled by the depths of her passion, at how easily she had bent to Gideon's will. His fervor and skill had made it anything but a hardship, unlike Thurmond's attentions.

She had tried to tell herself, during the course of their lovemaking, that the terms of endearment he whispered were merely words of the moment. Her heart soared at the knowledge that he had meant every syllable he had spoken.

Looking down at the book resting on her lap, she felt a shiver wash through her. Lucinda set the journal aside and rose, picking up the cashmere throw from the foot of the daybed and winding it tightly around her nakedness. She felt sinfully brazen – not wearing a stitch of clothing…in the midst of Gideon's study…at half past noon. It felt undeniably right for such an adventurous woman as herself.

Lucinda laughed, took up the journal and plopped onto the daybed. She turned pages, paying close attention to the exquisitely drawn artwork until she reached the images she had briefly viewed nearly a year prior.

She perused the pages, having the luxury of time to study them with the admiration of an artist's eye. The focus on detail was undeniable. On the left-hand page the artist had drawn an ostrich feather, its fringe just touching the edge of a perfectly formed breast. Lucinda's gaze drifted across the binding to the opposite page.

Her bosom swelled as she gazed down at the image. The tightly contracted nipple allowed no doubt as to the path and effect of the delicate feather. Her own flesh pebbled and a tingle twisted low in her belly and coiled downward. She crossed her legs against the ache and perused drawing after drawing, until she realized her breathing had become drastically uneven, the growing dampness between her thighs undeniable. She was about to slam the book closed when a passage of text caught her eye.

Mastering the art of orally loving your lady will most certainly assure her sheer and utter devotion and desire, no matter the hour of the day or how she might be otherwise engaged.

Lucinda would have pondered the "sheer and utter" presumptuousness of the statement if the phrase "otherwise engaged" and the familiar way in which the "r" and the "w" were connected had not caused her heart to miss a beat. She slid off the bed and rushed to the seating area to retrieve her purse. She worked the drawstrings open, fingers trembling as she pulled the crisp, cream-colored note free and stared unbelievingly at Gideon's bold handwriting.

* * * * *

"I've returned," Gideon announced. "With sustenance and Ann and Hastings' best wishes that we have a most pleasant afternoon." He set the tray on the corner of his desk and gave her a quick smile. "I continue to be amazed at how easily your maid relinquishes her duties when it comes to allowing her mistress to remain unchaperoned."

While he had been annoyed time and again at Ann's failure to be present when Lucinda was alone with her models, he found the woman's compliancy to her mistress's current demand a godsend.

"I'm afraid I had to offer them a bit of an untruth. I told them you were helping me catalogue some of these tomes," he said, waving his hand. He watched as she closed the journal around her finger, as to not lose her place.

"It's not like you to be deceptive," Lucinda said softly, gracing him with a feline smile. Had the mere thought that he no longer need deny his affection not distracted him, Gideon would have given her look a tad more consideration.

"Have you finished reading about the merits of feathers and bondage, my sweet?"

"No. I'm afraid I became a bit distracted." She swung her feet around and stood. The throw she had wrapped around her body hugged her luscious curves and his smile deepened as her swaying hips carried her to his side. His eyes drifted to the fullness of her breasts, pushed high about her makeshift toga, and his mouth actually watered.

"Did you learn nothing at all, then?" he asked, running his hands over her hips and then up her rib cage until his thumbs could reach the undersides of her breasts.

She rose on her toes and kissed the outer corner of his mouth. "I would not say that. A person could glean a wealth of knowledge simply from studying that magnificent artwork," she said in a sultry voice.

Gideon studied her upturned face, the narrow set of her eyes a clear warning.

"They are so detailed...so undeniably erotic." He felt her pull his shirt down his arms, uncertain as to when she had worked the buttons free. *Get a grasp, man!*

"They made me so very, very uncomfortably wet," she whispered against his chest and his balls all but slammed into his body. She kissed her way to one flat nipple and he watched, mesmerized, as her lush lips hovered over his hardened disc. "Do you know the artist?"

Her tongue rolled around his suddenly erect nipple and his cock began to throb in earnest. She looked up at him through her lashes and bit gently.

"Yes," he answered sharply, his hand moving of its own accord to dive into her silky tresses.

"Is there a chance I might meet him?" Her tongue darted out and lightly licked.

"Meet him?" Gideon asked, fighting to concentrate on the thread of her words. She chose that moment to close her lips and suck and his groan filled the room.

"I imagine," she said, releasing his nipple and giving it a final kiss, "that much like you, Gideon, he's oftentimes otherwise engaged."

"Otherwise—"

Her arm came up between them and Gideon stared at the journal, desire and puzzlement dueling at the forefront of his emotions. She opened the book and he saw the note he had sent her that very morning. Her finger held it in place beneath a row of journal text and he glanced downward at the exact phrase he had written in an attempt to anger her enough to bring her to his side.

"You wrote every word...sketched each drawing." Her voice was a mere whisper.

Gideon looked into her unreadable eyes as he eased the book from her hand and set it aside. He would not lie. "I did."

"Did Thurmond ask you to do so? Did he find the task of producing an heir so repulsive that he needed an outline on how to touch me?" Her gaze turned accusatory and he took her cheeks between his palms.

"He did not," Gideon replied honestly.

"Then why—"

Gideon stopped her question with a long, slow kiss.

"For you, Lucinda. You and you alone. I knew where Thurmond's preferences lay the last few years of his life but there was a time when he relished the sound of a woman calling his name. I believed all he needed was a gentle reminder, something to strike a chord on the shared pleasure to be had if he employed a bit of patience.

"I knew the day you stepped down from that train that you were a woman who deserved to be loved fully and I cursed the injustice that I would never be the man to do so. Thoughts of how very much I wanted you were present with each stroke of ink, each smudge of charcoal. In the recesses of my besieged mind I somehow thought if he were able to bring you pleasure through my efforts…it would be as if I had done so myself."

"He never made an attempt to please me," she said, voice cracking.

He knew her distress had little to do with Thurmond and more with the fact that she realized she was finally loved. Gideon stopped the wet trail of a lone tear with his lips, whispering in her ear. "He was a selfish man, Lucy. I'm so terribly sorry."

The quiet between them stretched.

"I am not," she said, finally and firmly, covering his hands with her own. "It allows you the distinction of being the only man who shall ever bring me pleasure."

"Truly?" he asked, the ache that had appeared in the vicinity of his heart quickly dispersing.

"Well and truly," she replied quickly. "In every fully detailed, perfectly drawn way possible."

"There was a moment, just yesterday as I recall, when you deemed my drawings crude."

"That was a moment—I'm sure there'll be more of the same—when I was trying to annoy you into doing exactly as I wished," she said, gracing him with a beatific smile.

He slid his hands down her neck until her little purr of contentment vibrated against his thumbs. "Your tactic seems to have worked. The journal is now yours to do with what you will. You have all you've wished for these past twelve months."

"It seems as if I finally do," she said softly, her smile turning utterly seductive.

Gideon chuckled as she trailed her fingers down his chest and over his taut stomach.

"You fibbed earlier, my lady, when you said you learned naught. Your hands have become quite talented," he said, tightening his muscles when her fingers brushed against his fastenings.

"Not so much as yours, my love." She stopped her motion and looked solemnly into his eyes. "Your talent is phenomenal, Gideon."

"To which talent does my lady refer?" he asked, winking, fingers drifting downward until he reached the knotted fabric at her breast.

"The one that makes me wet…but not screaming my release," she grinned.

"It is nothing."

"Misplaced modesty," she said, working his buttons free and pushing his trousers over his hips. "We shall find a discreet publisher and your work will be famous."

He tugged and the blanket fell to the carpet. There was never a finer sight than Lucinda naked before him, reaching out to take his cock with her soft caress. "I've no need for fame. I'm more than comfortable, as you know. One scandalous profession betwixt us is enough."

"In a roundabout way you would be providing women throughout all of Britain, perhaps the Continent in its entirety, with a most welcome service," she said, wrapping her fingers around his steely length.

"There is only one woman I wish to provide a service to, your ladyship. Come here."

"Not just yet," Lucinda said, placing her other palm against his chest. "Do you know the thing I adore most about you?"

"Dare I hope you're holding it in your fist this very moment?" he teased. She didn't return his grin and he inclined his head at her seriousness.

"You have always allowed me my freedom...my choices. Even when you did not agree—I am well aware there were times when you did not—yet you held your tongue. I would hate for that to change. I cherish that liberty."

His cock had lengthened in her hand and she eased his hardness upward until it was trapped between their bodies. She ran her thumb over his tiny slit, picking up the drop of pearly wetness and rubbing it slowly over the darkened tip.

"But I cherish you more, Gideon," she said, moving her hand up his chest until it rested against his heart. "I can be proper, if I must."

Her declaration had his breath abandoning his lungs and his heart swelling beneath his ribs.

Lucinda watched the play of emotion cross his handsome face, waiting for his response.

"I'd thought you the smartest woman ever created and you turn out to be nothing less than a complete simpleton. That will never do," he said sternly.

She was less than prepared when he yanked her onto her toes and ground her mound against his cock. His strong fingers flexed against her ass, forcing her hips into another roll that immediately had her insides clenching.

"What could possibly compel you to think I'd want you to change?" he whispered, lessening the pressure of their contact but continuing the sideways movement until she was short of breath.

"I would never want you to conform — to lose that spark of life that is definitively you, Lucy."

Lucinda wrapped her hands around his biceps, losing herself in his sparkling green gaze and the wealth of sensation he would always provide.

"I welcome your opinions," he said, brushing his cock head against her clit as he switched to an upward motion that had the embers of her banked desire suddenly flaring.

"I relish your stubbornness — your spiritedness. The last thing I wish from my old age is to be hampered with some simpering ninny."

He rocked their flesh together, his eyes never leaving hers and she nearly crested.

"Dear god, Gideon," she said, wrapping her legs around his waist and pulling herself into his arms. "Make me explode."

"I even adore your irreverent commands, which I shall endeavor to meet at every turn," he said, melding her pussy against his shaft until she dug her nails into his flesh and came, screaming in his arms. The tremors shook her and he held her all the while. "And I love the way you'll always come for me, my darling. Only me."

He turned his head and placed a light kiss on her shoulder before licking a path directly to her lips. "It would be easier for me to stop the rotation of this planet than to change you, Lucinda. It's quite fortunate that I have no desire to do so. Not now. Not ever, my love. Tell me you'll stay just as you are…and that you'll stay with me. I love you beyond reason, Lucy," he whispered huskily.

Lucinda floated back to earth, glorying in the fact that he desired her as much as she desired him — in an all-consuming manner that encompassed both body and mind and most definitely their very souls.

"We shall have to be very discreet," she said softly. "For an entire year."

"I can be quite stealthy, your ladyship," he replied, his deep voice riddled with mirth, offering up her own words from the previous day.

She cradled his face in her hands, gazing longingly into his gray-green eyes. "I wish to spend every remaining day in this life and those of eternity wrapped in your arms. I love you, as well, Gideon."

He gave her a smile so raw in adoration that Lucinda nearly wept. She blinked quickly and asked in a softly provocative voice, "After luncheon, might you consider the possibility of a journey to the lake?"

"I might," he said, kissing the tip of her nose.

"And while there, would you perhaps allow me to paint you?" she asked hopefully. How glorious it would be to immortalize every chiseled inch of his beloved form!

"Perhaps...if you allow me to sketch you in all manners the journal did not touch upon," he countered.

"There are more?" she asked incredulously.

"Many, many more," he said huskily.

"Might you enlighten me further, sir?" she asked with coy sincerity.

"Your ladyship," he said, inclining his head and offering her a wicked leer. "It shall be my pleasure."

MATING RUN

Tielle St. Clare

ജ

Trademarks Acknowledgement

ಖ

The author acknowledges the trademarked status and trademark owners of the following wordmarks mentioned in this work of fiction:

Jaguar: Jaguar Cars Limited

F-150: Ford Motor Company

Chapter One

ಬಂ

Cat reached for the front clasp of her bra, hesitating a moment too long.

"All of it. Off."

Her head snapped up at the command and she pierced the source with a deadly stare. The woman looking back wasn't intimidated. She was trying not to laugh.

Cat sighed and forced her fingers to undo the clasp. "I can't believe I let you bitches talk me into this."

Jen chuckled. "You made the bet."

Cat extended her glare to the other two women surrounding her, one of which was holding a terrycloth robe open, concealing Cat as she stripped.

"And you lost." The smug addition came from Mika.

The only one not exulting in Cat's predicament was Brandy. Cat wanted to believe it was because she felt guilty for making Cat do this, but though Brandy wasn't laughing, she hadn't backed down either.

Fuck, who would have thought the shy little bitch would be such a shark at cards?

During their twice monthly poker game, Cat and Brandy had run out of money and begun a high-stakes game of services. Cat had bet an oil change, tune-up and tire rotation. When Brandy couldn't offer anything to match that, she'd demanded Cat perform one task that she'd specify later.

Cat lost the hand and Brandy's demand was that Cat participate in the Pack's semiannual Mating Run.

"It's an archaic, barbaric, chauvinistic practice," Cat groused as she shoved her arms into the sleeves of her robe.

Once the terrycloth covered her body, she reached under and pulled down her panties.

All three women nodded.

Cat threw up her hands. "If you all agree, *why* am I doing this?"

"Because you need to get laid."

"Seriously."

"Oh yeah."

Cat folded her arms across her chest and glared at the three women she had considered her best friends until tonight. She was planning a change in associates. As soon as this dumb bet was finished. She wasn't a welsher.

"I don't see any of you getting all hot and heavy with anyone."

Mika and Jen had the grace to look embarrassed—or was that irritation?

Brandy spoke up. "Yes, but we don't get quite so crabby when we aren't having regular orgasms."

Mika and Jen contained their laughter for approximately four seconds before they lost it. Cat glared, feeling her cheeks warm. So she didn't do well when she wasn't having sex on a regular basis. If only she could find a man she could tolerate for more than a few hours of fucking.

Pack males were domineering, which, while intriguing in bed, sucked during everyday life. She wasn't about to become a full-time puppy breeder just because some male was good in bed. She had a job, a business, and damn it, she enjoyed it.

Too bad sex toys just didn't do it for her.

A voice resonated above the crowd, calling those participating in the Mating Run to come forward. In the past, werewolf packs had used Mating Runs to match the strongest males with the fastest, most cunning females. Nowadays, it was a social event. If a male caught a female, they fucked. But it didn't mean they were trapped together forever. Thank God, Cat thought, her wolf picking up the excitement.

"You'd better go," Jen said.

"Have fun," Mika smiled.

"Be safe," Brandy added. "We'll wait for you here."

"You will *not* wait for me." God, that would be mortifying, coming back covered in a male's scent.

Brandy nodded, looking slightly chagrined. *Good.*

"Fine," Jen sighed. "Call me when you get home. And we want details. Tomorrow, brunch at Murph's."

"Fine."

Tossing her bangs out of her eyes, Cat strode forward, joining the females gathering to one side. Her demeanor didn't exactly encourage conversation, so she wasn't surprised when the other women looked away. All except one. *She* smirked, standing there in the short, silky robe that covered perfect breasts and revealed long shapely legs. Candy—Alpha's daughter and prime bitch. Her eyes trailed up Cat's terrycloth-covered body.

"It's so sad. The poor little mechanic can't get fucked on a Friday night?"

Candy's crew turned around at their leader's snide remarks. They looked like carbon copies, even mimicking the sneer on Candy's face.

"Don't worry, Cat," Candy offered with mock sympathy. "I think there are a few old guys here that might catch you. If you run *really* slow."

Bitch. Cat pressed her lips together, preparing to verbalize the word, but a new sound stopped her.

"Cat."

She recognized the voice without turning around and groaned. Perfect. Just who she needed to witness her humiliation—Devon Sinster. And if Devon was here, Trejean wasn't far. Two gorgeous males she would have preferred didn't know about her participation in the Pack-sponsored orgy.

Forcing a breath into her tight lungs, Cat faced him. *God, he's beautiful.* Long black hair that hung to the middle of his back, blue eyes and shoulder muscles that just screamed for scratch marks—preferably created while he was over her, pumping his cock into her. His easy smile and sparkling eyes made him prime fantasy material.

Out of habit, Cat looked over Devon's shoulder to Trejean.

The only similarity between the two males was their dark hair. Trejean was taller and leaner than Devon, more serious. Cat was sure she'd never see him smile. Trejean's eyes were gray while Devon's were bright blue, usually sparkling with laughter. Where Devon flirted with every female he met, Trejean was reserved, almost aloof. But Cat sensed he was the stronger wolf, the more dangerous animal in a fight. More and more, *he'd* been the wolf filling her nighttime fantasies.

Betas from another Pack, they were staying in the area while Trejean, a carpenter, did some work for Cat's Alpha. She'd met them almost two months ago when they'd stopped by her garage for a tune-up on Devon's Jaguar. Since then, they'd visited almost daily, giving her plenty of ammunition for her lust-filled dreams.

Both men wore only shorts, leaving their chests bare. *Oh goodness, they're taking part in the Mating Run.* She gulped. Her pussy clenched and heat rushed through her core, her body instinctively preparing for sex. She squeezed her thighs together and hoped the heavy terrycloth covered the scent.

"Which way are you running?" Devon drawled, his eyes sparkling.

"Why?" Candy giggled. "Planning to *flee* in the other direction?"

Devon didn't react, ignoring Candy's question. He kept his eyes drilled into Cat's, waiting for an answer.

Her mind went blank. It was like he was flirting with her but that wasn't possible. Not when there were dozens of nubile, partially dressed females eager for his attention.

"Uh, I don't know," Cat stuttered.

One side of his mouth pulled up in a wicked half smile. He leaned down and breathed in her scent.

"Don't worry, baby. No matter where you run, we'll find you."

He straightened and stared into her eyes—the promise was clear.

He couldn't be serious, right? She so wasn't his type. Candy was his type—tall, blonde and gorgeous. Big tits, no body fat. Cat was medium height, her breasts were more modest sized and her legs were powerful, not sleek.

With a wink, Devon turned away, never acknowledging Candy's existence. Trejean approached. He too bent down and placed his nose inches from Cat's neck, inhaling deeply.

"Run east," he whispered so low no one else could hear, then stalked away.

Cat looked back at her friends. They hadn't heard the exchange, but they were watching, curious. She shrugged and headed to the far left of the females, determinedly ignoring the strange encounter. Males often flirted before a run, asking for directions or begging a female to run slow, but once the howl went up, it was every wolf for herself.

The scent of sex and desire filled the air, magnifying the ache in Cat's pussy. For the first time since agreeing to this stupid bet, she decided it might be a good idea. She needed to be fucked.

Long and hard. By a long and hard cock. And thick.

Her knees trembled and Cat felt her wolf coming through. The beast wanted free, to run and fuck. She pushed the animal back, but the wolf's hunger intensified Cat's. All she had to do was get on all fours, flip her tail up and they'd smell her cunt, know that she was eager and ready to be mounted.

Cat listened while the instructions were given. Any female caught by a male was expected to show her appreciation. The Pack didn't specify how that thanks was expressed but everyone assumed it would be sex.

The howl rang out. Cat ripped off the robe and ran. As she moved, she let the wolf take over. Her body changed, shifting, carrying her closer to the ground, her muscles stretching and bones cracking. It was done in a flash. And the forest raced by her, her paws devouring the distance.

Her wolf exalted in the solitary run, thrilling at the freedom. Heading deeper into the forest, she occasionally sensed a male's presence, but they never lingered, fading away amidst snarls and a random painful whimper.

Each time that occurred, her human mind was disappointed, but the sheer pleasure of running was almost as delicious as being fucked.

Well beyond the howls and barks of the Pack, her wolf continued the hard run. A male gray wolf appeared to her right, lunging at her, driving her to the left. Her wolf laughed silently as she danced out of the way. Though she wanted to be fucked, she wasn't going to make it easy. Any male had to prove himself worthy.

Cat burst into a clearing and skidded to a stop. The small opening between the trees was already occupied—by a big black wolf. She bared her teeth. The male snarled back. A shiver skipped down her spine—pleased with the strength of the male.

The tapping of paws interrupted their courtship and Cat spun around. The gray wolf leapt into the clearing.

Cat crept backward, opening the space for the two males, anticipating the fight. Though it was barbaric, she couldn't deny the thrill—that two strong males would be willing to fight for the right to fuck her. She crouched beneath the branches of a tree, waiting. The two wolves circled each other, not attacking, just feeling each other out. Cat watched, her human mind increasingly able to focus.

She gasped as she realized why. Her body was changing—without her consent. Her wolf was forcing the shift back into human form. Cat fought the transition. If she turned human now, it was tantamount to announcing that she conceded and would fuck one of the wolves.

And it was dangerous to be human in the presence of two fighting wolves.

Only they didn't fight. The black one padded over to the gray and they rubbed muzzles, friendly greetings that showed no aggression. Cat blinked, amazed. On a night like this—with the full moon and a Mating Run—the testosterone in the males should be rampant.

They began to shift, their muscles lengthening as they took their human forms. She recognized them before they finished changing.

Devon and Trejean.

Devon's hair fell across his face as he stood up. He looked at her between the long strands, his wicked blue eyes threatening, promising.

Trejean stood beside him, silently watching.

Her chest grew tight as if the invisible hand of fate squeezed it. Moisture rushed through her pussy as she looked at the two strong males. Their cocks grew long and thick as she stared. *Oh my.* Either male would fill her deliciously.

A brief moment of feminine modesty rose up, demanding she cover her breasts and hide her pussy, but she ignored the prompting.

Instead she lifted her chin and searched for the bravado that carried her through daily life.

"So," she asked. "What happens now?"

That half smile pulled Devon's lips again.

"Now? Now you get fucked."

Chapter Two

ഇ

Cat's skin came alive and heat invaded her pussy. She swallowed and squeezed her knees together, trying to conceal her body's reaction to Devon's blunt statement.

He took a deep breath and closed his eyes like he was sampling the finest perfume.

"Damn, she smells good."

Trejean agreed with a nod, licking his lips as if anticipating her taste. The simple action made her knees tremble and she struggled to stay upright. What had she gotten herself into?

Both males stepped forward and she held her breath, waiting to see who would stake their claim. Devon slid his hand around her hip and pulled her close, leaning down to rub his lips across hers. It couldn't really be called a kiss, more like a mouth to mouth caress. The fascinating sensation left her wanting more.

"Do you want to be fucked by us?" he asked against her lips.

She started to nod, captivated by the erotic touch...then his words penetrated.

"Us?" She stepped back. Devon let her retreat, but she didn't go far. She stared at him, then looked to Trejean, the sane half of the duo.

"If you stay, we're both going to have you."

"We'll *both* fuck you," Devon interjected. "Until you scream."

Her mind swirled, making her dizzy. Two strong, sexy male werewolves couldn't seriously want her. She'd have been thrilled with one of them. What was she supposed to do with two?

Fuck them. The intrusive voice of her wolf filled her head.

She couldn't do it. How could she do it? She caught sight of their cocks, both hard and breathtakingly thick. Damn, all she had to do was spread her legs and she'd get fucked. Her pussy throbbed, aching to be filled. She needed this, needed them.

Her brain frozen, she clung to the one point she could defend.

"I'm not much of a screamer," she said baldly.

And for the first time ever, she saw Trejean grin. He shook his head. "You shouldn't say things like that, honey. We might take it as a challenge."

Devon grinned. "And I do love a challenge. Before the night is over, baby, you're going to have at least one screaming orgasm."

Feeling cocky and a little sexy, she ran her tongue across her front teeth. "Just one?"

"You'll have others. At least one will make you scream," he vowed.

Panic raced through her brain screaming "what the hell are you doing?" but lust and need silenced the irritating bitch. No way she was going to miss out on this.

"So do I just lie down and spread my legs?" she asked, not quite able to let her defiance go.

Devon chuckled, reaching out and pulling her back into his embrace. "Not yet, baby. We've got things to do to your luscious body before we fuck you." He concluded the statement with a real kiss, covering her lips and sinking his tongue into her mouth. Cat moaned, grateful for his arm around her waist. God, he tasted good. She draped one languid hand over his shoulder, letting her fingertips trail through his soft hair.

Long, drugging moments later, he lifted his head.

Before she could protest, he shifted away, easing her into Trejean's arms. He held her close—not quite against him—and bent down, his lips moving across hers in a whispered version of Devon's overwhelming kiss. But Trejean's touch was no less powerful. He teased her, dipping his tongue between her lips, light caresses until she craved more.

"Trejean, please," she begged against his mouth. She expected to feel him smile, but he didn't. He meshed their lips together and drove his tongue inside. The heady taste exploded on her tongue—a different flavor that complemented Devon's precisely.

Heat singed her neck. Devon—his mouth, his tongue, his teeth, nipping and sampling. Every nerve in her body came alive, tingling, craving more contact.

Finally, desperate for breath, she drew back and gasped. Trejean's eyes glowed red. His lips were pressed forward, strained by the extension of his teeth.

Feminine power raced through her—that she could push him to the edge of his control. She reached up and slid her finger across his lips. He opened his mouth, sucking her inside, wrapping his tongue around her fingertip, biting down in a punishing nip. The delicate pain shot through her arm and into her pussy. And suddenly he was too far away. She moved closer, cuddling his hard cock between her legs, though she knew he had to crouch to get that alignment.

He tipped her chin up and took her lips in another conquering kiss. Sensation overwhelmed her. Trejean's lips on hers, his fingers stroking her breasts. Devon's mouth and hands, oh, his hands.

He cupped her ass in his palms and lifted, separating her cheeks and easing his erection into the tight space. He didn't try to enter her, just snuggled in tight. His teeth nipped her earlobe as if trying to get her attention.

"You've got a great ass, baby." He pumped his hips forward, pulsing his cock against her ass. Cat's claws extended and bit into Trejean's shoulders. "And I'm going to have it against me when I fuck you," Devon promised.

The low, hypnotic voice drew a whimper from deep inside her chest.

"But before he fucks you, I get to taste you," Trejean announced.

Breathless, she tossed her head back and stared boldly into Trejean's eyes.

"What did you do? Flip a coin to see who fucks me first?"

"Yes."

She had the strangest urge to cry. "And you lost."

Trejean shook his head. "I won."

"But—"

"He'll be the first inside you." He kissed her. "But your first orgasm with us belongs to me." He scraped his teeth along her neck, bent down and swirled his tongue around one tight nipple. Then placed a kiss on it as if promising more. "I've imagined hours with my face buried in your pussy." He knelt before her, kissing her stomach. "My tongue sliding into your sweet cunt. God, your scent has been driving me crazy." He finished with a moan that rumbled through Cat's pussy, tickling her clit. God, just a few words and she was ready to come.

Her knees trembled and she was grateful for Devon and Trejean's support.

Trejean's large hands replaced Devon's on her ass. The rough texture of his fingers sent a shiver down her spine that burrowed into her pussy like sparklers. Gentle and strong, he eased her forward. He scooped one hand beneath her thigh and lifted, draping her knee over his shoulder and opening her.

"Damn," he whispered, awe and worship filling his voice. Cat stared, not sure she could believe him. No male had ever looked at her like that. She rarely let any man go down on her. It was too intimate, too personal. And the thought of him staring at her pussy bound her muscles with tension.

Trejean massaged the tight muscle of her thigh. "Don't worry, honey," he soothed. "If you don't like it, I'll stop." With that promise, he eased her pussy lips open with his fingers. "So pretty," he murmured as he leaned forward. With one smooth stroke, he ran this tongue up the length of her slit. "Oh fuck," he moaned.

Pure sexual pleasure washed over his face. Like someone was sucking *his* cock, though she could see the hard rod between his legs and no one touched it. That pleasure was all from her taste. He watched her, his eyes glowing red, warning that his wolf was close to the surface.

His tongue flicked out, whipping against her clit. Her gasp echoed through the trees and came back to her. Devon pressed against her, warming her, holding her, skimming his hands up and down her sides.

"God, that looks sweet." He breathed the hot words into her ear. "I'll take my turn soon, baby. Have that delicious pussy cream all over my lips and tongue."

Her supporting leg wobbled as they worked together— one seducing her with words, the other with his tongue sliding across her wet flesh. Trejean lapped at her clit, teasing it to an almost unbearable ache, then retreating, not leaving her, but going deeper, licking and sucking her pussy lips. He slid one finger into her passage and moaned as her pussy gripped him. The powerful combination of penetration and his tongue rippled through her cunt until she was sure she'd come. One more touch and she'd break apart into a million jagged pieces. But Trejean backed off, as if he didn't want her climaxing too soon. He explored her flesh, finding those places that made her shiver and returning to them time and again, until she was vibrating.

She didn't know how much more she could take.

Finally, *finally*, he dipped his tongue into her opening and thrust, shallow and sharp. Oh, that was what she needed. To be fucked. God, it wasn't deep but it was precise, deliberately working that first sensitive inch.

Cat slammed her hand against a tree trunk and hung on, pumping her hips in time to Trejean's strokes. She was close. A few more and—

His head jerked back and he growled, turning and snarling across the clearing. His eyes were full red and the muscles in his back were taut and uneven. He was close to his change, more animal than human. Her mind fuzzy, Cat distantly recognized the approach of another wolf.

"I'm on it," Devon announced. He ran for the forest, changing as he moved, a full wolf by the time he reached the trees.

As if satisfied that the threat was neutralized, Trejean pulled her pussy back to his mouth. His tongue sank into her opening, fucking her again with sharp strokes, reasserting his claim to her cunt.

She moaned and grabbed his head, needing more.

"Tre, please."

He growled, but shifted, licking his way to her clit and easing his lips around the tight bundle. With slow rhythmic pulses, he sucked.

Cat thought her eyes would explode. She cried out and moved with his mouth, digging her claws into his shoulder, holding him in place, not willing to let him go until he'd given her what she needed.

He suckled at her clit, humming as he worked her. The delicate little vibrations combined with the suction and she couldn't contain it any longer. Bright little sparks shimmered through her pussy and spread into her limbs, pulling the last strength from her muscles.

The world spun around her and Cat realized she was tipping over. Her muscles wouldn't react even as she felt herself falling forward. Trejean jumped up, catching her, pulling her against his chest. Hating the weakness, but unable to stand, she let his strength support her as her muscles melted. Her whole body shook, her muscles trembling. And her mind was a mess. An orgasm was supposed to satisfy her body, not fuck up her head.

Trejean rubbed his lips on her neck, the scent of her pussy moving between them as he kissed and licked her skin. Cat sighed, content, satisfied, craving the heat flowing from his body.

His cock pushed against her stomach. Cat smiled and couldn't resist curling her hand around the thick shaft. Damn, he was big, long and thick. He'd stretch her perfectly. She moaned as her mind created the visceral images. She squeezed his cock harder and began to pump.

"Careful, honey," Trejean said. "Dev gets to fuck you first."

Captivated by his physical response, Cat ignored his warning and fluttered her fingers along his cock, loving the way his muscles tightened and clenched. A new rush of heat filled her sex. She stared at the cock in her hand, suddenly hungry, wanting to give him the same pleasure he'd given her.

"Did you draw straws to see who gets to fuck my mouth first?"

"No." His cock twitched in her hand.

"Hmm, someone likes the idea."

Knowing she had his full attention, she sank down. Pine needles bit into her skin as she knelt before him. Cat smiled. They'd promised her a screaming orgasm. Maybe she could return the favor.

She lifted both hands and wrapped her fingers around his erection, easing it toward her mouth. She didn't immediately open her lips. Instead she guided her fingers along the smooth flesh, sliding her hand between his legs and cupping his balls. A gentle squeeze made him moan and the sound reverberated inside her chest. God, he was delicious.

Kissing up the hard shaft, she flicked her tongue across the tip, capturing the drops of precum that dribbled from his hole. It was sweet against her lips and she wanted more. The urge to tease him was overwhelmed by the hunger to have him come down her throat, to feel him lose control and fill her mouth.

She opened her lips and let him push inside. Like everything else, he moved gently. He was so thick, she couldn't take much. She wrapped her hands around the base and worked them in opposition to her mouth, pumping slowly, letting those first sweet inches of cock slide in and out of her mouth. Trejean pressed his hips forward, nudging the back of her throat and almost gagging her.

As a punishment, she pulled back, sucking as she retreated, digging her fingers into Trejean's thighs, keeping him from thrusting back into her mouth. He struggled, but didn't overpower her. Instead of swallowing him again, she withdrew, swirling her tongue around the head, flicking the tip with her tongue.

Trejean groaned and she heard wood cracking. Not releasing her hold on his cock, she glanced up—and saw the tree branch in his hand. She grinned. And rewarded his hunger with another long slow lick from base to tip.

Alive to the night around her, she sensed Devon's return, the fresh scent of a strange wolf on his fur. He loped to where she knelt, sniffing the ground. As if satisfied that all was well, he changed, turning human and crouching beside them. His eyes wandered to Trejean's cock, pressed against her lips.

"Having fun?" he asked.

"Uh-huh." She licked Trejean's cock, then decided to tease him. She turned and offered her mouth for Devon's kiss. He accepted, plunging his tongue inside. Trejean's growl made her smile and pull back.

"Keep sucking him, baby," Devon teased. "But don't let him come too soon. Make him work for it."

"Bastard," Trejean grumbled, but the sound was followed by a moan. And a compulsive thrust of his hips. Cat smiled, thrilled that she was able to challenge his control.

Devon knelt behind her and placed his knees outside hers, his cock pressing against her back. His fingers skimmed across her hips and dipped into her slit.

"She's wet. I think she likes sucking you off, man. That's it, baby." He traced the insides of her thighs, spreading her pussy juice across her skin. "Feel his cock slide into your mouth. God, that looks sweet."

She moaned her agreement and pumped her mouth up and down. The intoxicating growls of Trejean's wolf echoed through the night.

"Honey, I'm going to come," he warned. "Unless you want me filling your throat, you'd better back off."

She hummed and took him deeper, wanting her prize, wanting to be the one to make him come.

His fingers slid into her hair, holding her in place as he thrust once and again. His shout echoed through the sky and cum poured out of his cock in fast heavy pulses. Cat swallowed quickly, wanting it all, thrilled by the almost sweet taste. She wanted more of that, more of him.

His cock slipped from her lips and he stumbled backward.

"Hmm, baby," Devon whispered, biting down on her earlobe. "You must have one wicked mouth." He looked up. "We're supposed to make *her* scream when she comes," he pointed out to Trejean.

Trejean leaned against the tree, his chest rising and falling in heavy pants. Pride bloomed in her chest. She'd done that. She'd made him come and now he could barely stand.

"You try her mouth and see if you can stay silent," Trejean muttered.

Devon just laughed. "Later. Now I'm coming between her legs."

Heat and moisture flooded her pussy and she started to turn.

"No. Don't move, baby. You're perfect. Just lean down." Devon's voice and cock pressed against her and she complied, following the sexual instructions. "On your elbows. Let me see that sweet ass tipped up." His palm skated across her thighs, hips, along the smooth skin of her ass. "So pretty. Since the first time you leaned over to look under the hood of my Jag, I've imagined bending you over any flat surface. Fucking you long and hard, riding you deep. Coming inside you."

His fingers slid into her pussy. "Oh, fuck, Tre, her cunt is hot. Come here." A second streak of fire moved across her ass as Trejean joined Devon, reaching between her legs. "Feel that liquid, man."

"Yeah."

She moaned and buried her face in her hands, embarrassed but unable to resist thrusting back against their fingers, needing something inside her.

Devon gripped her hips and held her in place, the blunt end of his cock tapping against her opening. "You ready to be fucked, baby? Ready to take some cock in this tight pussy?"

"Yes," she whispered.

"Sorry, baby, I didn't catch that." The laughter in his voice flipped a switch inside her. She glared over her right shoulder.

"Fuck me, damn it."

Devon grinned, and for one terrifying moment, she thought he might deny her. Might make her wait. Then his cock found her entrance and he thrust into her, filling her in one long push. There was no way to contain the cry. She dug her fingers into the soil and held on, holding steady as he crammed every inch into her. Oh God, she'd never had a cock this big before.

"Go easy, Dev. Don't hurt her."

Devon nudged his hips forward, as if wanting to go even deeper. "You hurting, baby?" She shook her head. Her heart pounded, her pussy ached from the sudden penetration—thank God she'd been so wet—but she didn't want him to stop. "No, she's not hurt," he whispered, scraping his fingers through her hair like he was petting her. "She's just so fucking tight." He slid out and immediately filled her again, slower, still deep, letting every inch of cock settle into her passage.

Devon retreated again, pulling out until only the very tip remained inside her. She wiggled her hips. Devon chuckled. "Hold on, baby, you're about to get fucked." That was her warning before he slammed into her. The heavy, stunning pressure was enough and she cried out, the orgasm ripping through her pussy. "Oh, fuck." Devon's groan shook the trees but he didn't stop pounding against her ass. "That was sweet, baby, damn sweet." He grunted and thrust into her. "But I want more. Want to hear you come again."

Yes. She didn't say the word out loud, couldn't find the power to make it audible. All her focus, her energy, was on the cock shuttling in and out of her pussy. Hard, long strokes that demanded she push against him, urging him ever deeper.

Animal growls filled the clearing and she knew Trejean was near, watching. The wolf's snarls rattled the night air and raced across her skin, a delicate touch that perfectly matched the hard, pounding fuck from Devon's cock.

Moaning, she pressed up on her toes, pushing her ass higher, harder into Devon's thrust. His growls harmonized with Trejean's and he moved faster, filling her, driving her until she lost all sense of anything except the cock fucking her. She heard whimpers and pleading and was pretty sure the sounds were coming from her, but she couldn't stop them.

Human warmth brushed along her side and she felt Trejean's arm slide around her waist, down to her aching pussy. His fingers slipped into her slit, surrounding her clit, stroking her softly. The touch was light and perfect and just what she needed.

Her cry echoed through her head, smothered by the ground beneath her as harsh almost painful shudders rippled through her pussy. Devon grunted and drilled into her one more time, hot streams of cum pumping into her as he slammed his hips against her ass, locking his cock inside her body.

Cat came back to herself, lying on the forest floor, aware that both males touched her, stroked her. Devon was still inside her.

"Damn, Tre, she's perfect." Devon's announcement was quiet, a private communication between the two men.

Trejean. She was supposed to fuck them both and she didn't think coming in her mouth was going to be enough. He was going to want to come in her pussy.

Her pussy twitched, her body responding to the memories of sucking Trejean's cock.

"Hmm, someone's waking up." Devon's teasing forced her eyes open. She stared into Trejean's intense gaze.

After long moments, Trejean nodded and announced, "We should go."

"But what about...?" *Fucking me.* That sounded too slutty to say aloud, so she kept it to herself.

Though his lips didn't move, his eyes glinted with a smile.

"I'm going to have you, honey, but I want to be more comfortable and I want to give your pussy a rest after Devon pounded himself into it." The serious tone returned. "I don't want you sore when I fuck you."

He rolled away and stood, disappearing from her restricted view.

Devon eased his cock out of her, moaning as if he hated to lose possession of her pussy. He kissed her cheek and scooped her up in his arms, lifting her in one strong motion. Sexual exhaustion chased her and her head flopped against his shoulder as he walked down a narrow trail she hadn't noticed before.

Where was he taking her? They were miles away from the Pack House where the run had started. Surely he didn't expect to carry her all the way back. She forced her head off his shoulder and looked around.

The trees abruptly disappeared around them and they stepped into a field. No, not a field. A backyard.

"Where are we?" she asked, trying to put the two-story house in context.

"This is where Tre and I have been living."

At the mention of Tre's name, she looked for the other man. Only he was back in wolf form, running ahead and circling behind, guarding them. The two males didn't take chances. Which made sense since this wasn't their Pack.

"So close?" she asked, her mind still tripping from recent orgasms.

Devon chuckled. "Why do you think we wanted you to run east? We'll go inside, clean up and eat." At the word, her stomach growled. "Yeah, you need to be fed."

She felt strange in his arms, like a romance heroine being carried across the moors to the castle.

"I can walk, you know."

"Yeah, but then I wouldn't get to feel your tits bounce against my chest every time I take a step."

The wolf loping beside them growled. Devon laughed.

"Your choice, man. You wanted to play guard dog, so I get to stare at the pretty nipples." He looked down. "Damn, your tits are perfect. I didn't spend any time sucking on them, but the night is young."

As if her nipples knew they were being discussed, they tightened and perked up, standing out to even more obvious points.

"Hmm, very nice." He lifted her and hunched over, licking one quick stroke across her nipple before straightening. "By the way, that didn't count."

She shook her head, trying to concentrate on what the hell Devon was saying. "What doesn't count?"

"That." He tipped his head behind them. "It didn't count as a screaming orgasm."

"But—" She'd made a noise.

"It was close," he admitted. "More than a gasp, but not quite a scream. And we want you screaming, baby."

Caught between laughter and dismay, she remained silent as he carried her into the house and up the stairs to the master bedroom. The room was bare, empty except for a king bed and a dresser. No pictures, almost no clutter…a clear sign these guys were only here temporarily.

He put her down on the floor of a large white bathroom. "Take a shower if you'd like. I'll leave a shirt for you to wear. Something of Tre's." His eyes twinkled. "He'll like that. I'll go downstairs and start breakfast." Devon covered her mouth in a long, leisurely kiss, more romance than sex, more affection than seduction. Finally, he lifted his lips and stared at her with a seriousness she wouldn't have expected from him. "Thank you for letting us have you."

Before her mind could process his words, he turned and walked away, closing the door behind him and leaving her alone.

Chapter Three

ဆ

Cat scraped her wet hair back and looked into the mirror. Her lips were pink and a little swollen and her eyes bright. Wow, she looked like a woman who'd been fucked by two gorgeous males.

Well, not two. Trejean hadn't technically fucked her. She tugged on the white shirt that was draped across the end of the bed and did up the buttons. Pans banged and crashed in the distance indicating that Devon was indeed cooking. Another shower was running somewhere.

That left Cat alone for a few more minutes. She didn't think the boys were going to leave her on her own for long. Kind of surprised they'd let her shower alone, but she had a feeling that had more to do with Trejean's desire to give her time to heal than any courtesy on Devon's part. Thankfully, werewolves, particularly female werewolves, healed quickly. A lingering soreness fluttered in her pussy, but it wouldn't be long before she was more than ready to fuck again.

She strolled into the hall, tempted to open doors to see who slept where, but didn't want to get caught snooping. Mika's house was a similar layout. Cat froze. Her friends. She was supposed to call.

She went downstairs, turning into the living room and finding the phone against the back wall. Feeling like she was breaking some rule, she lifted the handset quietly and dialed Jen's cell.

It answered on the first ring.

"Hello? Cat?" The panic in Jen's voice ignited a flurry of guilt in Cat's chest.

"Yeah."

"Where are you? Are you okay? Do you need a ride? Did—"

"Jen, I'm fine, and no, I don't need a ride. I, uh, got a little distracted and forgot to call."

Jen went from freaked to curious.

"Distracted? By who? What's his name and was he any good?"

Hot hands slid around her waist and pulled her hips back, pressing her barely covered ass against Trejean's cock.

"Uh—"

He slid his hand between her legs, cupping her mound and fluttering his fingers across her pussy lips.

"He was very good," Cat moaned, trying to focus on the conversation, but Trejean's fingers sliding into her opening were too tempting to ignore.

"Dev will appreciate that," Trejean whispered against her ear. He pushed one long finger into her pussy, holding her as he slowly thrust in and out. "Feeling better?"

"Oh yes."

"Cat?" Jen's voice barely registered.

"Hmm?"

"Are you okay?"

"Yeah. Oh." Trejean pulled back and added a second finger, thrusting into her pussy.

"So hot. Don't want to hurt you but I need to be inside you."

"Cat?" Jen's voice grew distant.

Trejean scraped his teeth across her neck, leaving delicious trails of heat. "Watching Devon's cock slide in and out of your cunt drove me insane," he whispered against her ear. "I loved watching you come but I wanted to be inside you. Fucking you. So wet and pink. You glistened in the moonlight." He rubbed his chin along her jaw. "Such a pretty, fuckable cunt." She moaned and rocked against his exploring fingers.

"Hell-oo, Cat, you still there?"

Cat blinked and looked at her hand. Why did she have the phone in her hand? Trejean pulled it from her grip and held it to her cheek.

"Tell your friend you'll call later," he said.

"I'll call you later, okay?" she repeated, her lips barely able to function. Trejean took the phone away and she placed her hands on the wall, bracing herself to move against his fingers.

"Fuck me," she moaned, pushing her ass back against Trejean's groin. He'd pulled on jeans so she couldn't feel his cock and she needed him. "Fuck me," she pleaded.

"Not yet, honey." He nipped at her shoulder again. "I want to be able to fully enjoy your pussy when I get inside." He continued to pump his fingers inside her, not hard or fast, just enough to bring her to the edge. His thumb slid over her clit, light, tiny circles that ripped her breath away. "That's it, honey. Come for me. Let me feel it. Spill on my fingers."

The wicked circles were too much and she cried out, collapsing against the wall as the climax radiated through her pussy.

Long moments later, she opened her eyes and stared at the wallpaper. Tiny cuts marked where her claws had bit into the decoration. She rubbed her fingers across the little tears, trying to smooth out the damage.

"Damn it, man, give the woman a rest."

Dazed, her body loose, she glanced over her shoulder. Devon stood in the doorway, a dishtowel in his hands, his bare chest gleaming in the low light. Trejean shifted, keeping his arms around her, still nuzzling her neck, like a kitten waiting to be petted.

"Now if you two are done *playing*, breakfast is ready."

Cat sat at the table—her physical hunger satisfied, her lust rebounding. The boys had been attentive through the meal, making sure she was well fed. Between bites, they'd kissed and stroked her, opening the shirt she wore and caressing her breasts. Their fingers wandered, dipping into her pussy until she learned to keep her legs apart, available to their touches.

Some portion of her mind still rebelled. She'd spent too many years on her own to allow easy access to her body. But they were so seductive, so compelling that Cat forced the concern aside and enjoyed their caresses. As one stroked her, the other ate. A bite was fed to her and they would switch, the other sliding his hand into her pussy or cupping her breast.

They worked in unison, keeping her aroused. At one point she'd actually been panting, ready to beg. They'd backed off, giving her time to recover, not letting her come.

If it hadn't been so erotic, it would have been quite irritating.

When they finished eating, both men stood and carried plates to the sink, dismissing her offers to help.

Cat relaxed in her chair, content to observe the two males. How many other women had they fucked like this? She wanted to ask but it seemed out of place. After all, this was just going to be one night and she wasn't going to mess it up with petty jealousies about unknown women from their past.

She toyed with her coffee cup, watching Trejean and Devon as they cleaned up. They stood close together, their movements synchronized, their bodies almost touching. There was an intimacy between them she hadn't noticed before.

"You two are lovers," she blurted out.

Trejean tensed. Devon didn't react, like he hadn't heard her, then slowly turned, leaning against the counter, putting his shoulder against Trejean's. Trejean hesitated before accepting Devon's weight.

"Does it bother you?" Devon said, his question daring her. Suddenly the power between the men changed and Devon took the lead. Without so much as moving, he revealed his readiness to protect Trejean. He would allow nothing to hurt the male.

Devon tipped his head to the side, waiting for her answer.

"I don't know. I've never thought about it. I don't know if I know any other gay werewolves."

"Not really gay," Trejean muttered. "We like women, obviously." His cheeks turned dark red. "I don't want to fuck any other male. Just Dev."

"We've only been lovers for six months." Devon chuckled and patted Trejean's arm. "He's still adapting. And while I might be interested in trying another male—" Trejean growled. "I've decided that's not an option."

Trejean glared, then turned his attention back to Cat. "Is this going to be a problem?"

Her chest rose and fell in long breaths, her body humming with a new desire.

"I want to see you kiss."

Trejean's eyes widened, just a fraction. Devon laughed. "A bit of a voyeur, eh?" He shrugged. "I don't mind." His sexy drawl was like a tongue whispering up her spine. "Watch all you want."

The strain in Trejean's shoulders gave her a moment's hesitation but then he cupped his hand around Devon's neck and pulled him forward. The two males moved together, mouths open, breath mixing before Trejean sealed their lips together. They moved with the confidence of lovers, their bodies shifting, matching each other's. She couldn't see but she knew their tongues were wrapped together.

God, it was the sexiest thing she'd ever seen. Even from across the room, it felt like they were touching her, stroking her. Trejean's hands slid around Devon's back and pulled him forward, their bodies pressing together, their cocks rubbing against each other.

Cat struggled to breathe. The scent of desire filled the room, capturing her. Trejean growled and bent down, placing his mouth on Devon's neck. The pleasure-pain on Devon's face made Cat's pussy melt. With a moan that was almost a gasp, Devon opened his eyes and met her stare. He released his grip on Trejean and held out his hand, inviting her to join them.

Part of her wanted to stay back, detached from the incredible power between them. The energy between the two males was more than sex. It was love and affection and sexual enough to make her pussy ache.

She couldn't resist.

She used the table to help her stand and took slow steps across the room. Trejean lifted his head as if he sensed her arrival. Devon's hand was still outstretched so she put her fingers into his palm, using his strength to keep her moving. He pulled her to him, his lips to hers. His kiss was gentle, welcoming. She groaned as he eased his tongue into her mouth. The faint taste of Trejean on Devon's lips sent new flutters through her sex.

Devon turned her so she faced Trejean. Trejean caught her against him and took over her mouth in a blazing, dominating kiss. Where Devon had been gentle, Trejean was aggressive, as if kissing Devon released the wolf inside him. Trejean palmed her ass and pressed her pussy to his erection. He ground against her, silently begging to be inside her.

Devon scraped his teeth across Trejean's shoulder. Trejean growled and dragged Devon back to his mouth, demanding his submission with that powerful kiss.

Hunger surrounded them, encompassing her, drawing her deeper. She stretched up on her toes and danced kisses down Trejean's throat, savoring the way he shifted, inviting her to taste him. But it wasn't enough. She wanted to mark him, the way Devon had. Her teeth extended and she bit down, not too deep, scoring his flesh.

Trejean groaned and stared at her, his eyes glowing again.

"Dev —" He glanced at Devon. "She bit me."

What? She wasn't allowed to bite?

Devon smiled. "Nice."

Trejean kissed her lips, slow and sexual.

"Let's take this upstairs," Devon interrupted. When both Trejean and Cat looked at him, he shrugged. "We're on a deadline. We promised her a screaming orgasm before the night is over."

Trejean flashed another rare smile but he nodded. "Let's go, honey. It's time for you to get fucked."

"Again."

Chapter Four

ஐ

Trejean and Devon led the way upstairs. They walked ahead of her, entering the big bedroom first, leaving Cat to make the conscious decision to follow. This was it. If she walked into the room, there was no way she could later claim "moment of passion". As Tre had said, if she walked inside, she was going to get fucked.

She hesitated at the door. Barely recognizable tension zipped between them and Cat realized they were testing her. To see if she would run.

It was decision time and she knew she had no choice. Her body, her hunger wouldn't allow any other response.

With both men watching, she stepped inside. She tugged one side of her shirt and shrugged, letting the material slide down. Her nipples were tight and peaked, aching from the attention during their meal.

Even though she'd been naked with these men for most of the night, this felt different. She felt vulnerable and shaky.

"Come here, honey," Trejean called.

Her knees trembled but she managed to cross the room, straight into Trejean's embrace. He met her, bending down and cupping her face, whispering kisses across her mouth, silently asking for access. She opened her lips, wanting to taste him. As he dipped his tongue into her mouth, Devon kissed her neck, cuddling her backside.

She moaned, loving the heat radiating from these two males. Her nipples tingled as she rubbed against Trejean's chest. She wrapped her hand behind her neck, holding Devon. The different atmosphere surrounded them, sensual and loving. Trejean moved his mouth to her throat, licking and tasting. Devon's hand slid from her hip to Trejean's, resting on the bare skin above his jeans.

Cat watched, fascinated by the male hand stroking masculine muscles.

"Does that bother you?" Devon whispered into her ear.

"No."

"You like it."

Cat nodded.

"Good girl. Hmm, I know how much you like to have your pussy licked." He kissed her shoulder. "And I've been dying to taste you all night." He dropped to his knees and spun her around, turning her hips and causing the rest of her to follow. She yelped, grabbing Trejean to keep her balance.

"Damn it, Dev, she's not a rag doll," Trejean groused.

"Sorry." Though he didn't sound it at all. She glanced at Trejean, sharing a "what can you do?" smile. The urge to grin disappeared as Devon plunged his tongue into her opening. This was no leisurely exploration like Trejean. There was no seduction, no teasing. Devon was intent on fucking her with his tongue, fast, hard thrusts that made her pussy crave deeper penetrations. He tongue-fucked her until she rocked against him, then he drew back, focusing his attention on her clit, licking and sucking until her knees trembled.

Trejean's strength supported her body. He cupped her breasts in his palms, rubbing slow circles, his breath growing deeper as he watched Devon's mouth between her legs.

She placed one hand on Devon's head, holding him in position as she rolled her clit against his tongue. She wrapped her other arm behind her, drawing Trejean around to her mouth, needing the powerful thrust of his tongue between her lips. It was perfect.

Drunk on sensation, it barely registered when Devon stopped. He stood and put his hand on Trejean's neck.

"Want a taste?" he asked, whispering the final word against Trejean's mouth. The sight of those two men, lips together, sharing her pussy cream, almost made her come.

Trejean lapped at Devon's mouth, kissing, licking, their tongues twisting together. "Damn, her cunt tastes sweet on you," he murmured.

"Tre, she needs some cock."

She shivered, her clit tingling from Devon's tongue and watching her males kiss. Trejean eased his fingers into her slit.

"Yeah."

"Let's get you on the bed," Devon offered, guiding her out of Trejean's embrace and lifting her onto the center of the mattress. He positioned her legs, keeping them spread. The visible lust blazing from the two men crushed any insecurity she might have. Devon stepped back and ran his hand down the front of Trejean's jeans, massaging his cock through the thick material. "Look at that pretty cunt, man."

Trejean nodded and licked his lips, enjoying the remaining traces of her pussy juices. Devon undid the front of Trejean's jeans and shoved them down, just enough to free his cock. Both males groaned as Devon wrapped his fingers around Trejean's shaft and began to pump.

"Want him nice and hard for you, baby," Devon explained, though his laughing eyes said he was enjoying it as much as she was. Amazed at the ease with which Devon touched his lover, she couldn't look away. It was beautiful. She panted as Devon stroked Trejean's cock, wanting that rod inside her.

"Please." The plea tripped from her mouth without conscious thought.

Devon smiled, a wicked grin that gave her no comfort.

"Greedy little thing, isn't she?" Devon released Trejean's cock and climbed onto the bed, lying beside her, his jeans teasing her sensitive skin. "You'd almost think she hasn't had cock in days, instead of hours." He rubbed a finger across her lips. "She's had cock fucking this sexy mouth." He skipped his hand down her stomach, dipping into her pussy. "And cock in this pretty cunt, but still she wants more."

She arched her hips up, trying to drive his fingers into her pussy.

"Hold on, baby. Tre's getting naked. Then he'll have you."

The end of the bed dipped as Trejean climbed up. She raised her head. From this angle, his cock looked huge. She remembered struggling to get it into her mouth.

Trejean crawled forward, moving over her, kissing her stomach, her breasts, finally her mouth. "Do you want me inside you, honey?" he asked against her lips.

"Yes, Tre, fuck me."

His tongue delved into her mouth, meeting hers for a fleeting moment before he drew back, shifting so he knelt on the bed, his thighs under hers, her knees bent and draped over his arms. He lifted her hips, pulling her close.

Devon's reached out took Trejean's cock in his fist, guiding it forward until the head slid into her opening.

"Fuck her, Tre. Push all that cock inside her." Devon's command sent a shiver through Cat. She tensed, prepared for a hard thrust.

But Trejean held back, entering her in slow inches, allowing her pussy to adjust. Still, every time he went deeper, the wet flesh of her pussy strained to take him. It wasn't exactly painful but the burning made her gasp.

Devon watched, his fingers roaming across her breasts, her stomach, his gaze locked on Trejean's cock sliding into her.

He moaned and put his lips to her ear.

"Wait until he fucks your ass." He licked the skin below her earlobe. "That's a slow, wild fuck."

The picture filled her head and Cat moaned. Her hips pulsed up, sending Trejean deeper.

"That's it, Tre. Give it all to her."

Devon's words seemed to reach Trejean. He drove his cock into her, sinking the final inches in deep and hard. He held himself still, watching her, looking for some sign that she wasn't ready for this, but Cat reached out, gripping his hand, telling him silently that she wanted this, needed this. That seemed to release him. He pulled back and plunged inside, filling her, just like she'd imagined he would—hard and fast. All the power in his body moved into hers, overwhelming her pussy.

Devon rolled off the bed and yanked off his jeans, as if he couldn't stand not being naked. His cock freed, he curled his fingers around the thick shaft and pumped, watching as Trejean fucked her.

She licked her lips and watched Devon manipulate himself, suddenly hungry to feel his cock sliding across her lips. "Devon." The word was quiet but both men heard it. Devon's eyes flared red. He climbed onto the bed, kneeling beside her head, holding his cock above her parted lips. Her breath heated his skin as he pushed the head into her mouth.

He fucked her mouth, gently, never going too deep or too fast. Working the first few inches of cock between her lips in time with Trejean's cock in her pussy.

Her senses took control. She sucked the cock in her mouth, humming and moaning around his shaft. The sounds seemed to drive Trejean on. He lifted her hips even higher, pushing her almost to her shoulders, his cock steady and strong in her pussy, teasing her clit every time he filled her.

Devon pulled his cock away and Cat chased it, unwilling to lose the delicious taste.

"Not this time, baby," he said. "I'll come in your mouth soon, but now, we want to hear you scream." He dropped down beside her and latched his mouth on her sensitized breast, sucking the nipple hard while his other hand pinched the other tight peak. With perfect precision, he sucked and pulled as Trejean fucked her.

She lost track of time, lost the ability to think. They controlled her body—loving it, fucking it, until the world exploded. She tipped her head back and freed the scream that clawed the inside of her throat. Matching male groans erupted and hot cum pulsed into her pussy—and onto her stomach.

She opened her eyes, barely aware of what she was seeing. Devon pumped his cock, spilling his cum across her stomach.

The moment passed into another and they all began to breathe again. Devon collapsed onto bed beside Cat. Trejean eased his cock from inside her and crawled up behind her. His hand slid across her stomach, rubbing Devon's semen into her skin, pushing his hand down until he cupped her pussy, claiming her.

A satisfied silence settled on the room and her eyes drifted closed. It would be easy to get used to sleeping between these warm, masculine bodies.

"That counted," Devon muttered, snuggling closer, sliding his knee between her legs and draping his arm around her waist and Trejean's back.

"Counted?" she asked.

"As a screaming orgasm. That one counted."

She grinned without opening her eyes. *Oh yeah.*

Chapter Five

ဢ

"I really have to go." Cat tried to put conviction into her voice but the words came out lazy and drawling. She looked down at the gorgeous man whispering delicate kisses around her nipple and saw he didn't believe her any more than she did. It would have helped if she could have moved, to physically show that she really did need to leave, but her body just wouldn't respond.

Her muscles were lax, long loose masses of languid, sexually satisfied flesh. Her mind wasn't functioning well either. Only parts seemed to be working and none of them at the same time.

She licked her lips, aware that time was passing but unable to get too stressed about it.

"I have to run home and put on clothes." The almost random words tumbled from her lips. In her disjointed thoughts she knew this was truth, but for that moment she couldn't remember why she'd ever want to get dressed again.

Tre rubbed his mouth in a slow circle just below her nipple, not really a kiss, just warm lips caressing her skin, light and seductive, as if he knew how sensitive her nipples were and knew any pressure would be painful.

"We'll drive you," he murmured, his tongue lapping a long delicious path around the curve of her breast. "Give you clothes."

She closed her eyes and smiled, imagining her friends' reaction if she showed up at the restaurant wearing Tre's shirt.

He lifted his head a fraction. "I like my clothes on your body." The possessive tone created two reactions in her — a delicious shiver down her spine and a knock of warning in her brain. But the hazy awareness of the warning disappeared as Tre's lips bent in a half smile before returning to their worship of her flesh. Cat reached out and ran the backs of her fingers along his cheek, the smooth touch of freshly shaved skin caressing her as she touched him.

"I think when we get home, she should never wear anything but our clothes." Devon fell onto the flat space beside Cat, his landing jolting both of them. Tre looked up and glared but quickly returned his attention to her breast. "Or go naked." Devon smoothed his hand across her stomach. "Naked is always good."

That got a response from Tre. He nodded and breathed a hot "yeah" across her skin.

Cat felt her smile widen, just thinking about being home and naked with these boys. The knocking in her brain grew louder. Devon leaned over and began licking and caressing her other breast and the sound faded into insignificance.

Neither man seemed to be touching her with the intention of fucking—they just wanted to touch her. And Cat was content, the sexual hunger she usually felt so completely satisfied she didn't know if she'd ever want to fuck again. She mentally scoffed as soon as the words appeared in her brain. She was definitely going to want sex again, and soon. Probably with these two guys. They seemed willing to see her again, as if the night had been as amazing for them as it had for her.

They'd touched, licked and fucked her until she'd come three more times. Only two of those counted as "screaming orgasms", Devon had declared, but Cat was sure the only reason she hadn't screamed that third time was because Devon's cock had filled her mouth, turning her scream into a long deep moan. Which, if she recalled correctly, had inspired Devon's orgasm and he'd come into her mouth.

She licked her lips at the memory. Even though her body wasn't up to any more fucking, maybe she could... Clock chimes sounded in the hall, penetrating Cat's brain as she counted. Eight, nine, ten.

She moaned. "I really do have to go. I'm supposed to meet my friends at ten thirty." Trejean lifted his head, turning and kissing the fingers that had been stroking his cheek.

Devon pushed himself up on his elbow and grinned down at her. "Are you going to talk about us?" He trailed his fingers down, guiding one finger into the top of her slit and sliding away. Laughter filled his voice. "Tell your friends about the incredible fucking you received from your two gorgeous, sexy mates."

The knocking in her brain turned to full on pounding, but again she ignored the sound, not wanting anything to interrupt her last few minutes with these guys. There might be more sex in the future but there was no guarantee of that.

"I might mention your names," Cat smiled back at Devon. He winked and she couldn't resist touching him as well, rubbing her palm against his chest. "Now one of you has to move so I can get up." There, that had conviction and just a hint of command. Trejean sighed and rolled over, freeing her leg that had been cuddled between his but not releasing her hand.

"What time are you done?" he asked, biting the tip of one finger as if punishing her for making him move. She could have told him her body already thought it was punishment enough to be separated from him, but his ego didn't need the boost.

"Probably about one thirty." Their brunches tended to be long, champagne-soaked affairs, followed by afternoon naps and lots of groaning about never drinking that much in the middle of the day again. And Cat had a feeling that her report from the night before—even knowing she wasn't going to provide details—would draw the meal out even longer.

Trejean looked at Devon and they both nodded.

"We'll start packing here." Trejean gave her fingers another kiss. "Dev and I don't have much so we'll be able to finish by two and come help you."

Devon chewed on the inside edge of his lower lip. "I should rent a truck."

"Yeah, we're going to need it," Trejean agreed. Both men shifted away, climbing off the big bed, their thoughts seeming to have turned from her and into whatever plans they were making. Trejean tugged on a pair of jeans and buttoned the fly. "How much of your garage are you going to want to bring?" he asked, looking at her.

Distracted for a moment by the sight of his ass disappearing beneath the denim, she blinked and shook her head. "My garage?"

"Yeah, will some of that equipment stay and you'll sell it? Or do you think you'll take it all?"

"Take it all where?" she asked.

Devon grinned and she noticed that he'd pulled on jeans as well. That left her as the only naked one in the group. "We live about two hours northeast. You know that."

She did know that. She'd spent a lot of time talking to Tre and Devon about their Pack and their home.

"But I live here," she pointed out, her chest tight.

"Our Pack is there—" Trejean jabbed his thumb over his shoulder in some vague direction of north. "And as our mate, you'll be with us."

Pack? Mate?

Oh my God, they think I'm going with them. They think I'm their mate.

It was like a door had burst open in her brain and her usually cautious self burst through screaming "finally"!

She shook her head, grabbing the sheet and pulling it up around her body. "I'm not moving. I'm not going anywhere." There, now that she'd said it, it felt more real. "I'm not..." She took a deep breath and looked at both males. "I'm not your mate."

Trejean's eyes squinted down. "Excuse me?"

"I'm not your mate."

"What do you call last night?"

"Sex. Lots of sex. Lots of really good sex, but still just sex."

Trejean growled and red flared in his eyes, warning his wolf didn't like the direction of the conversation.

"Last night was a Mating Run," Trejean said.

Devon nodded "We caught you. We get to keep you."

Cat shook her head. "No one believes that anymore."

"We do," Trejean announced.

Cat rolled over and climbed off the opposite side of the bed, putting some distance between her and her lovers.

Once standing, she clutched the sheet to her front and stared at the two men, their determination and intent blazing through their eyes.

"This is insane. You can't truly expect me to just pack up my life and move hundreds of miles away based on the random results of what was nothing more than a run through the forest."

Trejean straightened to his full height and folded his arms across his chest. "There was nothing *random* about it. The only reason we were there last night was because you were running."

That little revelation made her heart flip.

Devon nodded. "Sure. Or we would have just kidnapped you."

Her mouth dropped open and she stared at Devon.

"Kidnapped me?"

"Well, we had to do something," he answered. He also seemed to pull himself up, as if his physical strength would make his actions justified. "Our Alpha's been pretty sympathetic to our cause, but he wants us home and that meant mating you."

Her mind was firing again, but not on all cylinders because he seemed to be implying that they—Trejean and Devon—were here because of her. That couldn't be.

"But you're here working. For my Alpha." The words just fell from her mouth, her mind too busy trying to process information to actually control them.

Devon smirked and shook his head. "Tre finished that job weeks ago." He strolled around the end of the bed. Cat's mind warned her to back up, to not let him get close enough to touch. They were dangerous when they touched her. But her body was too attuned to them, even after just one night, and her muscles wouldn't respond. "By then," Devon murmured, his voice low, like he was calming a nervous animal. "We'd met you and we knew we couldn't leave without you."

She blinked and stared at him. His blue eyes sparkled with lust and laughter and some emotion that she didn't want to acknowledge. He lifted her hand and carried it to his mouth.

"Don't you like us, baby?" he asked against the back of her fingers, his lips curling into a smile. "We like you."

"That's just sex," she protested feebly.

"It's more than just sex," Trejean growled, his voice right next to her. Somehow he'd managed to cross the bed and appear at her other side without her notice.

She opened her mouth to speak, hoping her mind would come up with an appropriate response. Her heart pounded and her pussy fluttered. She hadn't even allowed herself to consider that this might be more than one night of great sex. It was too much to take in, that these males, gorgeous, strong and powerful, would want to be with her, exclusively, forever. Werewolf mates didn't stray.

She looked into Trejean's eyes and saw the same terrifying emotions that Devon's had revealed.

"I—I..." She couldn't come up with anything.

"Listen." Devon's reasonable voice interrupted her failed attempt at thinking. A soft smile formed on her lips. Somehow she never would have thought of Devon as "reasonable" before this. Flirtatious, sexy, yes. But not reasonable. "We've clearly surprised you with this." He waited for her nod. "We should have been more obvious in our intentions." This time he looked over at Trejean, who hesitated, then nodded, though she could see he wasn't happy about admitting that. Devon faced Cat, still holding her hand. "Give us the chance to show you."

"Show me?"

He kissed her fingers. "Show you that it's not just about sex. It's about love."

"Love?" The word barely slipped out of her tight throat. Were they saying that they actually loved her? It wasn't possible. These things didn't happen to women like her. She turned her gaze to Trejean, knowing his stare would give her the truth. That scary, undefined emotion blazed in his eyes.

"Love," Trejean said, drawing close, wrapping his arm around her back. "And sex. More." He pulled her up to his mouth for a slow, sexual kiss that made her melt. "We want it all, Cat."

"So, give us a chance," Devon said again. "Give us a chance to court you."

Cat drew back as far as Trejean's grip would let her and looked at Devon.

"Court me?"

* * * * *

"Court you?"

Cat nodded and took a sip of champagne. All three women stared back at her, in various states of shock and surprise. Their eyes wide and barely blinking since Cat had started her story.

Jen sighed. "Wow."

"Amazing," Mika murmured.

Brandy nodded. "What does he mean 'court you'?"
Cat shook her head.
"I have no idea."

Chapter Six

ଗ

Four months later, Cat knew exactly what he meant.

Four months of relentless, seductive pursuit—complete with flowers and candy, even a few love poems.

Though after the first box of chocolates, when Cat had complained that she didn't want her ass to expand exponentially, Tre and Devon had given her a few pieces of candy at a time. They'd also spent several hours showing her how much they appreciated her ass just the way it was.

She squirmed in her seat and pressed her knees together, trying to ease the ache the memory created in her sex. Three nights without Trejean gave her hunger an extra boost. Not that Devon hadn't done his best to fill the void. She moaned and gripped the steering wheel, forcing the sensations in her pussy to cool off for just a few minutes.

Trejean had spent the last three days—and nights—with his Alpha. More and more they were being called home to deal with Pack business and Cat knew it wouldn't be long before Caine demanded they return permanently.

And she'd be going with them.

It only made sense. They were Betas in their Pack and would have no standing in hers. And after four months, she knew Devon and Trejean weren't the typical dominant male werewolves bent on keeping their female pregnant and tied to the house.

As part of their "courtship", Trejean had built shelves for her garage and bought her a new lightweight socket wrench set that fit her hands perfectly. Devon had taken those new shelves and organized her tools, keeping everything tidy and in place.

And then there was the sex. Trejean hadn't been kidding when he'd said they wanted it all. Her body had been used and loved in ways she hadn't ever imagined. Almost nightly, they explored and fucked, loving her. And when that got to be too much, Tre and Dev would just cuddle her, watch TV, hold her while she slept.

She turned into her driveway, pulling up behind Devon's Jag. Trejean's F-150 was parked in the road. She smiled as she climbed out of her car. Tre had made good time. With a little extra lilt in her step, she skipped into the house.

Knowing that Trejean and Devon were waiting for her, she'd left her coveralls at the garage and driven home in a pair of tiny shorts and a spaghetti-strapped tank top.

She stepped inside. Both males were in the house. She leaned her head back, preparing to call out a greeting. A long, low groan stopped the sound in her throat. She froze. She recognized that sound. She'd heard it enough in the past four months. That was the noise Trejean made moments before he was about to come.

Setting her keys quietly on the entryway table, she moved silently toward the stairs, avoiding the step that creaked and skimming her way to the top landing. She listened, then followed the distinctly sexual noises—skin on skin, low breathy moans—to her bedroom. The door was open and Cat peered around the edge.

A tight band squeezed her chest. Trejean stood, leaning against the wall, his jeans down around his thighs, one hand braced on the dresser, the other buried in Devon's hair. Devon's lips were stretched around Trejean's cock as he worked the thick length in and out, holding Trejean still with a firm hand on his hip.

"Oh, Dev, please. Let me come."

Devon moaned around the cock in his mouth and Cat could see the noise shiver through Trejean's body. He tipped his head back, his eyes squeezed shut, and thrust his hips forward, an erratic pulse between Devon's lips. She watched, breathless, unable to look away. Devon's cheeks hollowed out as he sucked with each retreat. He sank his mouth around Trejean's cock and held it steady. Though Cat couldn't see what he was doing, she could see the impact. An almost painful tension ripped through Trejean's body. He cried out, his hips jerking as he came down Devon's throat.

Long moments passed as the tension slid from Trejean's body, his muscles going lax. Devon slipped Trejean's softening cock from his mouth and stood, moving close, their bodies coming together with the ease of longtime lovers. Devon tipped his head back, offering his mouth, and Trejean accepted, sealing their lips in a strong, loving kiss.

Cat felt her chest rising and falling in long breaths. She knew they were lovers, but rarely got the chance to watch them together. When it was the three of them, both males focused on her.

"Damn, Dev," Trejean groaned. "Cat's going to be home in a few minutes."

Devon chuckled and wrapped his fingers around Trejean's cock. "Don't worry. You won't have any trouble getting it up for her." He pumped his fist up and down Tre's shaft, quickly drawing back to hardness. "Oh yeah."

She must have made a noise because Trejean's head snapped up. Devon was a little slower to react and she got the impression he'd known she was there all along. Trejean actually blushed, embarrassed to be caught with his pants down. Devon tilted his head to the side and stared at her, his eyes glittering with challenge. This was a test. Devon had known she would walk in on them and was testing her reaction.

A slow inhalation calmed her nerves and she strolled into the room, letting her hips swing, knowing that would capture the boys' attention. She drew close, inching her way next to Trejean, pressing up on her tiptoes and kissing him lightly on the lips. "Welcome back," she said with a smile. She turned her head. Devon's eyes still flashed. She leaned forward and placed her mouth against his, her tongue licking his lips. A hint of Trejean's cum lingered on his mouth. "Hmm, you taste good."

The challenge in his stare turned to a twinkle. "So do you."

"And you really must show me that trick toward the end." She grinned. "I've never seen him come like that."

Devon smiled. "I'd be happy to, baby." He winked. "You can practice on me."

The momentary strain between them faded and she leaned her back against Trejean. She reached out and began unbuttoning Devon's shirt. He was the only one still fully dressed. She slid the shirt off his shoulder and he pressed closer, sliding his knee between her thighs. Masculine strength and heat surrounded her and supported her.

She tipped her head back. "That one counted, you know."

"What did?" Trejean asked.

"When I came in the room. That definitely counted as a screaming orgasm."

Devon laughed and slid his hand around Trejean's back, pinching his ass. Tre flinched but didn't deny it.

"How's Caine?" she asked casually. She'd met their Alpha a few times and found him a surly but attractive man.

Trejean bent down and placed a kiss on her shoulder. "He wants to know when we're getting our asses home and bringing our sexy little mate with us." Devon's lips skimmed across her collarbone.

She smiled, looking up so Trejean could see her eyes. "How about two weeks?"

Devon lifted his head. Trejean's eyes got wide. "Two weeks?"

"Sure," she said, enjoying their surprise. It wasn't often that she was able to put her lovers back on their heels. "The sale of the garage will close in about ten days and we have to have a garage sale and get rid of some of this stuff before we move."

"You've been planning this," Trejean accused. His fingers gripped her tank top, holding her in place when she would have moved away.

"Well, of course." She stepped back, forcing Trejean to either let go of her or...rip. The cotton material split at the side seam and the two straps snapped, leaving Trejean with a handful of cloth and Cat topless. The heat that flared in both men's stares was familiar now, but no less exciting. After four months of lust and love with these men, she'd lost any insecurities about her body. She took another step away. "I knew that once I was ready to move, you'd be pressing for it to happen immediately, so I did a few things ahead of time." She knew Trejean's impatience to get home. Home. Yeah, that sounded right. Wherever these two men were would be her home.

"I've been planning for it as well," Trejean announced smugly. He folded his arms across his chest. "I bought the piece of land right next to ours so you can build your garage there."

Cat smiled and her heart did a little flip. It was strange. Four months ago, she would have thought he'd done it to keep her close, control her. Now she knew the truth. Trejean didn't like the fact that she worked alone in the garage. He wanted her close to protect her, but he wouldn't interfere with her work.

"And since I work from home," Devon interjected. "I can watch your ass."

She looked at Trejean. "Why do I think when he says 'watch my ass', he's not meaning it in the sense of 'watch my back'?"

"No, he means he'll literally be watching your ass."

Devon shrugged. "Hey, a guy's got to have some entertainment."

Cat and Trejean shared a sympathetic glance. Devon was a pain sometimes but they both loved him.

She shook her head and turned around. There was a lot to do and two weeks wasn't much time, but first, she needed a few hours with her men. She hooked her fingers into the sides of her shorts and panties and slowly inched the fabric down, baring her ass. Bending forward, she slid the silky material down her calves until it formed a shiny blue pile around her ankles.

She didn't have to turn around to know they were both watching.

With a flip of her head, she straightened and walked to the bed, spinning around and hitching her hips on to the high mattress. Devon straightened, his fingers hooked on the front of his jeans, his tongue slowly licking his lips. Trejean had kicked his jeans off and stood there in nothing but his shirt, his cock hard in his grip.

She deliberately separated her knees, baring her wet pussy to their sight, knowing they could scent her arousal from across the room.

"We really should start packing," she said with a sigh, letting one finger trail slowly between her wet folds.

Trejean growled. And stepped forward, reaching for her. Cat rolled out of the way, turning until she knelt in the middle of the bed.

"Uh-uh," she said, shaking her head.

"You're not going to let us have you?" Trejean demanded, that stern look tweaking his eyes.

"Maybe. But I think first..." She let her words trail away and looked over at Devon. He waited apart, often content to watch her and Trejean before joining in. "I think it's Devon's turn to scream." The suggestion seemed to please Trejean. He nodded.

"I think you're right."

Devon sighed dramatically, rolling his eyes. "I don't think it will work." His lips curled into a smile. "I'm not much of a screamer."

Cat grinned. She'd said those words before and they came back to haunt her on a regular basis.

"He's challenging us, Tre," she said. Trejean nodded. He tipped his head toward the bed.

"Get your ass over there."

Devon hesitated for a moment then pushed away from the wall, sauntered across the room and threw himself on the bed. "Do your worst."

Two hours later, the bed a mess, their bodies sweaty and gasping for breath, Cat and Trejean dropped down on either side of Devon. He'd made them work for it. Finally, Trejean had fucked his ass while Cat had sucked his cock, both drawing out the process until Devon couldn't contain the shout of pleasure.

Devon struggled to lift his head. He looked at Cat and then at Trejean.

"Okay," he panted. "That one counted."

"Damn straight," Cat replied. That took all her energy. She collapsed on the mattress and whispered, "Love you."

Two drowsy "love you" replies came across the bed. It wasn't the most romantic of declarations, but exhausted and sweaty from good sex, it was the perfect whisper to guide her into sleep.

MIDNIGHT SEDUCTION

Dawn Halliday

જી

Chapter One

ᔆᓿ

Invite me in.

At that moment, if Kyle Turner had a way to bend a person's will, he would have done it. He stood facing the woman who rocked his world. But she didn't believe it, and he didn't know how to show her what he felt. Especially when she would hardly let him touch her.

Her face aglow beneath her porch light, she smiled at him, and the earth moved beneath his feet. *Goddamn.*

Lacey Marceaux. The woman he'd had his eye on for five years, since the day she stepped into the downtown San Francisco offices of Turner & Hannover Construction as their project manager. His partner Tom had hired her—without a doubt the best thing Tom ever did for the company.

"Thanks for tonight." Her voice ricocheted through him and he sucked in a breath.

Did she comprehend what she did to him? *No,* he thought wryly, glancing at her downcast eyes. *Clearly not.*

In the two months they'd been together, kissing was as far as she allowed it to go. As soon as he tried to take it a step further, she'd push him away. She took him from amazing, intense arousal to frigid rejection, again and again. Physically, it was like having ice-cold water thrown directly on his aching cock. Even worse was what she was doing to his head. Each time she did it, it was like she twisted a red-hot poker deeper into his gut. He wasn't used to rejection. But the way he felt about Lacey—damn, what could he do? He didn't want to walk away from what they had.

"I had a good time." He took a step toward the door and paused meaningfully.

Either she didn't get the hint or…something. He couldn't figure her out. He knew he was the first man she'd dated since her divorce was finalized, but if she kept it up much longer, he was going to go insane with wanting her.

Screw it. He slipped his arm around her waist and gently pulled her close. Bending down, he let his lips hover over hers, drinking in her sweet scent, belatedly realizing she would be able to feel his rock-hard erection pressing against her belly.

See how I want you, Lacey?

She gasped, stiffened, but before she could pull away, he captured her mouth with his.

Not good enough. She froze in his arms, her lips tightened, and she flattened her palms against his chest in an attempt to push him back. Kyle wrenched away, clenching his teeth to subdue the groan of frustration rising in his throat.

He couldn't do this anymore. This wasn't going to work, damn it.

Before he could slam his fist through the plastered siding beside her front door, she grabbed his hand. "Come over for dinner tomorrow."

Tangling his fingers with hers and squeezing tightly, he perused her body through narrowed eyes. He slowly scanned her curving, flared hips, her abundant cleavage, the clavicle where he could see her frantic pulse. His gaze wandered upward, to her auburn hair fanned out over her shoulders, her heart-shaped face, the pink lips he'd just kissed, and the blue-green eyes that had instantly entranced him five years ago.

She'd just—*literally*—pushed him away and now she was asking him to dinner. His pride told him to sneer at her and stalk off. But he couldn't. A big part of him was undeniably connected to this woman, and he wanted to make it work, as impossible as it seemed at this moment.

Tomorrow they'd be alone, in her house. He'd talk to her—get to the bottom of what was going on with her, with them.

Maybe he'd have to end it. His gut clenched. Damn, he didn't want that, didn't want it at all.

But he wasn't made to be celibate. He couldn't live like this.

Tomorrow he'd make love to her...or break this whole thing off.

* * * * *

Lacey switched off her bedside lamp and burrowed under her thick down comforter. Though more than an hour had passed since she'd thrust Kyle away at her door, she was still sick about it, annoyed as hell at herself for doing that to him.

Kyle...the man of her dreams. Successful, intelligent, and though he had moved to San Francisco six years ago from Texas, he was a Southern gentleman through and through. With his shiny black hair, dark eyes and toned, muscular body, he defined the image of tall, dark and handsome with just a touch of the exotic passed to him, no doubt, by his Native American roots. And he wanted to take her to bed, if the rigid length of him against her belly earlier had been any indication.

Who was she fooling? They'd been dating for two months and he'd wanted her since the first time they'd gone out. She'd wanted him, too, with every cell in her body. They'd kissed several times, but tonight the suddenness of it had thrown her completely off guard, and her instant reaction was to push him away.

Kyle was her boss but treated her more like an equal partner. First a partner, then a friend. And now he wanted more.

So what the *hell* was wrong with her?

She was blowing this. Spoiling the potential for a great relationship.

The worst of it was, she knew exactly what was wrong but she didn't know what to do about it. Frank, her ex-husband, had done this to her. He'd ruined her for any other man.

Thinking of their last argument, Lacey squeezed her eyes shut, blinking back tears.

"How could anyone be with you and not want to be with someone else?" he'd said on their four-year anniversary after she'd found kinky love letters addressed to him from a mysterious woman named "V". "You're a cold fish in bed, Lace. The worst lay I've ever had. How can you blame me for sleeping with Vanessa? At least she takes part in the experience."

Lacey turned to her side, hugging her knees to her chest under the weight of the comforter, staring at the shape of her dresser in the dim light.

She should let Kyle off the hook. Having known him for five years and seen some of the women he dated, she had no doubt that he was a virile man. By the look in his eyes she could tell that she was torturing him, that he was already dissatisfied by her frigidity. And where would this lead? It could only get worse. She would eventually force herself to give in to him, but she'd be terrified of not pleasing him, of disappointing him. She'd end up lying there paralyzed by fear, doing nothing, barely a participant.

Frank was right.

The last time she'd had sex was over a year ago, before things had gotten really bad between her and her husband. She remembered every moment of that encounter in sordid detail. It wasn't good for her. Apparently it hadn't been good for Frank either.

She didn't want to disappoint Kyle. She cared for him too much. But how could she avoid it?

Over and over, Lacey rehashed that argument with Frank, then tonight's awkward episode with Kyle. What could she do? How could she fix this, make everything right?

Kyle had always been understanding in the past. Maybe she could tell him how difficult all this was for her, to somehow try to make him understand.

No. No way. What would she say? "Sorry I won't let you touch me, Kyle, but you know, I'm really a cold fish in bed—a really unsatisfying lay, or so I've been told. I don't want to you to be disappointed with my lackluster sexual skills, so it's best we keep to kissing. For the rest of our lives. Will that work for you?"

She shook her head. He'd run for the hills. Immediately.

The only answer was to break up with him. She was being selfish, leading him on. But if she were honest with herself, this could never work. She was damaged goods.

She'd call it off tomorrow. Over dinner.

Heartbroken, Lacey cried herself to sleep.

* * * * *

"Kyle," she sighed.

He stood beside the bed, caressing her, soothing her over the top of the comforter before slipping in beside her and wrapping his arms around her torso.

Relax, baby. It's just a dream. It was Kyle's voice, his words and ideas forming in her mind without being spoken.

A dream? The word seemed to pour through her body like thick syrup, loosening all her knots of tension and leaving her muscles warm and languid.

"Mmm." It was so easy to just let go. Pleasantly aroused, she melted against him, her back to his chest, and his erection rubbed against the crack of her ass. It felt so good—better than she'd imagined.

If this was a dream, she didn't want to wake up.

"Mmm," she murmured again, wiggling her behind against the silky hardness of his cock. He was rigid and thick, just as he'd been earlier when he kissed her in the hall.

That's right, Lacey. Can you feel how much I want you?

Strong, masculine fingers curled over her thigh, setting off little fluttery explosions in her pussy.

You need this, don't you? You need someone to touch you. Fingertips glided up and down the outside of her leg.

If this was a dream, it was the most vivid she'd ever had. "Yes," she whispered.

Don't hold back, Lacey.

"I don't want to." She didn't. Oh God, how she wanted to let it go, to stop worrying about failing and just…just make love. Make love to someone—Kyle—with complete joy and abandon.

She never had…perhaps never would.

Let go.

"I can't."

The fingers continued up the side of her body, so gentle. Soothing and soft.

Yes. Yes, you can.

"Noo…" She didn't sound very convincing. He was wreaking havoc on her mind, just by touching her. But she wasn't freezing up. Why wasn't she cringing away from him? She could feel every contour of him against her back. Her nipples puckered and ached for his touch as his fingers trailed past her rib cage.

One palm curled over her breast. *Beautiful, Lacey. You're beautiful. I want you…I want to see all of you, make love to you. Don't hide yourself.*

She had nothing to lose in the here and now, in her dream. This dream Kyle would never be disappointed in her, would never reject her. As a woman who'd gone too long without, who buried herself under fear of failure, she needed this.

Kicking the comforter away, she rolled to her back. His big body covered hers, straddling her. She could only see the most basic curves and contours of his face—her room was much darker than normal.

Exhaling harshly, he cupped her breasts in both hands and flicked her nipples with his thumbs. *You have a body made for fucking.*

She gasped at his words. Nobody had ever talked dirty to her before. Her pussy tensed and then throbbed once, hard enough to make her squirm.

He pinned her down, one big hand on each arm, and his breath whispered in her ear. *You like that, don't you?*

"No."

A laugh rumbled through her mind. *Don't lie to me, Lacey.*

She wasn't lying. Was she?

She didn't know what it was, but something about his voice, his touch, the way he talked to her and held her, was making her pussy tight and hot. Her clit ached for his touch, for release. All of these were foreign, utterly shocking sensations.

You're wet, aren't you? Your pussy is dripping, weeping for my cock. Ready for me to pump into you, to ride you hard.

Unable to move, Lacey whimpered. Against her will, her hips undulated, and she felt the head of his cock stroking the curls at the juncture of her thighs. She opened her legs to encourage him.

His lips moved down the column of her throat, across her collarbone, featherlight, a contrast to the steel grip of his hands on her arms.

Just be, Lacey. Just be you, and you'll make me crazy. My cock can't wait to be inside you. It's dripping, begging me to fuck you just as much as your cunt begs to be fucked.

She groaned aloud. The dirty words swept through her mind like a flash flood, erasing what remained of her inhibitions. This would be what it felt like if she didn't have so many hang-ups about getting close to a man.

"Then do it!" she whispered from between clenched teeth.

Teeth grazed her nipple, and that laugh resonated again in her mind.

No. Not when you're asleep.

Something within her deflated. If she couldn't even control her own erotic dream, then how the hell was she supposed to control her life?

But I can give you a gift. Something to make you remember…and want more.

His tongue stroked a hot trail down her belly as his hands traveled down to her thighs again, pushing them wide open.

In her imagination, in her dream, she didn't have to worry that Kyle would think this was disgusting, or unnatural. Frank did. Frank thought oral sex was only meant to be performed on men.

Frank isn't here.

No, he wasn't. Kyle was here, or the dream version of him. She didn't know what the real Kyle thought, but in her dream, he wanted to explore every part of her with his tongue.

I do, Lacey. I do. Every pretty pink fold. I'm going to fuck you with my fingers, open you, suck you…

"Oh God," she whispered.

His mouth closed over her. She nearly leapt off the bed. Tingles of sensation ran through her, coalescing in her center, in her very core. A ball of sizzling electric heat seared through her.

He parted her folds with his fingers. *Goddamn, you're gorgeous. Your clit is swollen, taut, peeking out from its cave.*

After one flick of his tongue, she cried out. Then he was sucking her, making long, deep draws on her clit.

No man had ever made her come before, not even a dream man. But this one, with a few strokes of his tongue, was close. So, so close.

A fingertip stroked downward from her clit and circled the opening of her vagina. *You're so wet. So plump and wet and ready. So fucking beautiful.*

Lacey shuddered.

The finger moved lower, circling the tight ring of her anus.

Your ass is so tight, Lacey. You're a virgin there, aren't you? I want to fuck it, make you come while I'm deep in your ass.

Lacey whimpered out loud, spreading her legs wider.

That's right.

His tongue followed the trail his finger had just taken. All the way down, making her shudder and jerk with need, then back up to her clit again. He cupped her ass with one hand, and his thumb rotated around her hole in a soothing motion. The fingers of his other hand moved from her thigh to her pussy, circling gently.

If he didn't do something soon, she was going to scream. Or implode. Or…wake up and finish it herself.

Are you ready, Lacey?

Ready? Was he crazy? "Please," she murmured. "Please, please, please…make me come." *Make me feel normal again.*

I will.

All at once, he pushed his thumb past the tight ring of muscle. He thrust two fingers into her pussy. And he lowered his mouth over her clit.

He fucked her in her ass, in her cunt, and he sucked her brutally.

After two thrusts, the waves began. Hard, rolling pulses that Lacey felt deep in her ass and in her pussy, resonating up through her body, to her chest. Her body convulsed on the sheets.

He rode the waves along with her, expertly drawing out the orgasm until she was a gasping mass of flesh, completely relaxed, her muscles no more useful to move any part of her body than jelly.

She was done for, sated, completely and utterly finished.

His body moved over hers once again, and she thought fleetingly of his long, hard, unsatisfied cock.

That had to be the most gorgeous thing I've ever seen.

She couldn't answer. Gorgeous? Damn, but it had certainly *felt* gorgeous. And the feel of his cock on her thigh sent a frisson of renewed heat through her.

Show me. When you're awake. I need you, Lacey.

"Hmm..." she murmured. "Yes..."

Don't let him win, Lacey. Don't let Frank win. Don't let him destroy you.

"I don't want him to win..."

Until next time, Lacey.

"Next time?" Her eyes snapped open. "Wait..."

She reached up to him. She'd wrap her legs around his body and hold him close, let him seek his own satisfaction.

But she grasped at thin air. It was too late. He was already gone.

Chapter Two

ഔ

They walked barefoot along Ocean Beach in the cool summertime dusk of San Francisco. Lacey's sandals dangled from the fingertips of one hand and her other hand was entwined in Kyle's. Fog was rolling in, obscuring the sunset, and waves boiled offshore, whitecaps picking up in the breeze.

Last night's dream had given her a new determination to make this work. She'd awakened this morning refreshed and ready to try. The Kyle of her dreams was right—she couldn't let how Frank had treated her destroy her life.

"Thanks again for dinner. Best steak I've had in years." Kyle slid her a sexy sideways glance. "And mashed potatoes too. White gravy…Texas toast. How did you know those were my favorite foods?"

If only the true way to a man's heart was through his stomach. She knew better.

She squeezed his hand. "I'm a Southern girl at heart, you know. I was raised here in the city but I was born in West Texas." A grin quirked up the corner of her lips. "I think pleasing Texas men is in my blood."

She didn't miss the catch in his breath and she bit her lip and glanced away.

His voice was gruff. "Is that so?"

She could shoot herself for allowing such a blatant sexual innuendo emerge from her mouth. Ever since that strange, vivid, erotic dream last night, it seemed she hadn't been able to stop herself.

Since he'd walked through her door tonight, she couldn't stop thinking about sex. Sex with Kyle. What would it be like to let go, to have those strong arms wrapped around her, pinning her down? What it would be like to feel his cock stretching her mouth, to press her tongue over its head, to feel it pulse as he came deep in her throat? What it would feel like to have him explore her as intimately as he had in her dreams last night...?

She gave herself a mental shake and pressed her thighs together to ease the ache between them.

After what had happened between them before he'd left last night, the evening had started off a little awkward. But as it always was with them, they had fallen into an easy camaraderie. Their dinner talk had ranged from light to serious, but it was always comfortable and open. She'd never felt so in tune with a man before.

Well—except in one way. The way that mattered most. She curled her toes into the cool sand. If only she could be as *physically* open and comfortable with the real Kyle as she was with the Kyle of her dreams.

But dreams couldn't hurt her, couldn't destroy her. The real man she cared about so much, the man standing beside her, could.

What would it be like to let him make love to her on the beach, hidden in a cove but still at risk for being caught? An image of her on hands and knees pressed into the cool sand flashed through her mind. Kyle taking her from behind, holding her hips tightly, slamming into her...

"Oh God," she murmured.

Alarm flared in his eyes as he glanced down at her. "What's wrong?"

Drawing in a deep breath, she forced herself to meet his gaze and smile. "Nothing."

Just then, the wind whipped, blowing her skirt up Marilyn Monroe-style. With a small squeal of dismay, she tore her hand from his grasp and smoothed it back down.

The gleam in his eye sent shivers down her spine, and she knew he'd seen the lacy white thong she'd worn tonight.

She glanced to the end of the beach. About a half a mile away, it ended at the rocky cliff leading to the legendary Cliff House.

She turned to him. "Let's race."

He arched his eyebrows. "Oh yeah?"

"Mm-hmm. To the Cliff House. Loser buys dessert."

A grin tilted his lips, so sexy it made her mouth water for a completely different kind of dessert.

"You're on."

She motioned to her skirt. "I have a handicap, you know."

"Chickening out already?"

"Absolutely not," she huffed, already secretly gloating. He knew she jogged for exercise on occasion, but she'd never told him about her past as a track star. She was a middle-distance runner, and in her senior year of high school, she'd won the California state championship for the eight-hundred-meter run. That was twelve years ago, but she'd never lost the touch.

She thrust her sandals at him. "I have the long skirt, so you can carry the shoes."

"Deal."

Drawing a line with her big toe in the sand, she said, "Prepare for the ultimate defeat."

He laughed. "Taking this a little seriously, aren't you?"

"Not at all," she said, crossing her arms over her chest.

"I won't be easy on you, you know," he said, taking a step toward her. He infused a suggestive rumble into his voice, making it clear that his meaning extended beyond this race. Far beyond.

She cocked an eyebrow at him, keeping her arms crossed. "You'd better not, because I won't be easy on you either. Only wimps let women win."

"Oh, really?"

"That's right. Give me all you've got. I can take it." She carefully placed her toes on the edge of the starting line, fisted her skirt in one hand so it wouldn't fly into her face, then sidled a glance at him. "Ready?"

"Say the word."

"Get set...go!"

And she was flying. Never did she feel such ultimate freedom as when she ran. Her toes hardly seemed to touch the ground. She was light and carefree, like a bird.

Kyle was beside her, keeping up with her stride for stride, moving seemingly as effortlessly as she did. She felt her jaw drop in wonderment, and then noticed that in her distraction, he'd moved a pace ahead of her.

Oh no.

Now that was unacceptable. With a burst of energy, she moved beside him again.

Kicking up sand in his wake, he lunged ahead.

They moved like this until they were a couple of hundred meters from the rocks. Over and over, Kyle pulled ahead and Lacey caught up to run alongside him only to have him pull away again. She was growing frustrated and winded, which irritated her even more. She couldn't believe he could keep up.

The last fifty meters. Only a few more seconds to go. Lacey gave it all she had. She caught up to him again, then drew ahead. Elation filled her, that rush of euphoria she always experienced when winning a race.

But it was short-lived. He sprinted past her, arriving at the rocks just a second ahead of her.

She collapsed on the sand, frustrated beyond reason, dragging air into her exhausted lungs.

Kyle glanced at his watch, looking barely winded. "Less than two and a half minutes. Not too bad."

She flopped back into the sand, groaning. "You didn't tell me you were a runner. I mean, I knew you played basketball, but I didn't know — "

"It never came up in the office." He lay on his back beside her. "I used to run track in high school, but it's just a hobby now. Running really helps with my speed and endurance on the court, though, so I've kept it up."

She was silent for long moments, catching her breath.

He turned toward her, propping his head in his hands. "You're fast."

Her only response was a noncommittal puff of air from her lips.

"You mad?"

"No," she lied.

He grinned and touched her nose with his forefinger. "You're mad that I beat you, that I didn't warn you in advance that I could run."

She shrugged.

"But," he continued, his dark eyes twinkling, "you did the same thing. You were trying to trick me, show me up."

He was right, damn him. She looked up at the sky, lips pursed, refusing to answer.

He tweaked her nose. "Showoff."

She snorted. "I could say the same about you."

Moving a little closer to her, he chuckled and ran the rough pad of his thumb across her cheek. "That was fun."

She imagined running beside him again, not in a race but as partners, for exercise and companionship. She'd always liked to run with people, and hadn't had a running partner since she'd first moved in with Frank years ago. A smile threatened to quirk its way onto her lips but she held it back. "Would have been more fun if I'd beaten you."

"Maybe I should've let you win after all."

"Humph."

He tucked a loose strand of hair behind her ear. "I like you like this, all breathless and pink."

"You don't even have a runner's body," she groused, still gazing at the twilight sky. She still couldn't believe he'd actually passed her. He was too big to be a runner.

"Neither do you," he pointed out. Though she wasn't looking at him, she felt his gaze traveling down her body.

She clenched her teeth together to hold back the automatic defensive response. She'd always been large-boned and taller than her teammates, yet she'd worked her butt off for four years of high school and eventually surpassed them all.

"Thank God," he added. "I like you just the way you are."

Something warm flushed through her body. She turned to meet his gaze and saw the sincerity in his eyes. "I like you too."

He cupped her cheek in his big palm and moved even closer. He was going to kiss her. She didn't tense up like she had last night and in the past. She didn't care if other people on the beach were watching them. Right here, right now, it was what she needed.

His lips were warm, soft, but at the same time firm with the command of a man with confidence, a man who knew exactly how to take what he wanted.

And right now she wanted to give. She slipped her arm around his waist, feeling the muscles ripple in his side, and tugged him closer.

The world narrowed down to the singular sensation of Kyle's lips on hers. Every nerve in Lacey's body was attuned to it, the soft friction, the slow dance of their tongues, the hot, driven, all-male taste of him. Sensation skittered through her, making her tremble, making her toes curl. He sucked her lower lip between his teeth, and she gasped, holding him even tighter.

His lips trailed down to her ear, and he whispered, "I want you, Lacey."

The words, spoken low and filled with promise, made her weak with lust. She wanted him too. Madly, passionately.

Tonight.

She squeezed her eyes shut, fighting the sudden onslaught of fear.

I can do this. I can satisfy him. I can resolve this awful tension that has built between us.

Yet a part of her cringed and cowered, preventing her from responding to him.

Staying close, he rolled over to his back. The air was growing cooler as twilight faded into night, and she cuddled closer to his warm body to ward off the chill. One star already heralded the dark. "I wonder what star that is," she murmured.

"I don't know. Vega, maybe?"

"I dreamed of you last night," she said on impulse. Then regretted it as the heat of a blush crept across her cheeks.

"Did you?"

"Yes."

"What happened in your dream?"

The muscles in her shoulders tensed. Why had she opened her big mouth? "I...you...we..." How on earth could she explain the dream without sounding like a sex-crazed lunatic? "Can't remember," she finished lamely.

A fingertip brushed over her lips. "I dreamed about you too."

"Oh yeah?"

"Yeah."

She glanced at him, and by the intense look in his eyes, she guessed his dream had been as erotic as hers.

They lay there for several minutes longer in silence. Finally, she sat up and hugged her knees to her chest. "I guess I owe you dessert."

Kyle watched her glance up toward the Cliff House Restaurant. Not exactly the kind of dessert he had in mind.

"How about we go back to your place and have dessert there? I saw some ice cream in the freezer. Looked good." He fought himself to keep from touching her, from lifting her skirt and taking her right here on the beach, in public.

But it wasn't worth it to risk spending their first night of intimacy in jail. The preferable way to end this night would be by falling asleep with her naked limbs wrapped around him. Damn, he couldn't wait to get her back to the house. Everything about her — her flushed cheeks, her tentative smiles, the way he felt so comfortable, so natural around her — spoke to him on a cellular level. This woman was made for him.

She felt the same way, if her body language was any indication.

"Okay," she said softly.

They walked the several blocks back to her house in silence. He was burning for her. Memories of the erotic dream he'd had last night didn't help. He'd fucked her with his fingers, sucked her clit his mouth. He'd awakened to the most painful hard-on of his life, frustrated as hell that he hadn't fully taken her in his dream and found his release then. He'd grimly rejected the urge to finish himself off — instead he'd thought of her all day, waiting, anticipating.

Tonight was the night. He thought she might finally be ready. And he was raring to go. Every moment today had been driven by his lust for her. He could still taste her from his dream — her sweet musky flavor had lingered on his tongue all day.

Now with the real Lacey standing beside him, every step she took, every time the wind blew her hair, every time her eyes lit up when she glanced at him—everything she did stoked the flames. Each time she touched him, his blood traveled south and his cock hardened to steel.

They reached her house and went inside. She walked directly to the kitchen, calling out, "Rocky road or mint chocolate chip?"

He followed her, leaning against the doorway of her kitchen with his arms crossed over his chest, watching her backside wiggle as she stuck her head in the freezer.

Lacey à la mode. He grinned. He'd be sure to try that sometime. Not tonight, though. Not for their first time. Tonight was special.

"Rocky road."

She scooped rocky road into two bowls and set them on the little round table in the corner of her kitchen. He slid into the chair across from hers and watched her spoon a bit of the ice cream into her mouth.

The way her mouth puckered from the cold, the way her tongue flicked out to lick a drop off her lip, spoke of pure sex. Kyle imagined her flicking her tongue over his cock like that, running it up and down his shaft. It would be cold from the ice cream. His dick responded eagerly to the thought, tightening uncomfortably in his jeans.

She smiled at him, arching a curious eyebrow. "What?"

"Nothing." He bent his head and focused on the ice cream for a few moments. When he glanced up again, she was staring at him intently.

Enough of this. He pushed the bowl away and rose. She stood at the same time.

"I'm going to kiss you, Lacey," he said, some part of him understanding that she needed to be warned of his imminent touch.

131

"Okay." Her voice was no more than a breath of sound, and the white, tender column of her throat moved as she swallowed.

Holding her by the shoulders, he took her throat first, pressing his lips to the delicate, pale skin. He kissed upward to her jaw, finally reaching her lips, cooled by the ice cream, and chocolate-sweet. She was more relaxed than she'd been since they started dating. Her hands explored him greedily, shifting the material of his shirt over his body. He drew back, pulled it over his head and tossed it away. She sucked in a breath, and for the first time ever, reached for him and leaned forward to initiate a kiss.

Without taking his lips from hers, he reached behind her butt and picked her up.

She instantly stiffened.

"Relax, baby," he murmured against her skin. "I've got you. Wrap your legs around me."

Clasping her hands around his neck and her legs around his waist, she squeezed her eyes shut and made a visible effort to release her tense muscles.

"That's it," he crooned. He strode through the open door of her bedroom and, using his foot, shut it behind them.

He laid her gently on the bed and she sank into the puffy down comforter.

As much as he wanted to tear off his jeans, lift her legs over his shoulders and fuck her into oblivion, he knew he couldn't. He wanted to make this good for her, make it memorable, make it last. So instead of stripping down, he kicked off his shoes and joined her on the bed.

He touched his fingers to her cheek. He loved her face, the shape of it, her smooth, soft skin. Most of all, he loved looking at her eyes, that enticing mixture of intelligence, spirit and vulnerability. Not for the first time, he wondered what her ex-husband had done to her. She'd been engaged when she started working at Turner and Hannover, and from the moment of her marriage until now, what little self-esteem she had seemed to slowly melt away. What had that asshole said to her?

Kyle had never liked Frank Jones. When he first met the man, he'd rationalized it away as jealousy because he subconsciously wanted Lacey for himself. But now he knew his gut dislike had been well-founded. He felt like hunting the son of a bitch down and demanding to know how he had hurt Lacey. And then make him pay for it.

Kyle gazed at her face. He didn't want her to hurt, he wanted her to smile. He wanted her to be happy, to feel confident about her amazing, voluptuous body. He wanted to see her in rapture, watch the expression on her face as she came.

"The way you look at me..." Her voice trembled, then dropped altogether.

"How's that?"

"It's almost...predatory. Like you could devour me."

I could. He didn't break the lock of his gaze on her eyes. "Does it bother you?"

"It makes me tingle all the way down to my toes," she said breathlessly.

He kissed her, tenderly, sweetly, pressing his body against hers. Inch by inch, he tugged up her skirt, exposing her thighs, which he explored with his fingertips, then her hips, round, smooth and feminine. She was soft everywhere he was hard. It brought out a strange feeling deep within him, a desire to keep her safe, to protect her.

He'd never felt this way about anyone before. The realization knocked the wind from his lungs.

Ever so slowly, he tugged up her shirt, exposing the lacy bra that matched her panties. He moved his hands over it, reverently palming each of her plump breasts, skimming her nipples through the lace. She gasped and arched into his hands.

"Beautiful Lacey," he murmured. He lowered his mouth to her nipple, sucking it through the lace. Tugging aside the bra, he drew circles around her areola with his tongue, watching in fascination as her nipple darkened and puckered. Then he unclipped the front closure of the bra and exposed her entire chest, giving the same treatment to her other breast.

She panted, twisting in pleasure at the slow, torturous treatment. Torturous for him, anyway. His cock was in agony, throbbing to be inside her. He could feel every beat of his heart as his dick pulsed against the inside of his jeans. He wasn't going to last much longer, and goddammit, he didn't want to come inside his pants.

He moved one hand down to palm her pussy. As soon as he slid his fingers beneath the drenched silk of her panties, she went completely rigid.

No!

"Lacey, baby—" He'd gone too fast, damn it. He moved his hand away, skimming over her belly, but she twisted away.

Shit, he couldn't take a rejection. Not tonight, not now.

"I can't do this!" she gasped.

"Yes you can," he said through the alarm bells blaring in his head. "Lacey, just relax and—"

"I can't." She sat up, pulled her shirt down and tugged her skirt to her ankles. She wouldn't meet his gaze.

Slowly, Kyle moved to the edge of the bed, fighting the raging of his mind and body. After a long moment, he asked, "Why not?" His voice sounded stiff and unnatural.

She looked away from him, at the other wall. "It's just...I can't, I can't..."

"Lacey, you need to tell me why. I can't help you if you won't tell me."

Drawing in a ragged breath, she spoke softly. "I don't need your help. This just isn't me, okay? I can't be the woman you need me to be."

But she was. They'd had such a great night tonight. He'd never felt like he could be himself around any other woman but her.

She was everything he wanted. He flexed his stiff fingers. Why the *fuck* was this happening? God, she'd been so wet— her cunt was drenched with her arousal. Why was she doing this?

"It's been two months."

"I know."

He spoke quietly, trying not to let his frustration infuse his voice. "Every time I try to get close to you, you freeze and push me away. If I'm moving too fast for you, just tell me. I'm okay with slowing things down."

He hadn't wanted to admit that, but it was true. For her, he'd slow things down if he had to. Only for her.

"No." She shook her head helplessly. "It's my fault. We've been having a good time together, but I've been leading you on. This isn't...this isn't *me*. I'm sorry."

"I think it is you, Lacey."

"No," she said with finality. She turned to look at him, her eyes blazing green. "No, it isn't. I'm sorry."

"Are you saying it isn't going to happen at all?"

"Yes."

He had to concentrate on releasing the tension in his jaw before he could speak again. "Do you want me to leave?"

"Yes."

"I will. Just look me in the eye and say you don't want me. Say it, because otherwise I'm not going anywhere."

She flinched but raised her eyes to his. Eyes shining with tears. "Just go, Kyle."

"Say it. Say you don't want me to touch you. Say you can't stand it when I kiss you. Say the thought of us making love makes you cringe."

She spoke slowly, enunciating each word clearly. "I don't want you."

Kyle felt like he'd been shot. His throat closed. He surged up and strode to the door. With his hand clenching the doorknob, he paused.

He was shaking, with anger, with disappointment, with emotions he couldn't define. Nor did he want to. All he knew was that she'd rejected him for the last time. His pride couldn't take this shit anymore. And he remembered the agreement he'd made with himself if this happened again. How could he forget? He'd rehashed it over and over last night before going to bed frustrated and unsatisfied.

The fingers of his free hand curled into a fist. He gritted his teeth to keep from punching a hole in her wall.

"I can't do this anymore," he ground out.

She let out a little sob. "I know."

"Why are you doing this? Why the hell won't you let me touch you?"

"Just…please go. This isn't going to work."

His fist curled tighter. His back was rigid. He couldn't remember ever being so pissed off. "If I go out this door right now, this is it, Lacey. It's over between us."

"I know," she said softly.

"Is that it? Is that what you want?"

She finally glanced at him, her eyes full of pain. "This is my fault. I knew from the beginning it could never work—"

"What are you saying?"

"Nothing." She shrugged helplessly. "I'm sorry for leading you on for so long."

Anger boiled in his gut. She'd intended to lead him on since the beginning, to never let him touch her? What the hell?

"So you reject me then dismiss me. Is that what you had in mind all along, Lacey?"

"Just go, Kyle." Her voice was rising now, near hysteria. She was lying on her side, facing away from him, not even letting him see the expression on her face.

"Fuck." He grabbed his shoes and shirt and stalked out the door, not stopping until he was on the well-lit sidewalk outside.

He gripped the edge of the bed of his truck, leaning over to catch his breath. He couldn't get enough air. He'd known this might happen tonight, but the reality of it pissed him off to no end. He had given her time, tried to help, tried to be understanding. But he had limits. Especially when she wouldn't talk to him, wouldn't tell him what was going on. Just stiffen, reject him, agree that she'd never wanted him and tell him to go away. How the hell was he expected to deal with that?

He shoved at his truck, causing it to rock on its wheels. She was right. There was no fucking way this could work.

Chapter Three

ဢ

Fingers stroked Lacey's hair, gently tugging her out from a black abyss of sleep.

"Kyle?"

She choked back a sob, remembering. It was over. Kyle wouldn't come anymore.

He tucked a bit of hair behind her ear, and soft lips pressed against her temple. Lacey squeezed her eyes shut and remained limp.

As he traced the shell of her ear with his lips, one hand stroked her arm, and she relaxed minutely. It felt good. She didn't know what it meant, but it was just a dream, just an illusion.

That's right, Lacey. It's just a dream. Relax.

Kyle spoke to her in her head, the exact same way he had last night. Remembering what he had done to her, how he had made her come, a flush of heat bloomed between her legs.

Vaguely, she realized that she was magically naked again as his hand moved up her arm and down to her chest, gently squeezing her nipple as he laved the other with his tongue.

Why? Why could she do this now, in her mind, when she couldn't help freezing up with Kyle? The real Kyle, who clearly felt something for her, who even seemed to find her attractive.

Not attractive. Beautiful. Perfect.

He pinched her nipple harder and a jolt of pleasure-pain shot through her. She gasped, opening her eyes. Just like last night, it was so dark in her room that she could only see Kyle's outline moving over her.

A big hand smoothed up her chest and throat then down, rubbing roughly over her tender nipple, causing her to squirm. Then lower, down her stomach until he cupped her pussy. This exact action was what had made her slam the door shut on Kyle last night. If she wasn't such a screwed-up idiot, she would have admitted it felt damn good, and she would have spread her legs to give him access to do whatever he wanted to her.

That was exactly what she did now. She opened her thighs in invitation.

He burrowed his fingers between her sensitive inner lips, not gently, but with a roughness that made her cry out, that made her pussy clench and pulse, already on the verge of orgasm.

She reached up to hold him, grab him, but his strong hands locked her arms to the mattress.

No, Lacey. This doesn't work both ways. I can play with your delectable body, but you can't play with mine. It's against the rules.

"That doesn't make sense. This is my dream, my fantasy. There are no rules." She wanted to feel him, to pull him close. She wanted to touch his cock, the long shaft which rubbed against her leg. She wanted to explore this man.

I make the rules. His hands moved lower until his fingers clasped hers. *If you want to play, you will touch me when you're awake. Only me. Imagine me, Lacey. Imagine touching me. I'm hard beneath your fingertips. My cock is throbbing for you. Every muscle in my body aches for you.*

"Impossible," she whispered on a sob.

Even now I'm dreaming of you – imagining you naked, lying here, your creamy pussy crimson with arousal. I want to touch you, to give you pleasure.

He slid down her body, his muscles grazing sensuously over her skin. His breath whispered against her swollen folds, and then the tip of his tongue glided in a slow circle around her opening.

My cock is so hard it hurts. Gently, he took her clit between his lips. *A little bead of come slides slowly down my hot, painful shaft as I take your taut little clit into my mouth. Do you want to taste it, Lacey? Do you want to slide your tongue down my cock? Do you want to ease my pain, bring me satisfaction?*

"Yes," she gasped.

As his lips brushed her clit, his fingers explored her, circling through the slick cream. Teasing her until she quivered from head to toe.

Suddenly, he released her. *Turn over.*

It was a command, and she didn't hesitate to obey. She flipped onto her stomach.

On your hands and knees, Lacey. Show me that pretty, round ass.

She paused. She'd always been shy about her behind.

A sharp slap stung her butt cheek and she jumped, yelping in shock.

Don't ever hesitate, Lacey.

As warmth seeped from her butt to fan the fire in her pussy, she shoved herself up to her knees and elbows.

Good girl. You have an amazing ass. I love your ass.

She sighed. God, but this Dream Kyle did wonders for her nonexistent ego. She should ask him to come over every night.

No! Another slap, this one on the other cheek. Lacey gasped, wiggling her behind to soothe the wild hunger between her legs.

What kind of a dream was this? Rules, an opinionated and dominating dream Kyle, and…spankings? Never, even in her wildest fantasies, had she imagined being spanked. Her mind, with its limited experiences and observations, would never have come up with that one on its own.

"Why not?" she challenged, pressing her forehead into the mattress, trying to keep herself focused. "Why won't you come to me every night?"

His big hands palmed her behind. *I want all of you — the real you — in the day and in the night. I want you beside me. Under me. You belong to me, Lacey. And not just in your dreams.*

Those words flowed through her like sweet wine. Every nerve in her body jumped to life. A whimper burst from her throat before she could stop it.

She belonged to Kyle. Oh God. It was true, completely true.

Not only that, but she was in love with him. She buried her face in her comforter. A tear seeped from the corner of her eye, even as her lust raged on.

What the hell was happening to her?

He slipped a finger down the crack of her behind, slick from her juices. Moving down to her clit, he stroked over it gently with his fingertip.

Let it happen. Don't fight it. It's meant to be.

He played with her, mere wisps of touches, and it was driving her crazy. She wanted more.

"You're confusing me...teasing me...stop teasing me." Lacey arched her back and pushed her butt toward him.

No.

But even as he denied her, his fingers slid between her thighs. He tickled her clit, and she cried out. She was close to coming, so close.

Slowly, he caressed her hot, sensitive folds, making her shudder and squirm.

"God, no, no more teasing," she muttered.

He laughed. *I'm imagining I'm about to fuck you, Lacey, but you...I want you to imagine my cock.* His body curled over hers until she felt his breath in her ear. *My cock teasing you...bumping up against your clit...*

His fingers stretched her wide as they slipped in. Lacey gasped and squirmed, but he held her down firmly, his palm pressed against the small of her back. How many fingers was he using? He was stretching her to her limit.

It was easy to imagine Kyle sliding his cock up and down, finding her pussy, pushing slowly inside. The image in her mind made her moan, made her channel hum with little pulses, squeezing him tight within her.

It'll be far superior to this, Lacey. More. Nothing in your life will feel better than having me penetrate your body, nothing will feel more right.

It felt so damn good, but she knew, to the depths of her soul, that what he said was true.

Slowly, he pumped her pussy. The fingers from his other hand moved back to her ass, kneading her cheeks.

Lacey tossed her head back and forth. She drove backwards into Kyle, wanting, needing more.

"Fuck me," she murmured. "Fuck me, Kyle. Please."

She was close, so damn close.

He thrust into her, a little harder now. He curled his fingers, brushing over a sweet spot inside her. The sensation was so strong, it made Lacey freeze. She was going to come. She was on the edge, one foot stepped off the precipice—

No.

He withdrew. She heaved in a great gulp of a breath, on the verge of mindlessness.

Come to me, Lacey. In the flesh. Only I can satisfy you tonight.

"No!"

Drive to my house. Knock on the door. Trust me.

"Nooo…" she groaned. "I can't. I can't!"

I'm thinking of you right now, Lacey. I'm desperate, aching to be inside you. I need you.

"Why?" she moaned. "Why are you doing this to me?"

Big, comforting arms wrapped around her body. *I'm giving you what you need. Now come to me.*

Moon rays streamed in through her gauze curtains. She blinked into the dim light.

Realizing she was still naked, she took in great gulps of air, her pulse beating as fast as a frightened rabbit's. She hadn't gone to bed naked.

Come to me, Lacey.

But nobody was in her room. She sat up in the bed. Her clit hummed between her legs, still begging for release.

She needed…something. Someone.

She needed Kyle.

Come to me!

* * * * *

An incessant pounding drew Kyle from a deep sleep. He groaned, running his fingers lightly over his dick, trying to calm the intense ache. God, he was rock hard. A bead of pre-come had run down the side of his shaft, and he smoothed it away.

The memory of his dream slammed into him like a punch in the gut. Lacey on hands and knees, arching into him as he thrust his fingers in her pussy, kneading her round ass. Shit. No wonder he was so hard.

He'd commanded her to come to him, to trust him, to relieve his ache. He'd promised to give her what she needed.

The pounding sounded again. He blinked, trying to focus. Was someone at his door? He glanced at the digital clock on his bedside table. It was one thirty in the morning.

"Kyle?"

Lacey! His heart constricted in panic. Something was wrong. Was she okay? He leaped out of bed, shoved a pair of shorts on over his still-raging erection and ran down the hall, flicking on the porch light as he passed the switch in the foyer.

He threw open the door. "Lacey?"

She froze in mid-knock and stared at him, her lips parted. Then she stepped back, took a deep, sobbing breath, and, in full view of anyone who might choose to drive up Nob Hill at this hour, dropped her robe. It slid down her body as if it was caressing her pale, naked skin, and pooled at her ankles.

Trembling with cold or nerves, he couldn't be certain which, she stood on his doorstep, completely nude. His gaze raked down her body, from the intense blue-green eyes to the small cleft in her chin to her full breasts to the flare of her hips and the triangle of dark hair between her lush thighs. Stunning. She was perfect—a goddess. His cock throbbed painfully, tenting his shorts.

"Lacey, what...how...are you drunk?"

She gazed intently at him. "No."

He knew she was telling the truth. He knew from the look of determination mixed with vulnerability in her clear blue-green eyes. Steely and soft swirling in her gaze like a whirlpool.

Trying to shake off his confusion, he moved aside and motioned her in. He didn't understand what she was up to, but he didn't want anyone else seeing his woman naked.

His woman? Damn, he must be high. She wasn't his woman. She'd made that patently clear earlier tonight.

And now she was standing naked on his porch. Lacey Marceaux was the queen of mixed signals.

Slowly she stepped over her robe and breezed past him, her bare shoulder brushing his chest as she entered his house. Lust ricocheted through him.

He gritted his teeth and strode onto the porch. Whatever the hell was going on, he wouldn't touch her. He knew only too well where that would lead.

He retrieved her discarded robe and went inside, pushing the door shut behind him.

Thrusting the robe at her, he said, "Put this on, damn it."

That had come out more sharply than he'd intended. She flinched but held her ground. "No."

He tossed it aside. "Then why don't you explain what you're doing naked on my doorstep at one a.m.?"

She bowed her head. Her shoulders heaved once, then she looked up and took a step toward him.

Hell. All he wanted was to thrust her against the wall and plunge into her. Residual frustration coursed through him, mixed with crazy, all-consuming desire. His cock throbbed. His pulse pounded in his ears. He was fast losing grip on his thread of control. He stepped back, narrowing his eyes. "Don't tempt me, Lacey. Don't make me do something we'll both regret."

Her eyes flickered with renewed determination. She took another step forward, but he couldn't move back this time. The wall was right behind him.

"Fuck me, Kyle." Her voice was so low, he almost didn't hear. "Make me yours. Please."

Heat sizzled through him, but he stared warily at her. "You don't want that."

"I do."

"You don't know what you're saying. I won't stop this time." He clenched his fists at his sides, forcing himself to go on. "I don't—" He drew in a shuddering breath. "I don't think I can."

Silence for a long moment. Then, "Good."

He snapped.

With a growl, he launched himself at her, capturing her in his arms and hauling her up, crashing his lips against hers. She cried out but didn't push him away. Instead, she wrapped her arms around his neck. Her soft breasts pressed against his chest, her pussy rubbed against his cock through the fabric of his shorts. They were in the way, goddammit.

He continued forward until her back bumped into the opposite wall. Then he let her go so he could get rid of his shorts.

She slid down his body until she was on her feet, but she didn't stop there. She sank lower, grasped the waistband and tugged. Before he had time to blink, his cock was in her hands and her mouth was tickling its head.

He braced his hands against the wall to keep his knees from buckling and looked down at her. Eagerly, as if this was the most exciting thing she'd ever done, she took him deeper. Her fingers curled around his shaft, then slid lower, rolling his balls gently.

"Holy shit." He angled his hips, thrusting deeper into her mouth. Instead of drawing back, she pushed down further, humming her pleasure.

He was on fire, burning. His balls drew up tight against his body, his come boiling inside, flowing. He was on the edge already, damn it to hell. Just seeing her so eager, just having her sweet lips on him, was enough to make him explode.

She pumped him, swirling her tongue around his shaft, over the head.

"Stop," he ground out, withdrawing from her hot mouth even though it nearly killed him to do it. "I've got to fuck you, Lacey. I've got to have you. I can't wait."

Now, all his senses screamed. His humanity seemed to bleed away, leaving him in a raw, feral state, and all he cared about was mating with this woman. Marking her, making her his.

She looked up at him, her eyes blazing green in the dim light of the hall. "Condom?"

He blinked. "Yeah. In my bedroom." He paused, looking down at her wild auburn hair, her swollen lips, her trusting eyes, and emotion tightened his chest. Primal lust surged through his veins, hot and impatient. *Damn.*

"What are you waiting for, Kyle?" Uncertainty flickered in her eyes.

"Nothing." He pulled her up. Not willing to wait for her to follow him, he simply hooked a hand behind her knees and carried her to his bedroom. Slamming the door behind him, he tossed her onto the bed.

Her eyes sharpened as she stared at him, as if her need was as great as his own. She kicked the blankets away, cupped her breasts in her hands, then as he watched, slowly opened her legs. Her pretty pink pussy opened in front of him like a blooming flower, her juices making it glisten.

"I need you," she whispered. "Please, Kyle. I have to have you inside me."

Pictures crowded his mind. All the things he wanted to do to her, to that body, to that pussy, to that ass. He just stared for a moment, nearly bowled over by the intensity of the images.

But then his cock throbbed angrily, returning his focus to the matter at hand. He would taste her, suck her, tease her ass with his tongue and fingers another time. Maybe later tonight.

Right now, though, he had to fuck her. Nothing was more important.

Cursing in impatience, he found a condom, tore open the package and rolled it on. He crawled onto the bed, his body hovering over her. Immediately, her legs and arms entwined around him, tugging him close.

Now.

Easily, his cock found her slick entrance and with one hard thrust, he was inside.

He froze, staring at her in shock. For a long moment they stayed still, shuddering as one with the intensity of it, of their bodies finally locked together.

Nothing, not even five years of lusting after this woman, could have prepared Kyle for this. Nothing had ever been so perfect, felt so right. Her pussy clenched and rippled around him like a tight, pulsating fist.

Color rose high on her cheeks and she began to squirm beneath him. "Move, Kyle. Move. I'm going to come. Please!"

He moved. He yanked his cock out and then rammed into her, forcing the breath from her body in a puff. Again and again he thrust.

Her pussy tightened and contracted around him. Every muscle in his body was strung as taut as a rubber band pulled to its fullest stretch. But he sure as hell wasn't going to let himself come before her.

He didn't need to wait long. Her fingernails dug into his back. Her heels tightened on his ass. Then she arched beautifully under him, her body undulating. The sight of her mouth open in a silent "o" of a scream and her eyes clenched shut, the feel of her nails clawing him and her pussy spasming over his cock. All of it shot directly to his balls, to his cock, yanking him over the edge as well.

With a shout, he thrust hard into her one last time, and the world exploded. He saw stars. Otherwise, he couldn't hear, couldn't see. He could only feel the fierce river of semen bursting from his cock, the pleasure of it drawing a long, satisfied groan from his throat.

When the pulses finally subsided, he sank down, supporting his weight on his elbows so he wouldn't crush her. And he said the very first thing that came to his mind.

"I love you, Lacey."

Chapter Four

Lacey woke from a deep slumber. Kyle was behind her, his broad chest pressed into her back, his arm wrapped possessively around her waist. She sighed in pure contentment and snuggled more closely against him.

A figure came into her vision, but she didn't move, didn't even tense. She knew who it was. The Kyle from her dreams.

She could see him more clearly tonight than she ever had before. It really was Kyle, she realized, but he looked like a watercolor portrait of the man she loved, fuzzy around the edges, and wavering like a mirage.

"Hello," she whispered.

Thank you, baby. Thank you for trusting me.

Kyle didn't budge behind her. His breaths were deep, as if he was in a heavy sleep. Was she speaking out loud? Because he didn't seem to hear her. Or was she dreaming?

What did it matter?

"Why did you do it?" she murmured. "Why did you come to me like that?"

It was the only way...the only way to show you how I could make you feel.

"Who are you, really?"

He glanced at the still form behind her. *Him.*

"But how?"

I'm a dream walker.

"A...what?"

His fingers stroked down her cheek in a fluttering touch. *I can send my spirit into others' dreams.*

"But you...you touched me." Her body flushed, remembering what he had done to her—how he had made her feel.

He smiled. *Yes. In times of strong emotion, I can become whole.*

"I don't think he knows what you've done—what *he's* done."

You're right—I don't know. The conscious part of me has no idea what I can do. But he has some idea of what I've done.

Her mind was reeling. What would she do when Kyle woke up? How could she possibly explain all this?

Talk to me about it, Lacey. A part of me will rebel, but a bigger part will understand. Ask about my family, about my Comanche heritage. I've heard the stories. And when I hear the truth, I'll understand. I won't be able to deny it.

Withdrawing his hand from her face, he bent down until his soft lips tickled hers.

"Wait—"

His form shifted, then slowly disintegrated into the dimness, leaving her lips tingling with pleasure.

"Thank you," she whispered to the empty room.

Don't forget I love you, baby.

Lacey entwined her fingers with Kyle's and drifted into a contented sleep.

* * * * *

Kyle stood in the doorway of his bedroom watching Lacey sleep. A soft smile curved her lips upward, and her thick, dark eyelashes curved against her cheeks. He had never seen her sleep before, and he would have been content to simply stand there and watch her for hours.

"Mmm." She yawned, opened her eyes and pointed her toes, stretching languidly.

After a moment of just drinking her in, he walked toward the bed. "Good morning." The mattress shifted as he sat down on its edge.

She turned to him and smiled. "Good morning."

The sheets rippled, exposing her bare shoulder and the upper curve of her breast. His cock leapt to attention, but he had questions first, questions that had been nagging at him since he woke up this morning.

"Lacey…" His voice trailed off.

"What?"

He took a deep breath. "What happened last night? Why did you come here?"

She sat up in the bed, pulling the sheet to cover her chest. Scooting back against the wooden headboard, she gave him a rueful grin. "You wouldn't believe me if I told you."

Damn, it was impossible to be near this woman without wanting her. Unable to stop himself from touching her, he leaned down and his lips met hers in a hot, possessive kiss. When he pulled away, he sifted his hands through her hair and tugged gently. "I want to know. You told me it was over. Then you came here… God, Lacey…you were a different woman."

She lowered her eyes. "I was afraid," she whispered. "Afraid that I couldn't please you in bed." She gave a shaky laugh. "I was petrified that I would fail you."

His hand moved from her hair to cup her chin, tilting it so she'd look at him. "How could you say that? You must know how much I care for you—how much I want you."

She sighed. "Sometimes fears aren't logical."

"Tell me what happened."

"I…dreamed."

"You had a dream?"

"Yes. Well, two. Three, actually."

"Of me?"

"Yes. He—you—"

"Go on," he said softly, seeing the fear and confusion in her eyes. "You know you can tell me anything."

She took a deep breath. "The first night I dreamed about you touching me. My breasts. You said I was...attractive."

Kyle raised an eyebrow. "I could have told you that in person."

Her face heated in a flush, but she licked her lips and pressed on. She was so nervous she was breathless. "You...you spoke really dirty and you...well, you touched me...everywhere. Then you made love to me with your fingers and mouth."

Kyle stilled, staring at her, feeling the oddest sensation of mingling arousal and alarm. He was pretty sure he'd had the same dream. But that was impossible. They were just so in tune with one another, with what they'd been going through together, that they'd had similar erotic dreams. It could happen to anyone.

Still, he had to know. "How?" he demanded. "How did I fuck you in your dream?"

Lacey's breaths became even more shallow. "You were...licking between my legs and...well, you were penetrating me with your fingers...ah, everywhere else."

Shit. He closed his eyes, then opened them. "Then what?"

"Then...well, I came. And you left."

"Shit," Kyle said aloud, turning away from her and moving to sit on the edge of the bed. She reached out to put her hand on his shoulder.

"I'm sorry, Kyle."

Why was she apologizing? He shook his head, fighting the welling panic. How could two people have the exact same dream? And yet something nudged at him—some memory... "Tell me what happened in the second dream."

"You came back." She sounded like she was on the verge of tears, but he couldn't look at her, didn't want her to see the panic in his eyes. She continued, a note of desperation in her voice. "You said I turned you on. That I was yours, that I belonged to you. You began to make love to me again, but you wouldn't let me come. Then you ordered me to go to your house. You said the only way I could get satisfaction was to come to you. That you wanted me, that you were aching for me."

Kyle's shoulders shuddered uncontrollably. Behind him, Lacey made a small sound of distress.

"I woke up naked, and I knew I had to come here," she said. "I knew I needed you. I don't know what happened, Kyle."

Kyle sat silent for a long moment, his back to her.

She sighed. "I'm sorry — maybe I'm crazy, I don't know."

He turned and grasped her shoulders. "No! No. You don't understand."

"What do you mean?"

"I had the same dreams. Last night and the night before." He shook her slightly. "The same goddamned dreams."

She stared at him. "Are you…are you sure?"

He was breathing heavily. "Last night…I was fucking you with my fingers, right? You…" He sucked in a breath. "You were on your forearms and knees, pressing your face into your blanket. You were tossing your head back and forth. You said, 'Fuck me, Kyle, please.'"

God, even now, even with this weird shit going on, his cock was as hard as steel remembering it.

She stared at him in shock. "You were there," she murmured.

"Damn it, Lacey. This is just too weird."

She cupped his face in both hands. "You came to me again last night, after we fell asleep."

He felt like he'd been punched in the stomach. All of a sudden, he remembered that dream as well. Vividly.

"You came to me and said you were some kind of a dream traveler. You said the conscious part of you didn't know or understand it, but it's some kind of power passed down to you from your Native American heritage."

Kyle squeezed his eyes shut. "Shit. Shit, shit, shit."

"You had that dream too?"

"Yes," he muttered, feeling numb from head to toe. "I was here, watching you and me in bed. You were awake, but I was sleeping behind you. And I was telling you all these things as if they made complete sense—even though they were completely off-the-wall."

Lacey's hands fell away. They sat on the bed for a long moment, staring at one another.

He remembered his grandfather, who was half Comanche, telling him about the dream walkers with a canny gleam in his dark eyes.

It was all coming back in a flood. He bowed his head to stare down at his blanket, remembering that before he died, he and his grandfather had shared many an adventure together. In their dreams.

After his grandfather died, Kyle's father had moved them to Houston and he'd forgotten all about it. Or, as he said in the dream, he'd repressed it.

Even as he said the words, he realized he'd been lying to Lacey. His words in the dream hadn't been completely off-the-wall. He remembered every detail of their experiences together, everything he'd said and done to her. He'd awakened with his fingers wet from sliding through her pussy and her musk filling his senses. He'd been in control in his dreams. He'd decided not to fuck her, to save her for him when both of them were awake. He'd told her the truth about himself, even as the words surprised him. He'd chosen to come to her, make love to her and then be honest with her.

Because he loved her.

She cupped his jaw in her hands, forcing him to look up. "You helped me, Kyle. Somehow, you made me confident enough to come to you on my own."

He gazed at her for a long moment. Whatever had happened to him, to them, he loved her. He reached up and brushed his thumb over her cheek.

"If you hadn't come to me in my dreams, I wouldn't be here. That's what matters, isn't it?"

He reached up and brushed her hair back from her face. When he spoke, his voice was raw. "Yeah, baby."

She gave a slow exhalation of relief.

"Goddamn, you're beautiful."

"So are you."

"I'm going make love to you again, Lacey. I want to do those things I—we—dreamed about."

Her breath hitched in her throat. "I do too," she whispered. "All of it."

He wrapped his arms around her, bringing her to her back on the bed. He tugged the blanket off her body, and let his gaze rake over her beautiful, delicious body. He cupped her breasts, smoothing his thumbs reverently over her nipples.

"Kyle…"

"What, baby?"

"Did you mean what you said last night? Before we fell asleep?"

Keeping his hands on her breasts, his eyes snapped up to her face. He understood exactly what she meant. Did he really love her?

After a long moment of staring at her, he ran his teeth over his bottom lip. He felt completely exposed knowing all the need, lust…and love showed clearly on his face. When he bared himself to her, his voice was low. "Yeah, baby, I meant it."

Lacey blinked. She'd never truly imagined what it would feel like to be here in this moment with him. Her heart surged with love.

And something else. Triumph. She'd won, after all. She'd beaten Frank, beaten her own insecurities. And she'd won Kyle Turner, the finest trophy of them all. Nothing could be better.

She slid her arms around his neck and pulled him close. "Thank God."

He stiffened and pulled back, his eyebrows drawn together in concern.

She smiled, and though she knew her heart was on her sleeve, she wore it confidently. "I love you, too, Kyle Turner. And I'm pretty sure I'll love you forever."

He drew her against his body, his erection grinding against her hip. "I've got to make love to you, Lacey."

"Anytime," she whispered. "Anywhere. I will never shy away from you again."

His hand tightened on her waist, and his eyes narrowed. "You belong to me now. Nobody else is allowed to touch you. Only me. In the flesh…and in dreams. You got it?"

A thrill ran down Lacey's spine. "Yes, I've got it." Not that she wanted anyone else, or ever would again. The only man who could truly satisfy, her dream man, was real. And he was beside her, holding her in his arms.

"Good."

His hand slipped from her hip down between her legs, his fingertips brushing softly over her clit. "You're already wet and ready for me, aren't you?"

"I said anytime," she gasped.

He chuckled and pulled his hand away. "Now on your hands and knees, Lacey. Show me that pretty, round ass."

This time she didn't hesitate at all, because she knew he found her beautiful. She knew she could please him. Most importantly, she knew he loved her.

Lacey turned over, rose on her hands and knees and wiggled her butt in anticipation.

MOON MAGIC
N.J. Walters

જી

Chapter One

ะจ

"I need a man." Meghan Flynn's heart pounded as she extended her hand toward the dark opening of the ancient stone well.

"No. Wait!" She pulled her clenched fist back to her chest, the silver dollar still clutched tight. The sultry night breeze ruffled the hem of her nightgown, swirling it around her ankles. The air around her was redolent with the scent of lilacs and wild roses, which grew along the wooded path that stretched behind her grandmother's home. Her home now, she supposed.

Even though the gown she was wearing was held up with thin spaghetti straps and was made of the flimsiest of silk, a bead of sweat rolled down her neck and disappeared between her breasts. Her long hair lay like a heavy cape against her back and she wished she'd taken the time to pin the mass up before she'd left the house. She'd mistakenly thought that the air would cool once the sun had gone down. The night was exceptionally hot, even for July. She swiped the back of her hand over her forehead as she stared at the well.

It was magic, if one believed in such things. And on a night like tonight, who wouldn't? This was Ireland, land of the fairies, and the full moon was staring down from the sky, watching her, urging her to make a wish and seal it with the silver in the coin.

This had been her home until she'd turned eleven. That was when her mother had remarried and they'd moved to Boston with her new stepfather. Meghan had been heartbroken to leave her grandmother behind. Siobhan Flynn had been the most important person in Meghan's world, the last link to her father who had died when Meghan was just a girl of three. Her mother rarely talked about him, but her grandmother would spend hours talking about her son and showing Meghan pictures. What she knew of her father had come from the older woman. In truth, her grandmother had been more of a mother to her than her own had been.

Meghan had been born here and started school here. Heck, she'd even had her first eleven-year-old girlish crush on an older boy of fifteen her last summer here. She smiled softly at the memory.

He'd been visiting with relatives and she'd seen him in the village with some of the older boys. Tall and lanky with dark hair, he'd glanced her way and smiled. She'd been totally smitten. She'd seen him a total of five times, but never managed to even find out his name. There had been no way to ask without arousing attention and possibly getting teased, and that had been the last thing she'd wanted.

An owl hooted in the distance and the crickets began to sing. Sighing, Meghan sat down on the ground and pulled her legs to her chest, curling her arms around them.

She'd adapted to her new life in Boston because she'd had no choice and because she was young. The young always manage somehow. She'd made new friends, gone to school, grown up and started a career as a librarian at a small private college. Over the years, she'd written her grandmother, but had never managed the time, or the money, to return to Ireland for a visit. That thought shamed her and she buried her face against her knees.

She'd had her share of ups and downs, the worst of it beginning a year ago when her mother and stepfather had been killed in a car accident. Her life had gone completely downhill ever since. Eight months after her parents' death, the college had downsized their staff and Meghan had lost her job.

She might have managed to get past that and find another job if it hadn't been for the whole apartment fiasco. She'd given up the lease on her apartment to move in with her boyfriend of six months. In hindsight, it had been a mistake to take that plunge without being one hundred percent sure that Mark was the man she wanted to spend the rest of her life with, but she'd been lonely and feeling desperate with her thirtieth birthday looming in the distance.

When she'd found out about her job, she'd left work early, wanting to be with Mark and talk to him. She'd discovered just what a cheating bastard he was when she walked into his office and found him fucking his secretary.

Sighing, Meghan raised her head listened to the calming sounds of the night. The breeze brushed over her skin like a lover's caress, so soft and gentle that she moaned. Her nipples hardened into tight buds. Her breasts felt heavy and hot.

Groaning, she lay back on the ground and stared up at the stars in the sky. The grass welcomed her, lightly tickling her arms and bare legs. It had been more than a year since she'd had sex. She should have known there was something wrong between her and Mark when he suggested waiting until they were living together to have sex, but she'd thought he was just old-fashioned. What he'd been was gay and desperately trying to hide it from his boss and ultra-conservative family.

She felt naïve now as she remembered liking the fact that he had a male secretary instead of some sexy female. Meghan wasn't under any illusions about herself. She was tall, a well-rounded size sixteen, and her waist-length red hair had a tendency to curl wildly in any kind of humidity. Still, Mark had seemed to like her well enough. She hadn't worried about his secretary in the least and had rather liked him. That is, until she'd caught him and Mark in the act.

Her legs shifted restlessly, her sex swelling and dampening as images of the perfect man flitted through her mind. A dream lover was what she wanted — one who came to her in the dark of night and fulfilled her wildest fantasies. Her lover would be taller with wide shoulders.

She licked her lips as he began to take form in her mind. He would be dark in coloring, the exact opposite of blond-haired, blue-eyed Mark. His stomach would ripple with muscle and his waist would be firm. Long legs and strong thighs would fill out a pair of faded jeans to perfection. She couldn't quite make out his male attributes, but she knew they'd be as impressive as the rest of him.

Her feminine muscles fluttered and cream seeped from her core. She tried to think of something else, anything else, but it was impossible. The night was hot and so was she.

Closing her eyes, she gave herself up to the fantasy. It was *his* hands that pushed the straps of her gown down her shoulders and arms. *His* hands that cupped her ample breasts and teased the puckered nipples between his fingers. The silver coin slipped from her fingers and dropped to the ground beside her.

She gasped and opened her eyes, half appalled by the way she was wantonly spread across the ground, her hands on her breasts. Sure, she'd pleasured herself on occasion. What woman her age hadn't? But this felt different. Nervously, she glanced around to assure herself that she was alone. The hair on her body was standing on end and all her nerve endings were tingling. She could almost hear his silent voice, urging her to finish it.

She nearly got up and went back to her cottage, but for some unknown reason, she felt compelled to stay. There was magic in the air tonight and her body had been too long without.

While one of her hands stayed on her breast, the other slid down the silk of her gown and between her thighs. She could feel the dampness through the fabric. Slowly, she inched the silk upward until she was exposed to the night. She spread her legs wide and let her fingers dip lower, stroking over the slick folds of her vulva.

Pleasure hit her like a sledgehammer and she groaned and arched her back, reaching for more. As if her fingers were no longer under her command, they continued to play over her sensitive flesh. Two fingers slid past the opening of her core and plunged deep.

Sweat trickled down her temples and got lost in the mass of red hair that pooled around her head. She tweaked her nipples and plumped her breasts with one hand as the other one stayed busy between her legs.

Each sharp inhalation of air brought the lush scents of arousal, roses and sweet grass to her nostrils. She could feel the beginnings of contractions deep in her womb and began to thrust her fingers deeper, using her thumb to press on the hard knot of nerves at the apex of her sex.

So long. It had been so long since she'd felt this alive. This vibrant. This real. Her entire being reached for the orgasm that hovered just out of reach. She cried out in frustration and pushed her fingers harder and deeper, her hips thrusting mindlessly into the air.

The first faint fluttering began inside her. She cried out as pleasure slammed into her. Her pussy contracted hard around her fingers. Her hips jerked as cream gushed over her hand. Moments later, she slumped back onto the grass and sighed. Her fingers slid from her body and she lay there, gasping for breath.

When reality began to creep back into her brain, she shoved her gown down to cover her legs and quickly thrust her arms back into the straps and yanked them up until she was decently covered. Had she lost her mind?

Perhaps she had. After all she'd been through in the past year, the last straw had come just over three months ago when the lease had expired on her apartment and she'd had nowhere to go. She'd thought her life couldn't get any worse, but that was when the registered letter had come. Her beloved grandmother had passed away suddenly. Meghan had been devastated to lose the last living relative she had in the world. She'd also felt guilty for not coming to visit her grandmother since she'd left Ireland almost twenty years before. Yes, they talked on the phone every two weeks and wrote letters, but it wasn't the same.

Yet, once again, her grandmother had been looking out for her. She'd left Meghan her cottage and land in Ireland as well as a nice nest egg. With the money she'd saved on her own over the years and a place to live in that belonged to her, Meghan suddenly found herself with enough money to live for several years without having to even think about working.

Desperate for a new start and a chance to rest and reflect on how she wanted to spend the rest of her life, she'd sold off all but her clothing and personal belongings and moved to Ireland, leaving Boston and its bad memories behind her.

Maybe she had changed, she reflected. The woman who'd lived in Boston definitely wouldn't have had the nerve to pleasure herself in a woodland glen in the middle of the night. She shivered as remnants of her earlier pleasure rippled over her.

Barely stifling a giggle, Meghan rolled to her side and then sat up slowly, swiping a few stray bits of grass from her limbs. She glanced around and found the silver coin lying on the ground beside her, shining in the light of the moon.

Why not! Grasping the coin, she stood and strode to the edge of the well. Closing her eyes, she concentrated with all her being. "I want a lover who'll come to me in the dark of the night. A man who will want and accept me for what I am. One who will pleasure me and who will allow me to pleasure him in return. I want to share my body and myself with him and have him do the same. I want a special, forever kind of love. I want…" she trailed off as the reality of the situation hit her.

Opening her eyes, she gazed into the dark well. "I want the impossible." Letting her fingers slowly separate, she dropped the coin into the opening and listened. Moments later, she heard the tiny splash.

It was done.

Suddenly, she felt very silly and extremely vulnerable even though she knew she was alone and there was no one but perhaps a stray owl or a field mouse to witness her folly. Picking her way back down the path in her bare feet, she hurried toward home. Less than two minutes later, her cottage came into view and she breathed a sigh of relief as she closed the gate behind her and reached for the latch on the back door.

Rory Shaunnessey stood silently, not daring to move or to breathe as he watched the woodland goddess hurry away. He wanted to call out to her to stop, to wait, to stay with him. He could grant her wish she'd cast into the well if only she would give him the chance.

He followed her home, making sure to stay hidden in the shadows, wanting to make sure she was safe. He knew who she was of course. Everyone knew Siobhan's granddaughter had come back to Ireland to live.

Meghan. Her name was as lush and beautiful as the woman herself. He wished he had a better view of her face, but the view he'd had of her body had been more than enough to tempt a saint. And if he knew anything at all, it was that no one would ever mistake him for a saint.

When the door closed behind her, he turned and headed back to the small clearing. Hunkering down next to the flattened grass, he laid his palm on the ground, which still held the imprint from her body. He took a deep breath and, even though he knew it was impossible, he swore he could smell the faintest whiff of her feminine arousal.

His cock swelled against the zipper of his jeans, pressing for release. He stood and tried to adjust himself, but the pressure didn't ease. The memory of her curvaceous body almost naked except for the strip of silk pushed around her waist would haunt his dreams. Her long legs had been spread wide, exposing her soft reddish curls. He'd said a prayer to the moon, thanking it for shining on that particular part of her.

Her breasts had been more than a handful and they were very sensitive as well if he wasn't mistaken.

For once, he'd been glad he hadn't been able to sleep. His insomnia and the call of the full moon had lured him out for a walk. Never in his wildest dreams had he imagined coming across a seductive woodland nymph, one who lured him with her body and called to his very soul.

His mind worked furiously as he headed back to his own home, his long legs quickly eating up the distance. Maybe she would be back tomorrow night. The lure of the night and the magic would be too much for her to resist. At least he hoped it would.

And he would be there. If she wanted a secret nighttime lover, then he would be it. There was no way in hell he was letting another man near her. He'd found her and he was keeping her.

Letting himself in through the back door, he headed straight to his office. His computer screen was dark but came quickly to life when he hit a key. Ideas were flowing and he sat down and placed his fingers on the keyboard. The tapping continued long into the night until the moon whispered goodnight and the sun beckoned good morning.

Yawning, he saved his work and turned off his machine before stumbling up the stairs to bed. He had another moonlight meeting tonight and he wanted to be well rested for it. Hauling off his clothing, he crawled into bed, closed his eyes and dreamed of her.

Chapter Two

ဢ

As Meghan worked around the cottage early the next morning, cleaning and mopping, she tried to forget what had happened in the secluded glen last night. But it was impossible. Her breasts felt heavy and her core empty, reminding her vividly that she hadn't had a real lover to fulfill her needs. Muttering, she packed away the cleaning supplies and dug out her baking pans.

Ignoring the heat, she baked fresh sweet bread. Its delicious aroma filled the kitchen, making her stomach growl. She cut a slice when it was still hot, slathered it with honey and ate it while looking out the kitchen window into the garden beyond. It was going to be another scorcher of a day.

Wrapping one of the fresh loaves, she headed out to her closest neighbor, an elderly lady who lived about a five-minute walk down the road. She didn't know her neighbor who lived up the road from her. According to Mrs. Grady, it was some recluse who rarely went into town. A good-looking man in his prime, he created a stir among the single woman whenever he appeared. He was some relative of the late Mr. Collins who'd lived in the house for some eighty-plus years.

Mrs. Grady chatted more about their neighbor, giving Meghan every detail that she'd gleaned to date. When Meghan left, she strolled home. Pouring a huge glass of iced tea, she changed into a loose pair of shorts and a tank top, and puttered around the garden until it was time to eat her evening meal. Once again, she pleased herself, cutting a fresh slab of bread and serving it with a sharp yellow cheese, a crisp, tart apple and a half glass of white wine. She tried reading the new book she'd bought for herself, but not even the latest romantic thriller from one of her favorite authors could hold her attention. All she could think about was last night.

Feeling tired and out of sorts, she finally she gave up trying to do anything productive, took a quick, cool shower, pulled on her thin nightgown and fell onto her bed. The window was open, but there was hardly a breath of wind. The drapes didn't move at all. The weight of the heat was oppressive and Meghan finally gave up all pretense of trying to sleep after an hour of tossing and turning. Rolling off the bed, she stopped long enough to pin her hair up off her neck before heading down the stairs and out the back door, into the night.

Her bare feet moved swiftly on the hard-packed dirt path. She didn't even try to deny where she was going. Where she wanted to be. The path veered sharply and she left the dirt and felt the grass beneath her feet. The heavy perfume of the flowers hung in the air as it did the night before. Meghan breathed deep, pulling their scents into her lungs.

Stopping in the center of the clearing, she raised her hands to the sky. The moon still appeared as fat as the night before, even though she knew it was already beginning to wane. She felt a part of the night and its magic. A sense of anticipation shot through her.

Her legs clenched as a trickle of cream seeped from her core and slid down her inner thigh. Had she ever felt so aroused in her life? All day, her body had been remembering the night before. It was if she was preparing herself for the secret lover she'd wished for. Her breasts ached and when she glanced down she could see the outline of her nipples pressing against the fabric.

Lord, she was pathetic.

Sighing, she scrubbed her hands over her face. What was she doing running around half naked in the middle of the night? Maybe she was spending too much time alone. She didn't socialize much. Maybe it was time to change that.

Turning on her heel, she strode toward the path, determined to go home and go to bed and put her foolishness behind her.

"I was afraid you wouldn't come." The voice from the edge of the woods stopped her cold. Deep and masculine, it was tinged with an intense longing that shook her to the depths of her soul.

She froze, turning her head slowly as she tried to figure out where he was hiding. "Who are you? What do you want?" Her heart was pounding and she knew that she should be running as fast as her legs could carry her, not chatting with a strange man she couldn't even see. Yet, she wasn't afraid. Not really. There was more of a sense of anticipation than anything. Now she knew she was really losing her grip.

"I'm your dream lover. The one you wished for last night."

Oh God. Someone had seen her last night. Her common sense finally kicked in and she began to hurry away.

"Please," he called. "Don't go. I would never harm you, Meghan. All I want is to pleasure you."

She stopped in mid-stride, swallowing hard. For some unknown reason, something inside her was urging her to trust this stranger and she hadn't even seen him. Then his words fully registered in her brain. "How do you know my name?" Whirling around, she narrowed her eyes, trying to penetrate the darkness. "Show yourself."

"I know quite a bit about you, Meghan." The slightest rustling of the leaves gave away his position, but she had the feeling that he'd done it on purpose so as not to frighten her further. He glided forward, his strides fluid as he stepped into the moonlight and stopped, allowing her to see him for the first time.

Meghan almost swallowed her tongue. He *was* her dream lover come to life. He was so tall—at least eight inches more than her five-foot-eight—she had to tilt her head back to meet his gaze. She started at his feet and worked her way up.

Like her, he was barefoot. She licked her lips as she started upward. His legs were long, but heavily muscled. She could see the outline of his thighs through the fabric of his faded jeans. Even in this light she could see the long, thick ridge in the front of his pants. Heat blasted through her. There was no doubt in her mind that this stranger wanted her. No man could fake that kind of reaction.

She waited for the fear to kick in, but was only mildly surprised when she felt nothing but a growing desire. Rightly or wrongly, she felt a connection to this man. Logic told her that he was no phantom lover, but her unknown neighbor. He certainly fit the description that Mrs. Grady had given her. He shifted impatiently and she continued her perusal. He wasn't wearing a shirt, so she has a good view of the rest of his body.

His stomach was flat, but ridged with muscle. A light sprinkling of black hair dusted his chest before feathering down his abdomen, getting slightly heavier and thicker as it went. She imagined that his groin had a nice amount of the dark hair. Her fingers itched to touch him. To trace the path of the hair past his bellybutton and the button of his jeans.

Her breasts ached so badly that she wanted to cup them. No, that wasn't quite true. She wanted *him* to cup them in his large hands, which hung loosely by his sides. His chest was rising and falling rapidly as his breathing quickened. Her own breath was none too steady as she continued to study him. Broad shoulders, a thick neck and a stubborn jaw that was dark with evening shadow. She imagined he was the kind of man who had to shave at least twice a day if he wanted his chin to stay smooth.

His lips were full and sensual. The corner of his mouth was kicked up on one side, almost a smile, but not quite. His nose was large and appeared almost hawklike. Yet it suited his large face. His eyes were hooded, but even from here she could see his sinfully long lashes every time he blinked.

His hair was swept away from his face, accentuating his high forehead. The long, straight black hair grazed the tops of his shoulders. He was absolutely everything she'd imagined him to be and more.

"What's your name?"

There was no mistaking the slight upturn of his lips. "Rory."

He took a step toward her, but she felt no threat from him. If anything, her body swayed forward, wanting him closer.

"Now it's my turn to look." He took another step, bringing him within arm's length of her. She knew she should turn and run, but was rooted to the spot, unable to make her limbs function.

His eyes seemed to burn her flesh where they touched her. The color of fine aged whiskey, they seemed to almost glow in the moonlight. He appeared otherworldly, yet he was very much a flesh and blood man.

Butterflies fluttered in her stomach and her womb contracted with need. Pheromones. It had to be simple chemistry that was making her react this way. Never in her life had she felt so instantly drawn to a man and certainly not to a complete stranger. Except he didn't feel like a stranger, not exactly.

"How do you know me?" She tried to make her voice firm, but her question came out as more of a sultry tease.

He raised his hand slowly and grazed his thumb over the curve of her jaw. "You wished for me last night under the light of the full moon. Don't you know that there is magic in such things, Meghan?" The way he said her name, the lilt of his voice, made her knees weak. His voice alone was pure seduction.

"You saw me then?" She bit her lip, hoping against hope that he hadn't seen everything.

Her hopes were dashed by the flare of heat in his eyes. "Aye. I saw *everything*."

The way he said the last word left no doubt in her mind. He'd seen her pleasuring herself. Shame washed over her and she turned her head away. Catching her chin with the edge of his fingers, he tilted it upward until she had no choice but to look at him. She could feel the heat of a blush creeping up her cheeks.

"You were absolutely beautiful, sweet Meghan." He leaned down and she caught her breath as his mouth barely touched hers. "Magnificent." He licked her lower lip and she gasped. "Mine." His tongue swept into her mouth, coaxing hers to play with him.

All thoughts of running disappeared. This was what she'd wanted, wasn't it? A hot summer fling with a gorgeous man. She'd been sensible her entire life and where had it gotten her? She was thirty and she felt as if she'd never really tasted life, never taken a chance. What harm could it do?

She ignored the nagging voice that said plenty. She didn't want to think. She only wanted to feel. In a village this small, everyone knew everyone else's business. If he were dangerous, people would know.

Tonight would belong to them—a time out of time. Magic.

Only their lips touched, yet she felt as if his hands were stroking her everywhere. Rivulets of pleasure surged through her blood, finding their way to every part of her body from her toes to the roots of her hair. When he finally pulled away, they were both panting heavily.

"I want you, Meghan."

She sensed he was asking permission and would go no further without her consent. That gave her the courage to take the final plunge. To take what she truly desired. "Yes."

Satisfaction filled his face as he reached for the straps of her gown. He hooked his forefingers beneath each strap and eased them downward. They stopped just above her elbows. He stared down at her and waited. She knew that unless she shifted her arms from where they were tight against her body the straps would go no farther. She knew that the moment she moved, the straps and the bodice would fall, leaving her naked from the waist up.

Taking a deep breath, she slowly moved her arms. The fabric slithered down her torso, caressing her breasts and making her gasp as it teased her puckered nipples.

"Even more beautiful than I remembered," he whispered reverently as he raised his hands and cupped both milky-white mounds. Her breasts were large, but so were his hands. The sight of his tanned hands on her pale skin was very erotic and incredibly arousing. She arched slightly, pushing them deeper into his touch.

He tilted his head to one side and watched her as his thumbs grazed the swollen tips. A memory teased at her brain, nagging her senses. Maybe it was because she'd daydreamed about her dream lover so many times. There was a familiarity about him, but then it was gone. Lost in the present and the sensual longings he stirred within her.

"Let me pleasure you," he murmured, his sexy voice skating over her nerve endings as he lowered his head.

"Yes," she breathed as he placed a kiss on the curve of her breast. The ends of his hair felt softer than silk as they brushed across her chest. The dark stubble on his jaw was rough against her flesh. Her senses were heightened in the dark and she swore she could feel every individual strand of his hair that touched her.

His tongue rasped her nipple and she barely swallowed a cry of pleasure. She swayed and her hands flew out to clasp his shoulders. His skin was so warm it was almost hot and the muscles beneath were taut and thick. Her fingers curled inward, holding on to him.

He nuzzled from one breast to the other, taking his time as he licked and kissed both nipples until Meghan felt as if she couldn't stand the sensual torture any longer. He acted as if he had all the time in the world, but she knew that tonight was probably all they'd ever have. She knew that this was a time out of time. Moon madness. Perhaps in the light of day, she would question the choices she made tonight, but she knew she'd never regret being with Rory.

As if sensing her rioting emotions, he gave one final flick with his tongue and raised his head. "More?" His question made her shiver in spite of the heat. In answer, she gave her hips a shimmy and the fabric flowed down her hips and legs to puddle around her ankles. She wasn't wearing any underwear so she was now totally naked in front of him. She felt slightly self-conscious, well aware that she was not considered the feminine ideal with her ample hips and thighs. She was all curves and softness, not slender and willowy by any means.

Rory went to his knees in front of her and laid his head against her stomach. His arms went around her waist as he hugged her to him. Tears welled in her eyes and she swallowed hard. Without saying a word, he'd made her feel more cherished than any other man ever had.

Resting his hands on her hips, he turned his head and kissed the swell of her stomach. His lips were warm, the shadow of stubble on his face, slightly rough. His tongue snaked out to dip into her bellybutton. Her thighs trembled.

"I want to taste you, sweet Meghan. Spread your legs for me."

She felt almost lightheaded at his command. Could she do this? Before the thought was even finished her feet were moving, widening her stance. She'd never wanted a man more than she wanted the one kneeling in front of her. There was a solidness about him that drew her. Even though she had no basis for her belief, she trusted him implicitly not to hurt her.

He groaned as he nibbled her hipbones. "I wish I could see you better." His fingers sifted through her pubic hair. "You're a natural redhead, aren't you?"

"Yes," she gasped as his fingers probed a bit deeper, slipping over the wet folds of her sex. Personally, she was glad that they were in the moonlight. She was still feeling unsure of herself and her ample body.

"You are so damn sexy." His hands cupped her hips before sliding around to squeeze the globes of her behind. "I love your ass and your curves."

"I'm too fat." Oh God. She wanted to sink into the ground after blurting out that confession.

His hands froze on her butt and he raised his head. She could see the scowl on his face and the beginnings of anger in his eyes. Talk about a mood killer. *Way to go, Meghan.* She was even more self-conscious than she'd been before.

"You. Are. Not. Fat." He said the words slowly, spacing them out.

She shrugged. "I'm certainly not skinny."

"No, you're not," he agreed. "What you are is a woman. A real woman." His hands slid over her hips and down her thighs all the way to her knees before slipping inward and moving upward. "And you're mine."

"For tonight," she reminded him. His hands stilled and she thought he might say something, but then the moment passed.

"Aye. For tonight." He feathered his fingers over her sex. "And I plan to eat you until you come for me." His words and his touches were making her crazy. She was so wet she knew his hand was getting coated with her juices. She should be embarrassed, but she was too far gone to care. There was no hiding the fact that she wanted him. Badly.

His fingers parted her folds and he shifted closer, his breath hot on her already scalding flesh. She closed her eyes and just allowed herself to feel the sensations of pleasure washing over her. The slight night breeze, the sound of the insects buzzing and the hoot of the owl surrounded them. The scent of roses and lilacs mingled with her arousal, becoming a perfume all its own.

And then there was Rory.

She rested her hands lightly on his bent head. Her entire body tensed as his tongue swept out and stroked her slick folds. Her fingers curled, clutching at his hair. He laughed and then licked her again. She wiggled her hips, wanting his tongue on her clitoris, but he kept touching her everywhere but there.

"Rory," she moaned and tugged at his head again.

He raised his head, his eyes glinting in the moonlight. "Yes."

"Stop teasing me."

"But it's so much fun to tease you, my sweet." But he quickly bent his head and began to lick and suck. Two of his fingers slid deep into her tight channel and she sucked in a breath. Sweat beaded on her forehead and slowly slid down her back. She was burning up with need. Her entire body was focused on release, but it was just beyond her.

"Rory," she pleaded. Finally, the tip of his tongue grazed her swollen clitoris. Her entire body tightened. God, she was so close.

He separated his fingers and slowly slid them back out until only the tips were left inside her body. Then he thrust them deep. Meghan pumped her hips toward him, desperate now. She chanted his name again and again as he lapped at her clit, circling it with his tongue before taking it into his mouth and gently sucking.

Muscles tightened. Nerves tingled. Meghan tilted her head back and cried out as she came. Her body convulsed as pleasure rocketed through her. She tightened her grip on Rory. He was the only solid thing in her world. She swore she saw stars flash behind her eyelids as she shivered and shook.

When her legs buckled, he caught her, dragging her down into his lap and cradling her tight. She had no idea how much time had passed before she managed to pry her eyelids open. He was watching her much like a raptor watches its prey. His eyes were hooded, but glittering with intensity.

"That…" She swallowed hard before she could continue. "That was amazing."

"Aye." He gently tucked a lock of hair that had come loose from the knot around the curve of her ear. "And we've only just begun."

Chapter Three

ෂ

Rory stared down at the beautiful woman lolling in his arms. Her eyes widened at his words, but she didn't object, for which he would be eternally grateful. If he didn't get inside her amazing body soon, he'd explode in his pants. There was something about Meghan that sent his control out the window. He felt more like a callow youth than a man of some experience. Maybe it was because she was so real in every way. Her body was lush and bountiful and she held nothing back, giving him all of her passion. The effect on his senses was intoxicating.

The heat amplified the smells around them and the scent of her arousal was driving him insane. He wanted to toss her to the ground, thrust his aching cock into her and hammer his way into her heat and her heart until they both collapsed with pleasure.

He licked his lips, still tasting her on his mouth. She tasted sweet, like the finest clover honey. He shifted, trying to ease the throbbing pain of his cock, but it was no use. "I've got to get out of these." He lifted her out of his lap and stood. Meghan propped herself up on one elbow, staring up at the bulge in the front of his jeans.

"Oh, I'm sorry." She bit her bottom lip and he almost groaned aloud at the unintentional sensual action. He wanted to bite that plump lip and then soothe the sting with his tongue.

Instead, he unbuttoned his jeans and carefully lowered the zipper. The sounds of the metal teeth parting seemed unusually loud in the quiet of the night surrounding them. It was something man-made that didn't belong in this natural setting. He quickly shucked his pants and tossed them aside, glad he hadn't bothered with underwear.

Meghan's eyes were wide as she stared at his erection. The thick plum-shaped head bobbed toward her as if stating its intention. He was a large man and hoped she wasn't frightened by his size.

She blew that idea out of the window when she scooted closer and raised her hand to touch him. He groaned and his shaft jerked. She pulled back her fingers and glanced up at him, her teeth once again nibbling on her lower lip. "Can I?"

Could she? He swallowed hard, praying he wouldn't come the second she touched him again. He nodded. "Aye. You can touch me any way you want."

Taking him at his word, she wrapped her hand around his girth and gave an experimental pump. Rory gritted his teeth and counted to ten as she slid her hand upward.

"You're so hard, but so soft." Leaning closer, she rubbed her cheek up and down his length. It was torture. It was heaven.

He could feel her breath on him as her lips hovered over the tip of his cock. She parted her lips and he held his breath, willing her to take him into her mouth.

She blew lightly on the bulbous crown. The exquisite sensation made his head spin. He began to sweat. Could feel the rivulets of sweat slowly seeping down his back. He was surrounded by the heavy blanket of heat of the night as well as the heat from her mouth as she lowered it over the top of his erection.

The cavern of her mouth was warm and wet as it slipped easily down over his shaft. Rory cupped the sides of her head in his hands, desperately trying not to thrust himself deep. Her tongue swept over his skin as she pulled her head back. He'd had other woman suck his cock before, but never had it felt anywhere near as mind-blowing as this.

She smiled at him and then curled her tongue around the top as if she were licking an all-day sucker. He could easily imagine being sprawled out on his big bed for hours while Meghan sucked his cock. He'd probably die of pleasure, but what a way to go.

"Meghan," he groaned in warning when she cupped his balls in her hand. He could feel them pulling up tight and he knew he didn't have much longer. As much as he wanted to come in her mouth, he wanted to be inside her body when he came for the first time. He wanted her to come again. Wanted to feel her hot, tight pussy squeezing his cock when he came. And he had to stop thinking those things or it would be over before it even began. "You have to stop." His voice was rougher, but he couldn't help it.

"Why?" She pulled back her head long enough to ask, but then went back to licking off the pearly drops of fluid that were seeping from the tip.

"Because I'll come if you don't stop."

She paused and smiled up at him. "That's okay."

He almost fell to his knees, but he managed to stay upright. He knew what he wanted and he'd have it. "Next time. This time I want to fuck you until you scream with pleasure. I want to be locked inside your hot, wet body when you come. When we both come."

Meghan gave his cock one last long pull with her mouth and then sat back, licking her lips. "Okay."

The last thread of his control slipped away and he went to his knees beside her. "On your hands and knees. I want to take you from behind." The emotions pumping through him were hot and primal. He wanted to fuck her hard from behind, getting as deep inside her as he could. He wanted to mark her as his so she'd never want any other man but him. He was partly appalled by his lack of finesse, but he didn't care. He had to have her and he had to have her this way.

But only if she wanted it.

His hands were fisted at his sides as he waited for her to decide. She leaned forward and kissed him then. He opened his mouth, inviting her to take whatever she wanted from him. He slanted his mouth across hers, devouring her, tasting himself on her lips. His cock pulsed and throbbed. His balls ached.

She pulled away, took a shaky breath and then turned. He waited in agony as she hesitated briefly and then almost let out a shout as she knelt on the ground in front of him.

"Lower your head and raise your ass up." He watched as she did as he asked, exposing herself totally to him. "You're so pink and pretty." He dipped his fingers between her thighs. "And so damn wet."

He grabbed his jeans and dug into the back pocket, grabbing the foil packet he'd placed there earlier. He quickly ripped it open and rolled the latex over his shaft. His need to fuck this woman was overridden by the need to protect her at all costs. The last thing he wanted was for her to be worried in the morning. She raised her head, turned and smiled at him. "Thank you." Her soft words seeped into his heart and he nodded.

He made a place for himself between her thighs, sliding them farther apart to accommodate his size. His cock was poised at her entrance, but he paused. "Are you sure?" As much as it might kill him to stop, he'd do it if she wasn't one hundred percent sure.

"Yes." It was slightly muffled in the soft grass, but he heard her. Gripping her hips with his hands, he slowly began to push his way inside.

Meghan bit her bottom lip to hold back a scream of pleasure as she felt Rory's cock begin to slide deeper into her. He was so big and it had been such a long time for her that she honestly wasn't sure she could take all of him. His shaft stretched her as he rocked his way into her an inch at a time. He paused occasionally, his breathing rough.

"That's it," he crooned softly. "Just relax. You can take all of me." It was hard, but she took one deep breath and then another and felt more of him fit inside her. "Please, Meghan," he groaned as he pushed harder. Her inner muscles contracted and relaxed, coaxing him deeper.

She felt totally surrounded by him, filled by his cock as he finally seated himself to the hilt. God, he was large everywhere, but she wanted it all, every last inch of him. She could still taste his essence on her tongue—salty and warm.

He withdrew slightly and then surged back into her. It was easier this time and felt incredibly good. When he did it again, she pushed her behind back to meet him, driving him deeper. She moaned as he filled her.

His thrusts got harder and deeper with each one he took, eventually getting faster and faster until he was slamming into her. His hands slipped from her hips, one of them sliding up to cup her breast, while the other slipped between her thighs, resting on her clit. Every time he stroked forward, his finger brushed the bundle of nerves, sending lightning bolts of pleasure shooting through her.

Time seemed to stand still as he fucked her. Encircled by the enchantment of the night and the place, the ground was warm beneath her knees and hands and the sweet smell of the grass mingling with the more pungent smells of sex and sweat. It was primal. It was wild. It was pure magic.

He was driving into her so hard now that she felt the slap of his balls against her pussy with each stroke. Her entire being was focused on release as his fingers pressed against her swollen clit. She dug her fingers into the ground for leverage as his thrusts threatened to drive her forward. Her feminine muscles twitched and tightened, signaling the onset of her orgasm.

"Harder," she cried, needing more, needing everything from him. And he gave it. He practically lifted her off the ground as his hips slammed against her butt, the slapping sound of flesh against flesh adding to her excitement.

It came crashing down on her. Her back bowed as she cried out. Her muscles tightened around his cock and she could feel him jerking inside her, knew he was coming. For a brief moment she resented the condom, the barrier between them even though she knew it was sensible. She wanted to feel his hot cum flooding her, but had to be content with the spasms of his release rippling through her.

She thought he might have called out her name, but she couldn't be sure. There was a *whoosh*ing sound in her ears that blocked out all other sound. She collapsed onto the ground and Rory all but fell on top of her, managing to shift his body to one side so that he wasn't crushing her but they were still intimately joined.

Meghan concentrated on trying to breathe, but it wasn't easy as the air was hot and heavy. Her entire body was sweaty and her hair had mostly come down from its knot and was plastered against her face and neck. She wanted to reach up and try to move it, and she would. Just as soon as she got the energy.

Rory moved first, shifting backward to gently remove his semi-erect cock. She stifled a groan, but couldn't stop the involuntary action of her muscles tightening around him as he withdrew. She turned her head to watch him as he fished a tissue out of his pocket, removed the spent condom and wrapped it up for disposal.

She knew she should probably move or at least say something, but she honestly didn't have the strength. Rory sprawled back down beside her, his large body crowding her as he propped himself up on one arm. "How do you feel?" He began to smooth the damp strands of hair off her face and she sighed in pleasure.

"Great. Amazing. Incredible." There weren't enough words.

He chuckled. "All of that."

She gave him a mock scowl. "You know you're good."

He shook his head. "I know that we're good. Together."

She shifted uncomfortably beneath his stare. She didn't want to talk, didn't want reality to intrude on their special night, didn't want to dream beyond the moment. She'd had enough disappointment in the past year of her life. Right now, she wanted to feel.

She reached up to stroke his cheek, sensing his disappointment. Maybe it was wrong not to talk about what was happening between them. But the moment was gone when he began to kiss her. He licked at her bottom lip, biting it gently and then licking away the sting. "You have the sexiest mouth."

She could feel his cock swelling, pressing against her hip. He'd recovered amazingly fast. "Again?"

"Again," he nodded as he swooped down and captured her mouth. All thoughts of tomorrow vanished beneath the onslaught of their rising passion.

They made love twice more before he walked her to her garden gate. "Tomorrow?" she dared to ask, wanting more of what they'd shared tonight.

He stared down at her for so long, she feared she'd made a mistake in asking. Finally, he nodded. "Tomorrow."

And so it went for the next six nights, each one more breathtaking then the last. He encouraged her to tell him her sexual fantasies and desires, so she did, shyly at first, but then with more confidence. Not that there were many, but what few she did have, he fulfilled.

They talked some, but never delved into territory that was too personal. Her choice, she knew. Not his. She sensed his growing frustration, but still he came to her every night in the glade. Meghan prayed for the heat wave to last.

She knew she was being a coward, but couldn't quite find the courage to take their relationship beyond the physical, beyond the dark of the night. It was safer that way—at least emotionally. Or so she thought until she made her way to their spot by the well on the seventh night only to find it empty except for a note.

She picked up the scrap of paper and carried it home to read. Curling up in her bed alone, she unfolded it, her eyes scanning quickly. She'd been right. He was tired of being her nighttime lover. Her vision blurred, but she blinked her tears back. He wanted more from her. Much more.

He wanted her to come to him in the light of the day, but only if she was willing to give him more. Otherwise they were through. He signed it with his full name and his address. Not that she needed it. She'd known from that first night he was her elusive neighbor.

Meghan lay back on the mattress and stared at the sliver of the moon through her window. Tears seeped from her eyes and rolled down her cheeks to land on her pillow. She'd thought she'd been so smart, protecting herself from emotional entanglement. She should have known better. There was no way she'd have allowed herself to stay involved with Rory if she hadn't felt something for him.

She threw her arm across her eyes to block out the moonlight that seemed to mock her. There was no kidding herself any longer. She was half in love with the man. If asked a couple of weeks ago whether she believed in love at first sight, she would have said no. Now she wasn't sure. She'd felt something for Rory the first time she'd seen him that had gone beyond the physical. Whatever it was, she wasn't sure, but there was only one way to find out.

Did she have the courage to take the next step, knowing it would mean leaving herself more than just physically bare, but emotionally bare as well? She lay there all night thinking, finally falling into a light, fretful doze as the sun was rising.

Chapter Four

ಌ

The midday sun bounced off his computer screen, distracting him from work. Rory turned off his computer in disgust. He hadn't slept at all last night. He'd known he was taking a gamble when he'd left the note for Meghan, but he'd taken his chances and obviously lost. He glanced at the clock, noting it was ten minutes after twelve. He'd told her he'd wait until noon for her answer. He guessed he'd gotten one, just not the one he'd been hoping for.

Raking his hands through his hair, he sighed. Maybe he'd pushed her too soon, but there was no going back. He wanted more from Meghan. He wanted to know all about her life and not just the bits and pieces he'd managed to glean from some of the neighbors.

Pushing away from his desk, Rory stood and stretched before heading out of the room and down the stairs. A sharp rap sounded on the front door and he almost ignored it. He wasn't in the mood to talk to the neighbors. But he went to answer it anyway, unable to stifle the hope that it might be Meghan. He noted with disgust that his hand shook as he turned the knob and opened the door.

She stood there on the other side of the threshold, looking nervous and uncertain as she shifted her weight from leg to leg. "Hi."

"Hi."

She cleared her throat. "Ah, can I come in?"

He stepped back and motioned her inward. She came inside and looked around, her curiosity evident. He wanted to know for sure why she'd come before his hopes got dashed again. "Why are you here?"

She turned, startled by his voice or his words, he couldn't say. "Because you asked me to come."

He needed more. Crossing his arms to keep from hauling her into them, he watched her fidget with the buttons of her pretty yellow sundress. He tried not to notice how the low bodice cupped her breasts to perfection or how the fabric slid enticingly over her curves, but failed miserably.

She licked her lips and he stifled a groan of need. His cock was already responding to her nearness, lengthening and thickening in anticipation. But he wanted more from her. He wanted everything.

"What do you want?" His stark words lay between them.

She wandered into the living room and perused his bookcase. "I want you."

"I already know that." He watched as she examined the spines of several books before turning to face him.

"I'm afraid." Whatever he'd been expecting, it hadn't been that.

"I'd never hurt you."

She glanced away. "Not intentionally." Haltingly at first, she told him about the last year of her life, all the upheavals and the changes. "I'm afraid." She blinked back the tears that shimmered in her eyes. "Afraid to hope that we might work. But I'm more afraid of losing what we might have together by being a coward."

His heart ached and he knew in that moment that he loved her. She'd bared her soul to him, holding nothing back, offering him all that she was. He opened his arms to her and she walked into them. He held her tight, her heart against his, both of them pounding in rhythm.

"Come with me." He eased his arm around her shoulders and led her toward the back door. She sent him a quizzical glance, but went with him. He hurried them outside the house and around to a small stone patio with a wide chaise lounge and a matching fabric-covered chair sitting in the center. Turning, he reached for the buttons of her dress.

Meghan's head was spinning from the quick change of events. She'd gone from pouring her heart out to him, to being whisked outside. But she understood what Rory was doing. He wanted to reconfirm their commitment under the full light of the sun at the height of the day. No more skulking around in the dark, under cover of the moon. Either she was in this relationship or she wasn't. And she definitely was.

His long, thick fingers made quick work of the row of buttons that ran down the front of her dress. She hadn't worn a bra with it. Hadn't been able to due to the thin straps that held the dress up. She'd also felt more daring, more sensual going without one.

"Oh my lord," he breathed reverently as he slipped the last few buttons from their holes.

She hadn't worn any underwear either.

He slid the fabric over her shoulders and let it slide down her arms. She kicked off her sandals and stood there totally naked, letting him look his fill. The sun was hot on her shoulders, but not nearly as scorching as the look in his eyes as he surveyed her from head to toe and back up again.

She'd never stood outside in the daylight with no clothes on. It was different from their nighttime escapades. There was more of a "look at me" statement. She was no longer hiding from him or from their relationship. No matter what happened, she was determined to give what they had between them a chance to grow and flourish.

"You are so fucking beautiful." His voice was hoarse, his words raw, but they filled an empty spot deep within her. She knew that she wasn't beautiful, not in the classic sense. Not with her untamed red hair and her pale skin. Not to mention the extra pounds and curves. But she no longer cared about it.

Not when Rory looked at her like he did. With him she felt wild and free and, yes, even beautiful.

"You next." Her own voice was none too steady, but she wanted him naked. Wanted to see him. To touch him.

Reaching his hands behind his head, he grabbed his shirt and ripped it over his head, never taking his eyes off her. He was barefoot, so he didn't have shoes or socks to dispose of. His hands went to the button and zipper on his jeans and flicked them open. Then he shoved his pants and underwear over his long, muscular legs. Meghan licked her lips in anticipation as his cock sprang free from its confinement. Lord, the man was gorgeous.

Rory kicked his clothing aside and stood there with his legs spread and his hands on his hips. With his black hair touching his shoulders and the devilish grin on his face, he looked like some conquering marauder surveying his spoils of war.

"Sit down in the chair." His accent was thick now, like it always got when he was aroused. A shiver skated down her spine, but she eagerly did as he asked. The fabric was warm against her back and behind, but not too hot. "Now hook your legs over the arms."

Sweat popped out on her upper lip as she imagined what that position would do to her. She'd be totally exposed to Rory with no darkness or shadows to hide her. Licking her lips, she slowly hitched her right leg over the arm of the chair. Then she did the same with her left. With her legs spread wide, her pussy was totally exposed.

Rory fell to his knees in front of her and stared. She could feel her skin getting warmer and knew that it was more than just the rays of the sun heating her. "Touch your breasts." He picked up her hands as he spoke and placed them on the plump mounds. "I want to watch you pleasure yourself."

Embarrassment and arousal warred within her, but arousal won out easily. Cupping her breasts in her palms, she used her thumbs to circle her nipples, moaning as the pleasure shot straight to her core.

"Yes," he praised as he reached out and skimmed his index finger over her slick folds. "You're already hot and wet, aren't you, Meghan?"

"Yes," she groaned as she watched his cock jerk forward. "You want me too," she countered.

His whiskey-colored eyes were ablaze as he pinned her to the chair. "More than you can even imagine." His fingers sifted through her pubic hair, tugging lightly on it.

Meghan could feel thick cream sliding from her slit. Could feel the dampness on her inner thighs as he leaned forward. He spread her wide with his thumbs so he had nothing impeding him as he licked up one side and down the other. Her hips tilted forward. She wanted those thick fingers sliding in and out of her.

"Don't stop playing with those pretty puckered nipples, Meghan, or I'll have to stop what I'm doing to give them proper attention." The man was diabolical. No way did she want him stopping what he was doing. She plucked at her nipples with her fingers, crying out in pleasure at the sensation. Rory tongued her swollen clitoris before sucking it gently into his mouth.

Her toes curled as she tilted her head back, raising her face to the sun. There was something almost healing about the heat of the sun on her body and the heat of Rory's mouth on her sex.

She cried out his name when he slid two fingers inside her. Her feminine muscles tightened and relaxed rhythmically as he began to move them in and out at a slow, measured pace. His tongue kept licking and sucking at the slick folds of her pussy and clitoris. Meghan's nipples tightened painfully and she plucked at them with her fingers.

"Don't stop," she moaned just before her body convulsed with pleasure. Rory never even paused, continuing to stroke her body with his fingers and his tongue until her orgasm was finished and she was all but purring with contentment.

He pushed away from her and licked his lips as he stood. Sliding his arms beneath her legs and around her back, he lifted her easily from the chair. Her head lolled against his slick shoulder and she licked his warm flesh, savoring the salty taste of his skin. He shuddered, so she did it again. Laughing, he lowered himself to the chaise lounge and, with her help, arranged her on top of him so that she was straddling his stomach, her legs on either side. The head of his cock poked her in the behind.

"Your turn." He lounged back in the comfortable chair like a pasha. "Whatever you want."

What did she want? Well, one thing was for sure, she wanted to see him, to touch him and to taste him. Placing her hands on his shoulders, she slid them down the hard planes of his chest, testing the hardness of the muscles just below the skin. She could feel his muscles twitch as her hands passed over them. Scooting forward, she lowered her head closer and flicked his flat nipple with her tongue.

Rory sucked in a breath. Thick fingers threaded through her hair, knocking aside some of her hairpins so that a few of the locks tumbled down her back, as he held her mouth closer to him. Smiling, she flicked his nipple again as she scraped her nails over his belly.

"Meghan." She could hear the warning in his voice and almost laughed.

She raised her head and plastered what she hoped was an innocent look on her face. "What? You said I could do whatever I wanted."

The corner of his mouth kicked up in a grin. "Aye, I did. But remember that payback is a bitch."

"Promises, promises." She fluttered her eyelashes at him before lowering her head again. She left a trail of openmouthed kisses on his flesh as she moved down his belly, tasting and touching him everywhere except where he wanted it the most. His cock flexed and stretched, but she worked her way down his sides without touching it.

Finally, she sat back on her heels between his spread thighs and cupped his heavy sac in her hands, rolling his balls carefully. His eyes were almost closed, but she could still see the glitter of lust shining from them.

Bending forward, she licked his shaft from root to tip, taking care to swirl her tongue around the head. His fingers tightened in her hair again as she opened her mouth and took the tip inside, sucking hard. She could feel his sac pulling tight to his body and she rubbed the sensitive skin just behind it.

Sweat trickled down her back as heat surrounded her and filled her. The day was alive with smells and sounds. The bees hummed gently as they flitted from flower to flower. The perfume of about a dozen varieties of flowers, including roses and lavender surrounded them. The heat from the sun enveloped them. But Meghan barely noticed any of it. All her senses were attuned to the man sprawled out on the lounge beneath her.

Her body ached for his. She wanted him inside her. Needed to feel his heat and his power as he surged within her. She moved her mouth up and down his shaft a few more times before raising her head. When she released him, he shuddered. His hands fell from her head and dropped down beside him.

She tasted his essence on her tongue and her lips as she licked them. She didn't say anything as she positioned herself on either side of his hips, bracing herself with her knees and her hands. His cock was probing at her moist entrance.

"Protection," he rasped out.

She shook her head. "I'm safe and I'm on the Pill. I started when I thought that Mark and I were moving in together. I never stopped taking them and I'm clean."

"I'm healthy." He wrapped his hands around her hips. "I've never made love without a condom before."

"Never?" She was shocked and thrilled all at once.

"Never."

"Okay, then." Meghan began to lower herself, taking him into her body one slow, wonderful inch at a time. Without the condom as a barrier between them, the sensations were more intense. She felt the glide of his skin over hers and gasped at the deliciousness of it. Because of her earlier orgasm, he slid easily into her heated depths. When he was seated all the way in, she wiggled around to situate herself better. They both groaned at the wonderful friction between them.

"Move," he gasped and she could see the strain on his face. Sweat rolled down his temple, disappearing into his hairline. Her body was slick, inside and out. She'd never felt more alive in her life than she did at this moment.

She pulled herself upward until just the tip of his cock remained inside her and then lowered herself again. His fingers dug into her hips as he guided her up and down his shaft. Her breasts swayed as her body moved. They felt heavy and ached with need. Without thought, she cupped them in her hands and massaged the tight nipples.

"Yes," Rory hissed as he urged her to pick up the speed.

Tipping her head back to the sun, she quickened her pace, rising and lowering herself faster and faster. She could feel the familiar quivering low in her belly and knew she was close.

Rory watched Meghan move over him, enthralled by her unrestrained sensuality. The moon maiden had been replaced by the sun goddess and was just as captivating. Her long red hair glinted in the light as it spilled over her shoulders, like a fiery cape. Several strands were stuck to her forehead and cheeks, but she didn't seem to care. All her concentration was on their joining.

He tightened his hold on her hips, loving the feel of her lush curves beneath him. He knew that she thought she was overweight, but he thought she was perfect. He'd have all the time in the world to convince her of that now that she was committed to giving their relationship a chance and he was looking forward to the challenge.

His balls were so tight against his body, he was surprised he hadn't already exploded. He wanted to come, but he wanted it to last. The clasp and release of Meghan's cunt as she slid up and down his cock sent shocks of pleasure shooting out to every cell of his body. But the inevitable would not be delayed. He could feel her inner muscles grasping him tighter and knew she was close.

She plucked harder at her nipples. He wanted to taste them, but knew they were both too far gone. Later, he promised himself. At the moment, it was enough to watch her pleasure herself as she rode him.

Keeping one hand tight around her waist, he slid the other to the apex of her thighs, fingering her clit with every downward thrust she took. She sucked in a breath and screamed his name. Her cunt gripped him so tight it was almost painful. It drove him over the edge and he felt his own release rise up from his balls to shoot out the top of his shaft.

Gasping, he held her tight as he yelled his own release. His cock pulsed as he spewed his hot seed within her tight depths. Meghan cried out again, her hands clutching at him for support as she arched backward, driving him even deeper.

When she slumped forward, he caught her in his arms. She fit perfectly and he never wanted to let her go. Closing his eyes, he savored the feel of her slick skin against his as aftershocks of pleasure made both of them shudder. He would have stayed there forever except that now that his body was sated he began to really notice the heat.

"Meghan." He tried to rouse her, but she just mumbled against his neck. He managed to slip his semi-erect cock from her body, groaning as her muscles tugged at him one final time before releasing him. Gathering what little was left of his strength, he managed to shift them both so that Meghan was in his arms and he was sitting on the side of the lounge.

It took him three tries before he staggered to his feet and in through the back door. He didn't pause, but managed to get them up the stairs and into the bathroom. Meghan shivered when he propped her up against the cool tiles in the bathroom. She opened her eyes and blinked several times as if she wasn't quite sure how she'd gotten here.

"We both need a cool shower." He studied her pale skin and cursed himself. "I think you might have gotten a bit too much sun."

She smiled sleepily at him. "You too."

He turned away from her long enough to get the water running, making sure it was lukewarm. Still, she shivered again when he helped her beneath the spray. The water seemed to revive them both as they soaped each other's bodies. Rory didn't know where either of them found the strength, but they managed to make love standing up in the shower before the water ran completely cold.

After they toweled off, Rory took the time to soothe some aloe vera gel over Meghan's face, shoulders, back, chest and legs before tumbling her into his big bed and taking her into his arms. The heat of the day and the exhaustion from their activities washed over them both. He could hear her steady breathing and knew that she'd already fallen asleep. Shutting his eyes, he settled her closer and followed her into sleep.

When she awoke, Meghan felt absolutely and utterly replete. She knew that she had a slight sunburn, but she didn't care. It had been totally worth it. She'd awakened two more times during the afternoon and early evening to find Rory's hands and mouth already making love to her. The man did love to touch her, seemingly content to spend hours just stroking her body. Not that she was complaining. She loved every single moment of it.

The sun had gone down hours ago and the room was dark with shadows. Rolling to her side, she stared at the man sprawled on top of the covers next to her. His hand was wrapped tight around hers as if even in sleep he didn't want to let her go.

The moment she turned, she sensed his alertness. A second later, his eyes opened. "Can't sleep."

"Hmmm." She nuzzled closer to him, loving his unique smell. "I wouldn't say that. We've slept most of the day away."

He turned on his side, facing her and slid his free hand over her hip. "Not all day."

She laughed. "No, not all day," she agreed. The man was insatiable when it came to her and she loved it.

But instead of making love to her again, he continued to stare at her. "I remember the first time I saw you."

"That night at the well."

He shook his head. "No. The first time I saw you, you couldn't have been much more than eleven or twelve years old. I was fifteen and was visiting my great-uncle who owned this very house."

Meghan stilled. It couldn't be. Sitting up in bed, she flicked on a lamp and studied him in the dim light. Now that she was looking for it, she could see the features of that boy stamped on the man he'd become. "You."

He grinned at her and she caught a glimpse of the cocky young man she'd had her very first crush on. "Aye, me. Don't think that I didn't see you watching me when you came to town. I found out your name, but my vacation was over. You seemed mature for your age, but you were too young for me back then." He winked at her.

"Maybe you're too old for me now," she retorted.

He shook his head and chuckled. "When I returned the following year, you were gone to the States with your mother and new stepfather. I hadn't thought about you in years and then you were back. I was still trying to decide what to do about it when I came across you that night at the well."

"I've been living here more than three months." She was charmed that he remembered her and had apparently had noticed her as well. But she was also slightly peeved that he hadn't approached her in the three months since she'd been back since he'd known who she was.

He raked his hand through his hair. "You're not the only one who's relationship shy."

She guessed she could understand that. She was still pondering it when Rory sat up and reached around her, flicking off the light. When he lay back down, he urged her down into his arms.

"We both have pasts that have shaped who we are, but what matters now is the future."

She nodded, teasing his chest hair with her fingers. "I just realized that I don't even know what you do for a living."

He laughed. "I'm a writer. I write mostly fantasy novels with a touch of mystery and romance."

She sat up again. "You're serious." Everything fell into place suddenly. "You're *that* Rory Shaunnessey?"

He pulled her into his arms and rolled until she was beneath him. "I'm the Rory Shaunnessey who loves you."

Meghan froze beneath his body, not quite sure she'd heard him correctly. She was still reeling from the fact that he was a famous writer. Heck, she'd read some of his books.

His large hand gently pushed a lock of hair out of her face as he leaned closer until their noses were all but touching. "I mean it, Meghan. I don't know how or why it happened so fast. Call it moon magic if you want, but I know it's more than that. Your wish that night at the well echoed something inside me."

"I love you too." Even as she said it, she knew it was true. Whether it was magic or fate, she didn't care. They were together and that was all that matters. The future lay before them, uncharted territory for them to explore together.

She turned her head and could make out the moon, which was little more than a quarter now. Silently, she gave thanks to whatever deity had answered her prayers that night at the well. She'd gotten a man who wanted her for who she was, but she'd gotten so much more.

His lips caressed hers and she parted them, letting his tongue slide inside. They sealed their pact with a kiss, their bodies joining together to celebrate their future.

PRACTICALLY PERFECT

Allyson James

ഔ

Chapter One

ꙮ

"How long will you be staying with us on Level 20,000, sir?" the small, gray-haired man in his glass-walled booth asked Walker. He spoke with an ultra-cultured, old-world English accent, though Walker knew the man had probably never left the space station in his life.

"Couple of days," Walker answered.

Station 358 was the perfect place to lie low. Its soaring, transparent steel walls stretched upward to infinity, each level offering a world of limitless food, drink and entertainment, as much as you wanted depending on how much you could pay.

"Sir has not stayed on Level 20,000 before, has he?" the concierge asked, his slender fingers dancing over a touch screen.

"No, Sir hasn't."

Walker spent a lot of time in dumps, going without sleep or food while he stalked his prey. If he was going to take a few days off, he might as well do it in style. A hot bath, soft bed and mindless digital entertainment sounded good about now.

"I can put Sir in Suite 37,928, but it's a bit pricey." The concierge ran his gaze down Walker's rumpled space jacket and the very obvious pistol in a battered hip holster.

"Fine. What I want is privacy. Can you give me that?"

The concierge blinked. "Sir, on Level 20,000, you can have whatever you want."

Walker glanced at the railed walkway that encircled the inside of the station, stretching into misty distance. Wheeled carts and hover transports, mostly chauffeured, zoomed along with their privileged passengers. The good life.

"All right then, give me thirty-seven thousand…whatever it is."

"Thirty-seven thousand, nine hundred and twenty-eight." The concierge stamped a tiny chip under the skin of Walker's forefinger. "This key will last seven days. If you need to stay longer, simply return here and I will renew it."

"Thanks."

"Does Sir need any help with his baggage?"

Walker hefted his beat-up duffel bag. "Sir has it covered."

"Then can I offer Sir a Guide to the levels? Station 358 can be quite confusing—even if you stay on Level 20,000."

"Is the guide extra?"

The man's eyes widened in shock. "Oh no, sir. It is complementary."

"Fine, I'll take it."

He expected the man to slide over a handheld or stamp in another chip, but the concierge merely nodded. "I'll have one sent to Sir's room. Go to the left, take our hovercar a mile and a half to the Ambrosia corridor, then along to the third suite on the right. Enjoy your stay."

"Right." Walker slung his duffel bag over his shoulder, gave the concierge a tight nod and strode away.

He shocked the hovercar chauffeur by electing to walk the mile and half down the hall, which was barely a stroll in the park to him. Simple enough to find the Ambrosia corridor and his suite. His chip key soundlessly opened the door.

The first room was larger than some of the apartments he'd lived in, and that was only the foyer. An arena-sized living room opened off that with a transparent wall overlooking an atrium. Greenery and a misty waterfall completed the ambiance.

The bedroom beyond was no less large, with a bed measuring at least ten-by-ten feet. Three couples could have sex on it and never touch each other.

He wasn't in the mood for orgies, although he guessed the obsequious concierge could arrange one for him. Walker was a private man, and liked his sex without another couple screaming away in the same room, though he didn't mind the occasional threesome.

Right now, he wanted a bath. He stripped down, carrying his holstered pistol with him to the massive bathroom that included a soaking tub large enough for five. There were easier ways to clean his body—the bathroom provided a sterilizing booth—but nothing beat a good soak in hot water.

He told the bathtub what temperature he wanted and lowered himself in. Walker was a big man, nearly seven feet tall. He'd grown up on space stations and in low-G ships, which had contributed to his height, and he'd exercised like hell to keep his bones from becoming brittle. The result was a massive chest, broad shoulders, tight thighs and long runner's legs.

The mirror on the ceiling showed him in the clear water, a brown-skinned man with dark brown hair brushing his chest and curling around his thick cock. The brown hair on his head was sun-streaked, and a two-day beard prickled his sharp cheeks and jaw.

A gadget attached to the tub scraped off the whiskers, another scrubbed him all over. Then he simply soaked.

The smugglers were heading here, as Walker's trusty tracking robot reported, so there was no need to chase them. Lane would be an easy bounty.

He usually preferred a bigger challenge, but he was tired and ready to be bone-lazy for a while. After this he'd go after something more difficult, something that would bring him shiploads of cash and leave a terrific taste in his mouth. The euphoria of landing an elusive bounty was close to what he got from a good, hard-pounding fuck.

Not that he'd had one of those in a while. Bounty hunting could be a lonely life.

The front door chimed. Walker automatically reached for the pistol on the ledge next to him, though he reasoned it was probably the concierge with the promised guide. He touched a lighted screen to speak into the intercom. "Just leave it by the door."

There was a short silence then the door chimed again.

Walker let the intercom reveal a picture of who stood outside. He sucked in his breath.

The lens focused down on a woman with sleek, dark hair leaning toward the speaker, the camera angle letting him see a cute butt in a tight skirt. "Your Guide, sir."

Much better than the concierge. Should he let her in and have a little fun? Tempting, but Walker truly was exhausted.

"I said just leave it by the door."

She hesitated again. "I—can't, sir."

He growled. "All right. Hang on."

Walker heaved himself from the bath, grabbed a bathrobe and slid it on. The material was thin but silky soft, and it soaked up some of the water. He snatched up the pistol and hid it under the robe, ready and charged.

It took him a while to walk all the way through the massive bedroom, sitting room and foyer. When he opened the door, he stood to one side in case the young woman or any hidden friend decided to rush him. Old habits kept him alive.

The woman peeked around the corner at Walker. "Sir?"

Fucking damn. Walker's balls tightened.

She was tall enough that she could tuck her head under his chin if she wanted, so he could inhale the cinnamon scent of her glossy black hair. Long legs were set off to perfection by a slim skirt that ended halfway down her thighs. Her shirt was a little loose, showing the hollow of her throat and a shadow of round, cuppable breasts.

She walked all the way in and turned to close the door, giving him a full view of the sweet ass he'd glimpsed before.

He imagined sliding his hand over that nice behind to enjoy its firm feel.

Her eyes were brown. Walker had seen eye color from every part of the galaxy—black, silver, gold, blue, green—but nothing compared to the coffee-dark gaze of this beauty. Her face was neither too round nor too long, eyes, nose, mouth in perfect proportions.

Her mouth was red-lipped and sensual. He could dip his tongue behind the full bottom lip and swipe up her goodness.

His cock was swiftly lifting. It had been a long time since he'd gotten a hard-on just by looking at a woman, but she was something special.

Or maybe it had just been too long between fucks.

"Concierge send you?" he asked. Maybe the little man had sensed that Walker needed good-smelling female company. Level 20,000 really did anticipate every need.

"You ordered a Guide to the station, did you not, sir?"

Walker felt a bite of disappointment. She was a delivery girl, not an amenity. "You can drop the *sir*. It's Walker."

"Of course, Mr. Walker." Her sensual gaze skimmed his bathrobe-clad body. "Will you need assistance finding clothes? I can direct you to several tailor shops on this level."

"I have clothes." He could think of several entertaining ways to get dressed with her. Or her running a tape measure all over his body to measure him for a suit.

He stopped his thoughts before his skin started to smoke.

She needed to go before he slung her over his shoulder, hand on her nicely shaped ass, and carried her to bed. If he wasn't arrested he'd get kicked out of this plush lodging and find himself down with the lowlifes.

"Just leave the guide. I'll figure it out myself."

She smiled. Damn, she was pretty when she did that. Her smile was lopsided, ruining the perfect symmetry of her face, but that made it all the more beautiful. Her eyes got sparkly too.

He imagined her smiling that crooked smile while she floated in the pool-sized bathtub with him, arching her body back so he could squeeze his cock inside her pretty little pussy.

"You misunderstand, sir," she said. "I *am* the Guide. Your Personal Guide to Station 358. I can show you everything from the top of the dome to the trash compaction area, if you should so wish. You have but to want something, and I will give it to you."

Chapter Two

౭

This couldn't be real. This was a man's wet dream, a female who smiled and said she'd do anything he asked. *Go down on me? Play dress-up for me? Just let me fuck you until I can't see straight?*

His erection gave a nice, hungry throb. "And how long do I get to keep you?"

"Seven days, Mr. Walker. If you need to stay longer, just tell the concierge and he'll renew me."

Well, shit. "Let me get this straight—I want something, I ask for it?"

Her smile deepened as though she were pleased he'd finally caught up. "Exactly, Mr. Walker."

"What about sex?"

He couldn't help the question—his hammer-hard penis made him ask.

She didn't bat an eyelash. "Of course. Level 20,000 has some of the best and most discreet services anywhere. I can lead you to them or arrange for them to come here. Would you prefer male or female?"

Some of his ardor faded. He knew men who would drool on themselves when offered a sex smorgasbord, but her clinical answer took some of the enjoyment out of it. Besides, he wanted *her*, not a faceless professional service.

Sex should be basic and fun, spontaneous and wicked. No-holds-barred, however far either party wanted to go. No rules, no forms to sign, no menu.

"Never mind. I'll just eat and get some kip."

"Kip?"

"Sleep." He started the trek back to the bathroom. "Go on back to wherever you work. I'll call you if I need something."

He heard her soft shoes on the rug as she followed him. Even her footsteps were sexy. "You have me for seven days, Mr. Walker. I stay with you."

He swung around. She was a foot behind him, her sweet-scented hair nearly under his nose. "You're kidding me."

"Guides never kid, Mr. Walker. Although I do have a number of jokes I can tell if you'd like, and amusing puns about what we'll find on the station."

This had gone far enough. She was tempting but too clean and pretty for the Walkers of the universe. He wasn't just rough around the edges, he was rough all over.

He spent his time hunting down the most dangerous men in the galaxy not because he had a moral streak, but because it was so much damn fun. Plus, he'd hate to see defenseless people like pretty Miss Guide here mowed down by them.

"Look, sweetheart, run along back to the concierge and tell him I canceled my order. I don't need a sweet thing following me around. In fact, it might be dangerous if you do."

She looked stricken. "Cancel?"

Great, now he'd hurt her feelings. "It's nothing personal. I'm not the tourist kind of guy." He hauled his pistol and holster out from under the robe. "You see this?"

Her eyes narrowed as she took it in. "It looks like a model H28 X-charged, though you've modified the firing device."

Walker blinked. "That's right."

"I have an amazing store of knowledge, Mr. Walker. I've never used a pistol, but I know all about them."

With effort, he pulled his thoughts together. "The point is, you're too sugar and spice for me. I'm a bad man. I've killed with this gun, and I expect to do it again. I'm staying here because I'm between jobs, I can afford it and I had a bet with myself that a place like this wouldn't let me in. You're a sweetheart, and you don't deserve to be stuck with me. Understand?"

Her eyes were wide, stricken. "Please don't return me, sir — Mr. Walker. I'll sit quietly in your living room the length of your stay if you want. You don't have to use me if you don't wish, but please don't send me back."

This was getting more complicated every second. "Why? What, you'll get fired if I cancel the order?"

She shook her head. "No. Terminated."

He gaped at her. Even flummoxed, the tall man with the brilliant blue eyes was doing things to Tierre's insides she'd never felt before.

He was very tall, his hard body not well hidden under the clinging robe. He tried to hide it like he'd hidden the pistol, but his erection prodded the fabric full force. His cock must be huge.

Tierre liked that — and she wasn't supposed to like it. She was a Guide, not a Pleasurer. He shouldn't be turned-on by her, but it warmed her to know he *was* turned-on.

"They'll *kill* you if I send you back?"

"Yes. I have failed one too many times."

His eyes narrowed. "That's fucking barbaric."

"It's the rules. The concierge is kindly giving me one more chance, but if you don't want me, then I'm finished."

"Why the hell wouldn't I want you? Why were you sent back before?"

She shrugged, pretending his rejection didn't hurt. "The others said I was too — perky." Her flesh warmed as his gaze instantly flicked to her breasts. "Too helpful, too eager to please. I suppose that's annoying."

His face was absolutely still, but she saw in his eyes that he was trying to get his emotions under control. He didn't look like a man used to having to control his emotions.

"I won't send you back," he said, his voice calmer. "Let me get dressed and you can show me a place in this steel nightmare that serves ribs. *Real* ribs, not synthetic, rubbery gunk. All right?"

Tierre blew out a sigh of relief. "Yes, I will. Thank you."

Walker turned around and headed for the bathroom again, and Tierre followed silently on his heels. He wouldn't send her back. She had a chance.

She paused in the bedroom to rummage through his duffel bag. Really nothing there worth keeping—she'd have to show him to the tailor shops. She pulled out the least worn of his clothes and entered the bathroom with them just as he dropped the bathrobe.

She got an amazing view of his sculpted back, tapered waist and tight ass. She suddenly wanted to walk to him and draw her tongue over the taut mounds, tasting his skin.

She started forward on silent feet, unable to stop herself, and he abruptly swung to face her.

His front was even better than his back. Smooth, brown skin lay sleek over his chest, which was brushed with dark, curling hair. Droplets of water the robe had missed glistened on his skin.

His cock was thick and dark, swollen from base to tip. She longed to feel the weight of it in her hand, and the sudden need jolted her.

He didn't scream or dive for his bathrobe or plunge back into the water. He simply planted his hands on his hips and gave her an admonishing look.

"Never sneak up on me...what's your name?"

"Tierre," she said softly.

"Never sneak up on me, Tierre. It isn't healthy. I don't want to hurt you by accident."

She shivered in pleasure at the sound of her name on his lips. "I will remember. I brought your clothes."

She held up the pants and jacket. He stared at them incredulously and she wondered what she'd done wrong. Then he threw his head back and laughed. His laughter was warm and made her tingle all over.

"Damn, woman, do you know what those are?"

Tierre studied the matching pants and jacket, which were scarlet with gold slashes. "They are—colorful."

"It's a costume for a Tarkhanian circus performer. I did one a good deed, and he paid me the only way he could. I haven't had the chance to unload the suit, but I might hang on to it for the amusement value."

"I thought you'd look good in it."

He stopped laughing. Still naked, he came to her and gently took the clothes from her hands. "You are too sweet to be real."

He snaked his hand through her hair, pulled her forward and kissed her.

Tierre let her head rock back, taking the bruising kiss and his tongue spearing hard into her mouth. Fires ran through her insides, threatening to melt her into a pile of goo.

She tried to answer with her own tongue, but couldn't quite match his masterful strokes. It was wonderful and dizzying, his hand in her hair tight but not painful. He'd never let her fall.

Walker suddenly jerked back, taking his wonderful lips away. He peered down at her with eyes like chips of ice.

"You've never done this before."

Tierre's face burned. "Not really, no."

This wasn't what she was made for. She was not for pleasuring, she was for talking, looking good in a short skirt and helping people in a friendly fashion.

She suddenly regretted she wasn't a Pleasurer. She'd have enjoyed pleasuring every inch of his body, from his bath-tangled hair to his beautiful cock.

He continued to peer at her, then his hand softened on the nape of her neck and he caressed her there. "Sorry," he said gruffly. "I thought you were...something different."

"A perfectly natural mistake, Mr. Walker." Her own voice was strangled and all wrong. "If you would like a Pleasurer, I can call one. I assume female?"

His lips compressed. "No. Let's just go get those ribs."

He turned away to the bedroom, snatching up clothes she'd left loose on the bed.

He dressed without looking at her, as though he didn't care one way or the other if she watched, but Tierre watched with great enjoyment. His hard muscles worked as he slid on his pants then pulled a shirt over his head. He settled the shirt and combed fingers through his damp hair.

He was not at all like her other customers, who were very clean, wore knife-sharp suits and doused themselves in cologne. Most of them were rude to her. She'd been hit on more than once, and she always offered to call for a Pleasurer for them, making sure she smiled a wide smile when she said it.

Not one of her clients had ever kissed her. Walker's kiss had been masterful, as though he knew exactly what he was doing and what would arouse her. He hadn't been wanting free sex, he'd wanted to take her completely.

For the first time in her life, she wished she could comply.

Tierre waited, smiling on the outside, until he was ready. She led him out of the suite, her insides still sizzling over the kiss, feeling a deep stab of regret that she could have nothing more than that.

Walker strapped on his pistol before he left the suite. When she pointed out that the upper levels were so secure he didn't need a weapon, he only grunted and didn't answer.

He liked the ribs at the restaurant Tierre took him to. They came sizzling on a plate, a row of bones with meat covered in a sticky sauce. Tierre ordered a glass of water, since she could consume very little that this restaurant offered.

"Not eating?" he asked, licking his fingers.

She liked watching him lick his fingers. He'd pop one in his mouth and suckle all the sauce from it, then slowly draw it out. He might suckle a woman's nipples like that.

"No, I'm fine."

His gaze flicked over her, lingering on her breasts. He looked back up at her again, his smile sinful and slow.

If she heated any more, she'd corrode.

"What else of the station can I show you?" she asked hurriedly. "There is an art gallery at the end of this corridor with paintings from the Venusian colony of 3006. Classic."

When he looked blank, she rushed on, sifting through things that might entertain him. "Level 760 has some famous exotic dancers. Thirty oiled women sliding all over each other—some of them have five arms and legs. They can form the most interesting shapes."

Walker choked on his next bite and hastily gulped down the tall glass of beer he'd ordered. "No thanks."

"What then? I can hardly be your Guide if you have no idea what you want to see."

He shook his head. "Returning to my suite is fine. I don't get much chance to live in luxury in my business."

"What is your business? You—kill men, I think you said."

Fortunately the booths in this restaurant were very private. "I'm a bounty hunter. When men do bad things, I hunt them down and bring them in. Dead or alive. I get paid, I go out and find more."

"And you enjoy this?"

"Pretty much. It pays."

Tierre had never met anyone like him. She usually got assigned to fat merchants or reed-thin aristocrats who were bored with the universe and wanted spectacle to keep them from thinking about their ennui.

She'd never met anyone so full of life as Walker, who thought eating *ribs*—whatever those were—and staying in a lower-end suite of Level 20,000 was enough.

After dinner, she took him along the walkway, pointing out the beauty of the structure above and far below them. Walker listened politely, but she could tell he wasn't interested. When she finally asked him point blank what he wanted, he looked her up and down and said he wanted to go back to the suite.

They walked side by side, Walker close enough to her that their arms brushed. She found that oddly pleasurable.

When Walker closed the door of the suite behind them, he switched his blue gaze to Tierre. "You can go if you want to. But if you stay…" He glanced into the bedroom and back at her. "You know what I want."

"What?"

He cupped her face in his hands, his eyes going dark. "You in my bed. You know that."

Her knees went weak but in a good way. "I told you, I'm not a Pleasurer, Mr. Walker. That's not what I'm for."

"I don't give a crap." She sensed his body hardening, his attention intense on her. "I want *you*, Tierre. I won't coerce you. You stay or go, your choice."

"My—*choice?*"

"Yes. What, are you a slave to that concierge? Slavery's illegal in all corners of the galaxy. You don't have to answer to him. Or to me. You choose."

He filled her head with so many confusing thoughts, she thought she might overload. No one had ever given her a choice before.

"I want to stay, please, Mr. Walker."

"Just Walker. I don't have a surname."

She wanted to ask why but he was leaning toward her to devour her mouth with another hard kiss.

Chapter Three

&

Tierre was a sweet armful. Walker kissed her for a long time, savoring the taste of her—spice and the cool water she'd drunk at dinner.

She didn't argue when he swept her up and carried her to the bedroom, just smiled as though happy to go along with what he wanted.

Good, because he'd been hard all evening. He supposed he could have taken her up on her offer to watch the thirty oiled women who could undulate into fantastic patterns, and sate himself by thinking about being in the middle of them.

What stupid entertainment would people come up with next?

No, what he needed was a good fuck with a real woman like Tierre. He needed to bury himself in her softness, suck up her taste, slide into her until he came.

He laid her on the bed and unbuttoned her blouse. She wasn't wearing underwear beneath it, which he'd suspected by the enticing way her body had moved. She had firm, lovely breasts in perfect apple shape, nipples rising to his touch.

He kissed her throat then leaned and sucked one nipple into his mouth.

It tasted a little unusual, not the salt-velvet taste he expected, but perhaps she'd coated herself with lotion.

He didn't care. He'd like her if she were covered with radioactive oil.

He shucked his own shirt then skimmed off her skirt and the silver panties underneath. She lay before him bare but for her shoes, not wearing stockings or anything else. She had a chain around her waist, thin links that he leaned down to catch in his teeth.

She made a noise of pleasure. He looked her over, firm, upthrust breasts, slim curve of waist, triangular patch of dark hair between her slender legs. Most of the women he had sex with shaved themselves, but Tierre's coy patch of curls was very erotic.

He tugged the chain with his teeth again then licked a slow circle around her navel.

Tierre laced her hands in his hair. "Don't I get to see you bare?"

Walker chuckled. "You already saw me, remember?"

"Yes, but I'd like to see you again."

Walker licked across her bottom lip. He'd never thought of himself as much to look at, and her interest in him was flattering. Where would he find such a sweetheart again?

He unfused the binding of his pants and kicked them off along with his boots. He stood beside the bed, one hand on his hip, hoping she liked what she saw. He warmed as her gaze crawled over his body and lingered in a satisfied way on his long, fully hard cock.

"Touch it," he murmured when he saw her hand move hesitantly toward it. "Get to know it, love."

Tierre's eyes rounded as she closed her fingers around his cock.

"*Damn.*"

She began to explore it, fingers growing bolder as she ran them along his shaft. He stood still, letting her stroke it to his base, trying not to groan when she cupped her hand around his sac.

He was too excited. He didn't know why—he should have plenty of time for mutual pleasuring before he got down to the business of actual fucking. But her fingertips on his flange were driving him crazy, and that little smile made him want to shove his cock between her red lips.

He wanted her bad, and he didn't want to wait through foreplay.

Walker disengaged her hand and climbed on to the bed, pressing her legs apart. Her chest rose and fell with her excitement, and her cheeks flushed.

"Are you going to fuck me now?" she whispered.

He liked the word on her lips. "Yes, sweetheart, I am."

"Good." She threw her arms around his neck. "Good."

He kissed her. He dug hard with his tongue, stroking inside her mouth as he'd done in the bathroom. She pressed her tongue against his, getting better with every lick. She was a quick learner.

He lay down on top of her, nuzzling her cheek. "Don't worry, Tierre, I won't give you a child or a disease. I have the microchip." A must for someone who traveled as much as he did.

"I know."

Level 20,000 thoroughly researched its guests. "I'll try not to hurt you," he murmured. "But I'm big, and if it's your first time..."

She looked up at him with excitement in her eyes. "You won't hurt me. I am resilient."

"Good to know." He stroked her hair back from her face, loving its silkiness. "Spread your legs a little more, love."

She did, sliding her legs around his, rubbing the back of his calf with her foot.

Walker positioned his tip at the slick opening of her pussy and slid himself partway in. He lay still a moment, letting her get used to him—he was plenty big and he didn't want to scare her.

He just wanted her. He wanted to lick his way over her body, hold her close, fuck her until they both screamed.

"Sweetheart," he whispered. "You're beautiful."

"Am I?"

"Hasn't anyone ever told you that?"

"Not really."

"Then they're blind." He kissed her lips, a rough kiss, because he was beginning to lose control.

"Thank you, Walker."

"We're not finished yet, sweetheart. Not for a while."

"Thank you for saying I'm beautiful. And for not sending me back."

He stilled her words with a kiss. "You're too cute, you know that? Relax now, all the way, so I can get inside you."

Tierre drew a breath then her body went slack and pliable. Her eyes widened slightly as he pushed farther inside.

"You all right?" he asked her.

"I don't know."

He stopped, though his cock screamed at him to get on with it. "We'll take it slow, baby. I promise."

She nodded, but looked worried. His cock throbbed with need and impatience but he willed himself to wait. He wouldn't force her.

"Lie still, and I'll make it all right," he said. He kissed her forehead. "Once we get used to each other, it will feel so good."

She nodded, but her frown wouldn't go away.

Walker drew a breath and slid another inch inside her. He moaned with it, loving the feel of her hot sheath. She was wet, her juices making everything beautifully slick.

She gasped. "Walker."

He kissed her, stifling his groan. She clenched him in the best way and he wanted to pump in and out, feeling her clamp down on him.

"You have to get out of me," she whispered suddenly.

He didn't want to. Not for hours. "Does it hurt, sweetheart? We'll wait until it doesn't hurt."

"No, Walker, you have to get out, *now*."

She pushed at his chest. Walker's body did not want to obey, his cock sending signals of rage to his brain.

But Walker didn't hurt innocents. He withdrew, trying to go slow, trying not to groan in protest as he left her tight, hot pussy.

Tierre snaked out from under him the instant he was fully out and flung herself from the bed to the middle of the room. She stood still, breathing hard and looking terrified.

"What's the matter, darling?" he asked, keeping his voice gentle. "Did I hurt you? I'm sorry."

She shook her head. "No, no you didn't hurt me, it's—"

She screamed suddenly and shoved her hands against her stomach. Walker leapt to his feet, his cock deflating with his panic. He reached for the emergency button on his bedside console.

"No!" she shouted at him. "Don't tell anyone." Tears ran down her cheeks and suddenly her body began to jerk sideways, in a way no human's could.

Walker sat down hard on the bed, his libido dying a swift death. "Holy shit."

"I can't...I can't be with you. It's overloading. I thought..."

She kept jerking then suddenly her body went very still. She remained upright but looked like a dead thing, her perfect breasts unmoving.

Her lovely brown eyes clicked as they swiveled to look at him. "I'm sorry."

"Tierre, what the *fuck* are you?"

"A model PP-29," she said, her voice weak. "Of the Practically Perfect line."

"*Model?*" He stared at her body, the beautiful limbs twisted at wrong angles. "Model of *what*?" But in his heart he knew.

"Android," she whispered. "I'm so sorry."

Tierre's body quickly returned to normal now that the strange sensations had stopped flooding her feedback loops. PP models were expert at self-repair, and in a few minutes she could move again.

But she thought Walker would never return to normal. His face was red with rage as he glared at her, fists planted on his hips.

"I was doing it with an *android*? A robot?"

"An artificial life form," Tierre corrected him. "Not a robot. It is different."

He didn't seem to hear her. "Who put you up to this? I thought that guy at the desk was too accommodating to be real."

"He is an android too. We all are—the Guides, the Pleasurers, the concierge."

Walker put his hands to his hair and spun away from her. Since he was still naked, this gave Tierre a delectable view of his taut backside and muscular back.

"You had me fooled," he said, voice tight and angry. "Your sweet smile, your kisses—I thought you really wanted me."

"I *do* want you. But…"

He spun around again, giving her a terrific view of his equally muscular front. His pecs and abs were tight, and his cock hung thick and long between his thighs.

"No, you don't. It's just a program. You're designed to please."

She shook her head, her hair bouncing over her bare shoulders. "I'm designed to show people the best of the station. Pleasurers are designed for sex—I'm not."

"Then why did you want to go to bed with me?"

"I don't know." She wiped the tears from her face. "I just wanted to. But I'm not made for it. That's why my computers overloaded when I started to...enjoy myself."

His tone softened a fraction. "You can't have been enjoying yourself. You can't feel."

"I'm an artificial life form," she repeated. "The most sophisticated in the known universe. That's why I can cry, and why I enjoy looking at you even when I'm hurting. It is very confusing."

Walker stared at her, brown hands on his lighter brown hips. "When you told me you'd be terminated if I returned you, you meant shut off, not killed."

She nodded. "Stripped down for parts."

Walker looked down at the ground and cursed low and viciously. When he looked up again, his blue eyes had gone cold.

"Who's doing this?" he demanded.

"Doing what?"

Walker waved his hands. "*This.* Sending an android to seduce me. Is it to kill me or make a fool of me?"

He stopped abruptly and grabbed a handheld from the nightstand. He tapped it a few times, peered into it then relaxed. "No, Lane is still on his way, and he doesn't know anyone on Station 358. I checked." He swung back at Tierre, his gaze still suspicious. "So who was it?"

"I don't understand you. You wanted a Guide, and I was the only one available."

She wished she would stop crying. There was an ache in her chest she'd never felt before, a hurt that made her want to sit down and weep for hours. Walker standing near her didn't help—she could smell his sweat and his male scent, and she only wanted him to kiss her again.

But the Pleasurers had told her that no matter how perfect a Pleasurer might be, some men were repulsed by the thought of having sex with an android. It seemed that Walker was just such a man.

"Tierre." His voice had softened another notch, though his eyes were still hard. "Tierre, stop crying."

"I can't help it. I'm not what you want, and I so wish I could be."

"Damn it," Walker muttered. "If they had to send me a robot, why did they send me one with feelings?"

Tierre raised her head and glared at him. "I am *not* a robot. Robots are machines. I am one of the most sophisticated AI models in existence."

"Except you've been malfunctioning, which is why the concierge is threatening to terminate you."

She stopped. "Well, yes."

Walker blew out his breath. "And if I send you back tonight, it's the scrap heap for you, right?"

"Yes." She shouldn't be afraid. Being switched off was just that—switching off. There should be nothing to fear.

But she didn't want to be "switched off". She loved life, loved her job and she wanted to get to know Walker—everything about him, not just what he looked like naked.

Of course, he was stunningly gorgeous naked, and she'd prefer to get to know him *while* he was naked.

Walker rubbed his hands through his hair again, a gesture she'd come to like. "When you told me you'd sit quietly in the living room my entire stay, you meant it. You could just sit here the whole time, not eating or sleeping. That's why you didn't want to eat at the restaurant."

"I can eat. Just not ribs."

"Shit."

She swallowed. "I won't pester you, Walker. If you don't want me, then you don't want me."

That was one of the most difficult things she'd ever said in her existence. The tears started coming back, and she swiped them from her face.

"Damn it, Tierre, stop making me feel like I just kicked a puppy."

She wiped her eyes again as he came toward her, large and powerful and unhappy. "Not a puppy, an artificial—"

His fingers on her lips stopped the words. "Yes, I get it." He held his fingers there a long moment, as though wondering if he should even touch her. She restrained herself from kissing his hand.

Walker caressed her cheekbone with his thumb, touch soft. "What the fuck am I going to do with you?"

Tierre knew exactly what she wanted to do with *him*, and fucking was involved. "You like to swear," she said.

"It makes me feel better."

He took his hand away, which made her want to cry out in disappointment. They were both still unclothed, but he acted like he didn't notice anymore, like she was no different from his handheld.

"I can still be your Guide to the station," she said. "I did find the ribs for you, and you liked them."

Something flickered in his eyes then they went cool again. If she had a heart, it would be breaking.

"All right, you can still be my Guide." Walker put his fingers under her chin, his touch light. "I won't send you back and let you be terminated."

"Thank you." Relief swept through her, but it wasn't full relief. She could be with him, yes, but only at a distance.

He turned his back and walked away from her, giving her another great view of his ass. He tossed on his shirt and pants then stripped back the bedcovers.

"I'm going to sleep now. Or at least try to sleep. You can go sit in the living room if you want."

"You sleep in your clothes?" she asked.

Walker slid under the covers and rested his hands behind his head. He wouldn't look at her. "Best way. I never know when I have to leave in a hurry. Do you mind if I turn out the light?"

"I can see in the dark," she said.

He gave her a long look, and her face heated. She'd just betrayed another way she was different from him.

Walker turned off the light and the suite went pitch black. Tierre's sight adjusted quickly to the conditions, and she saw Walker lying on his back, hands behind his head again, staring up at the ceiling.

She walked to the other side of the bed. "Do you mind if I sleep with you?"

Walker turned unerringly toward her, though she knew he could see nothing. "You sleep?"

"I need to recharge, just like humans do."

He thought for a long time, rubbing the bridge of his nose with his strong fingers. "All right," he finally sighed. "But just sleep."

"Thank you, Walker."

She climbed into the bed without donning her clothes, happy that she could at least have this. She curled herself into a ball, her forehead resting an inch away from Walker's shoulder.

He said nothing, but she sensed his tension. He resumed his study of the dark ceiling, his anger and confusion palpable.

Whenever he left the station, he'd leave Tierre behind and probably be happy to. She would have to soak up his warmth, his strength, the gravelly sound of his voice while she could.

She tried to stay awake as long as she could to enjoy being next to him, but even androids had to sleep—recharge—eventually.

She drifted into oblivion—and when she woke again, he was gone.

Chapter Four

ಐ

"Here in the atrium we can grow species of plants from seven hundred planetary systems."

"Is that right?" Walker replied absently.

He could care less about flora from seven hundred systems, many of which he'd seen firsthand, but Tierre seemed anxious to show him.

She'd been anxious to show him everything after she'd rushed into the bathroom this morning to find him taking a shower. He wished she still didn't look so hot to him, her breasts round and beautiful, tips of her nipples hardening when she saw him standing in the sterilizing shower.

Programming, that's all it was. Not real.

She'd exhaled in relief when she found he hadn't left her behind then became the brisk and businesslike Guide again. She'd taken him to breakfast then led him on a whirlwind tour of the station. The atrium, she said, was a must-see.

"Bamboo from old Earth," she said, pointing out green, ringed stalks rising beside a pool. A little waterfall inside the greenery cooled the air and made a calm, trickling sound.

"Looks like it."

"You've seen bamboo before?" She sounded disappointed. "Most people are fascinated by it."

"I've been in jungles in what they call the Far East on Earth. Bamboo all over the place."

"Oh. Perhaps then you'd be more interested in the giant fungi of Apollyion Six?"

"Sorry. Spent three months on Ap. Six while I was tracking a guy. I got sick of giant fungi for breakfast, lunch and dinner, not to mention having to sleep in it. Couldn't get the stench out of my clothes for weeks."

"Well, then perhaps..."

He reached down and took her hand in his. "Why don't we just walk around and enjoy the quiet?"

She fell silent instantly, her brown eyes grateful.

She was such a beautiful woman, and what she called "perky" he found refreshing. Walker was used to living alone or sharing space with men and women who were either burned out or too on edge. The women he encountered were wary and wanted sex without bonds, which Walker himself had preferred.

Tierre was trying to be his friend. She quietly walked with him, her hand in his, observing the greenery she must see every day with evident enjoyment. She relished every second of her un-life, he realized, in a way human beings rarely took the time to.

Walker worried what would happen to her when he left the station. Maybe the next client she led around would complain about her, and the concierge or whoever would use that as an excuse to terminate her. Something twisted in his gut when he thought about that, and he knew he couldn't let it happen.

He couldn't take Tierre with him—his life was far too dangerous for a cute sidekick—but he could find out if the station was willing to sell her to him. She could continue being a Guide, but the station couldn't terminate her without his say-so if he owned her. She'd at least be safe.

"Why is he doing that?" Walker asked curiously, pointing to a bent, elderly man who was sweeping leaves from the path with a palm frond. "Can't the station get him a vacuum?"

Tierre laughed. He wished he didn't love her laugh so much.

"He's a mystic," she said. "They live on the bottom level of the station and believe that manual labor is the way to enlightenment. They work for free, so the station lets them stay here in return. They seem to be very happy, though they don't talk much."

"Interesting."

The wizened man looked up. He had a long, thin beard and an equally long ponytail, both dark gray. He gave Walker a knowing smile then bent back over his task.

Walker and Tierre moved on, the encounter forgotten. She led him through the last of the atrium then took him to lunch at a restaurant she said he'd like—one that served lots of charred meat.

She was right, it was good, and he enjoyed a chilled glass of beer. He felt relaxed in her company, and Walker was never relaxed.

After lunch Walker talked to the concierge while Tierre "freshened up", whatever that meant, and discovered that Tierre was damn expensive. She was a top-grade model, the little man told him with wide eyes. A PP. Practically Perfect.

It would take the whole of the bounty Walker got for Lane to buy her, but what the hell? He'd find a bigger catch and make it back in no time.

When Tierre returned they strolled the walkway that circled the inside of the station. They stopped to gaze over the railing at the upper levels which stretched several miles above them and five times as many below. Station 358 was one of the wonders of the galaxy, built before space stations had become small, functional and boring.

Walker had been here before, but never had he appreciated the beauty of the place. He usually stayed in cramped holes on the lower levels a day or so while his ship was refueled or repaired, and then he was gone.

Lane would arrive tomorrow. Walker would nab the man, stun him and put him into stasis for the haul to the planet that was paying the most bounty, and then take off. He'd come back and pay for Tierre, instructing the concierge that he was to take the best care of her possible while he was gone.

Then Walker would be able to spend time with her whenever he wanted. So he couldn't have sex with her...but he could be with her. She was like balm to his battered soul—

"Walker!"

Walker swung around. Instincts taking over, he shoved Tierre behind him and had his pistol in his hand, humming with energy, in an instant.

He feared Lane had arrived a day early and found him first, but Walker's tracking robot had showed Lane still half a day out, and his tracker was never wrong.

It wasn't Lane. Instead Walker faced a man he'd taken in a couple months ago, a vicious fucker named Ridgley who'd vowed revenge if he made it out of prison alive.

Guess they released him.

Lane wouldn't have called out. He'd have shot Walker in the back, because Lane was a coward. Ridgley—*what a stupid name*—wanted Walker to know exactly who was going to kill him.

"Pretty girl," Ridgley said. "I think I'll take her."

No way in hell. "They let you out?" Walker asked conversationally.

The pedestrians on the walkway had either scooted away or stood with mouths open, shocked that such things were happening on such a respectable level. He noted someone down the walkway surreptitiously pushing the silent alarm for security.

"I escaped," Ridgley said, sounding proud. "I lived to track you down."

"That's all I needed to know."

An escaped felon, especially one like Ridgley, would bring in a good bounty, and Walker could double his effort on one trip. Easy meat.

He shot. Walker's energy bullet bounced off some kind of shield surrounding Ridgley, likely emanating from the thick belt around his middle. Walker paused a moment in surprise—and that pause was fatal.

Ridgley laughed and shot back, the energy bullet coming straight at Walker.

Time seemed to slow to a crawl. *Well*, Walker thought. *It's not been a bad life.*

He heard Tierre screaming. Damn, he would have liked to say goodbye to her. He'd kiss her and taste her like he had the first night and tell her everything he truly felt.

Then Tierre launched herself in front of the bullet.

"No!" Walker shouted. He grabbed for her, but suddenly everything was moving too fast again.

As Tierre shoved him out of the way, the bullet caught her full in the chest. Its impact launched her upward and slammed her body on top of the railing surrounding the walkway, a gaping hole in her chest. She hovered on the rail a single instant while Walker lunged for her, her lovely brown eyes wide with pain.

I love you, Walker, her red lips formed—then she fell backward over the side.

Walker screamed. He'd never heard a sound like that come out of his throat.

He swung back to Ridgley. "*You mother-fucking son of a bitch!*"

He shot and shot, some part of him reasoning that Ridgley's shield wouldn't hold against a repeated assault. He was right. After four shots it shimmered and dissolved, and Ridgley died when the fifth bullet went through his head.

Walker's throat was raw. He slammed himself against the railing and peered over it, but there was nothing to see, only emptiness and mist.

Tears rained down his cheeks. He smelled burning, his own arm where one of Ridgley's shots had hit him, but he barely felt the pain.

"Tierre," he whispered. He laid his head on the railing and closed his eyes.

Walker's journey to the bottom of the station took an hour and a half, but he didn't care. He felt empty and hollow, and time moved oddly for him.

It had taken Walker a long time to explain to the station police that he was a licensed bounty hunter, which meant it was perfectly legal for him to kill escaped prisoners like Ridgley. He directed them to put Ridgley's body in stasis—another expense—until Walker could leave the station.

Then more time for a medic to patch up Walker's arm and give him a painkiller he didn't need. The pain in his arm was nothing to that in his heart.

The concierge had approached him apologetically and said that since Tierre had been destroyed as a direct result of working for Walker, he'd have to pay for her replacement.

She wasn't destroyed, he wanted to scream at the man. *She sacrificed herself to save my worthless fucking life.*

Finally he got away from everyone and took a slowly descending car to the bottom of the station.

Tourists never came down here, Walker decided as he waded through piles of junk. The place reeked. Garbage that hadn't been disintegrated or that had simply fallen from one of the thirty thousand levels came to rest here.

Walker swore in every language he knew. He knew that Tierre could not have survived the fall, no matter how well she'd been constructed. She might have been repairable if she'd only taken the bullet, but the fall must have completely obliterated her.

But for some reason, he thought if he could find the parts, or even one piece, he could give her a funeral, a memorial—*something* to indicate what he felt for her.

"I am a stupid fucker," he said. He said it again, louder, liking the echoes coming back to him.

So what if she'd been an android? Walker had felt something for her the moment he saw her, and his liking for her had only grown. She'd liked *him*. He could count on one hand the number of people who liked him, and he wasn't even sure of them.

He could have taken her with him, treasured her, enjoyed how she made him laugh…

"Can I help you?" a raspy little voice said.

Walker looked down to see one of the mystics in front of him, complete with bent back, long, wispy beard and palm-frond broom.

"Did I see you in the atrium this morning?" Walker asked him abruptly.

"No, I imagine it was one of my brethren. What brings you to the bottom level?"

"Did you see a girl fall down here? An android? She had dark hair and eyes. She was…beautiful."

"Ah, that one. Yes." The mystic bobbed his head in a nod. "Poor thing."

"Where is she?"

"In a million pieces, I am afraid. I cleaned them up and threw them away."

"You threw her away?" Walker grabbed the front of his robe. The man weighed nothing, but he just smiled as Walker shook him. "You can't just throw Tierre away!"

He felt tears on his face. The old man simply looked at him until Walker set him down and fiercely rubbed his eyes.

"You cared for her?"

A dozen thoughts went through Walker's mind. He could argue with himself for eternity, but he knew the answer. "Yes."

"Why?"

"Why? I don't know—how can I know a thing like that? She sacrificed herself to save my worthless hide, and now you're telling me I can't even say goodbye."

The mystic put a surprisingly strong hand on Walker's wrist. "I am sorry. Loss is something we can never brush away." He reached into a pocket of his tattered robe and pulled out something that glinted. "I did find this."

He pressed a thin gold chain into Walker's hand. Walker had last seen it around Tierre's petite waist, gleaming against her bare skin.

The sight made his throat hurt. He bunched the chain in his hand and thrust it into his pocket. "Thanks."

"You are leaving the station?" the mystic asked him.

"Tomorrow. Still something I have to do."

Walker turned to pick his way over the debris again, ready to find the elevators. He could care less about the bounty on Lane now, but he knew that burying himself in his work would be the only way he'd get over this.

When he reached the elevator, he looked back to nod a goodbye to the mystic, but the man had disappeared.

Walker went back upstairs, moving like a dead thing, checked his handheld for Lane's progress, tried to eat and couldn't and fell into bed. It took a long time for sleep to find his exhausted body.

"Walker."

It was her whisper, Tierre's sweet, low voice right in his ear. Walker smiled in his sleep and reached out to brush her luscious hip.

The dream was cruel to him, offering him what he could never have again, but he clung to it, wanting to feel her. He could smell her too, a womanly smell, clean and ready for him.

"Tierre," he murmured. "Damn it, I'm so sorry."

"Shh."

She brushed his hair back from his forehead and ran her fingers down his chest. Walker jumped a little as her fingertips snagged his nipple. He jumped even more when she bent down to take the stiff nub between her teeth.

If this dream was out to torment him, he'd let it. His mind was giving him what life could not—Tierre as a real woman.

She felt real, she tasted real as he pulled her up for a kiss. When he'd first taken her to bed he'd ignored the subtle signals that screamed something was wrong, because he'd simply wanted her. His body had known, no matter how perfect she was, that she wasn't real.

Now he tasted her deeply, the true taste of woman, the feel of warm lips against his. He bunched her hair in his fists, loving its silken warmth.

Walker tried to say her name but she shushed him again and trailed kisses down his throat. She opened his shirt all the way as she went down until she ran her tongue around his navel.

He groaned. He caressed the nape of her neck, his heart flooding with happiness. A dream, that was all, but in a dream he could express what he felt.

"I wanted this with you," he breathed. "Ever since I first saw you, I wanted you. You walking next to me was the best thing in the universe. I was falling in love with you."

Walker always kept his emotions close to his chest. He had to, in his line of work—there wasn't room for pity, remorse or guilt.

Or love.

He'd blocked love out so long that even the vestiges of it, in this dream, prickled his chest like a shot from a stun gun.

Tierre opened his pants then leaned down and licked his cock.

"Aw, fuck," he moaned, and she giggled.

"You like to say bad words."

"They're expressive. You feel so damn good."

She laughed softly, her breath warm on his skin, and then she wrapped her lips around him.

He wasn't sure what he said then. Something like, "Suck me, sweetheart, you're a fucking angel."

She sucked and tickled him with her fingers, moving down to fondle his balls, which had hardened like rocks. It made sense that in his dream she knew exactly what he liked.

Tierre licked her way down his staff and sucked one of his balls into her mouth.

"Shit, Tierre. I can't take any more."

Walker gently pushed her aside then skimmed off his pants and shirt. Stark naked, he drew her on top of him and his cock waited, dark and hard between them.

"You on top of me, sweetheart."

She nodded eagerly and slid her thighs around his hips. He held his cock steady with one hand, his other guiding her to him. His tip found her warm pussy open and wet, her delicious curls of hair tickling his skin.

He lowered her slowly onto him, his cock happy that it was sliding once more into the snug, slick place that was made for it. Walker's head went back into the pillows as she squeezed him, the sensation driving his entire body wild.

She made a noise of pleasure, an *oohh* that made him answer with a growl. Her eyes grew heavy, her body rocking as she sought to pleasure herself with him.

Walker arched up into her, thrusting hard while holding her thighs, driving as deep as he could. He knew she wasn't used to it, but hell, this was a dream. He could fuck her as hard as he wanted, and he wanted it hard.

Her round breasts moved with his thrusts, and he splayed his hand over one, loving her pebble-hard nipples rubbing his palm. Both he and Tierre were sweating, the perspiration trickling from her cheek another sign that she was real.

He wanted to give her all he could. Walker snaked his middle finger between them to find her clit in the wet, hot madness. He felt it, the nub swollen for him, and she jerked and cried out when he made contact.

He pleasured her, pinching the little bead, rubbing it, tickling it, feeling her blossom under his touch. She cried out, her buttocks bouncing on his thighs, her dark hair dancing on her shoulders.

She started to come. He felt it in her pussy, which clenched his cock, and in the scalding liquid that poured over his fingers.

"I love you, Walker!" she cried. "I love you, love you!"

Something tore in his chest. At the same time his climax surged through him and he came hard, shooting his seed high into her beautiful body. She continued to squeeze him, getting wetter and wetter.

She screamed his name and he dragged her down to his chest, where they panted and laughed together.

"Fucking hell, that was good," he gasped.

Tierre raised her head and kissed him with swollen lips. Her eyes were half closed, the brown of them warm and welcoming. "You wanted me."

"Hell yes." He stroked her hair with shaking fingers. "I wanted you from the first second I saw you."

"I wanted you too, even if I wasn't supposed to." She kissed his cheek and snuggled down into his shoulder.

They lay in silence awhile, Walker easing his palm over her hair, drawing her against him. His body wound down but his cock was still hard, even in the exhausted afterglow.

"Walker," his dream Tierre murmured. "When you go, will you take me with you?"

"I'd love to have you with me. Part of my life. Always."

"Will you show me the worlds you talked about?"

"Of course, babe. Every single one."

How wonderful that would be. He'd seen some beautiful and exotic places, and he imagined Tierre's delight when she encountered them for the first time. She was innocent and full of wonder, while he was hard-bitten and universe-weary. But the thought of seeing it all again through her eyes made him wish he could show it to her.

"Thank you, Walker." She kissed him once more, her eyes heavy with sleep. "I won't let you regret it."

"I don't regret a single second, love."

He felt his body moving toward deeper sleep, the dream dissolving. He tried to hang on to it, savor her as much as he could, but his body had other ideas. He drifted down into sleep with his arms around her, his face buried in her neck.

Chapter Five

ഌ

Walker woke up alone.

That was the bitch about dreams—you were happy for a while only to wake up and break your heart all over again.

He lay in bed for a long time, not giving a damn about his life. Lane was due in today—Walker still had a job to bring him down and collect the bounty, then deliver Ridgley and collect the bounty on him too.

Big fucking deal.

He'd have to leave the station and the memory of Tierre. He'd go back to being the stoic, hard man he was and forget about the beautiful young woman and his fleeting moments of happiness with her.

Like hell.

He could never forget her, not a strand of her hair or her sexy brown eyes or the way her smile was just a little bit lopsided. He'd never forget the feel of her lips on his, the glow on her face while she blatantly admired his body.

He'd not forget what it was like to walk through the atrium with her, holding her hand and listening to her chatter about so many things.

He'd never forget how she looked at him when Ridgley shot her, and she knew she was dying for him.

He pressed his thumb and forefinger into his eyes, cursing softly when his fingers came away wet. A man like Walker didn't have time for emotion.

But emotion was taking time for him. He couldn't stop his eyes from stinging, his heart from burning, as he rolled out of bed and pulled on his clothes…

Which were crumpled on the floor—even though he remembered going to bed *in* them as usual. He must have torn them off during the very erotic dream with Tierre. Thinking of the dream made him want to dive back into bed and close his eyes tight, hoping it came back.

Instead he fastened his pants over his aching cock and walked toward the bathroom.

He heard a splash on the other side of the bathroom door and froze. Quietly he retrieved his pistol from the holster next to the bed and cradled it, finger on the trigger.

He stood to the side as he slid back the bathroom door, but no one charged him or shot him—he heard only another splash and a woman humming. Walker peeked around the doorframe, wondering which of his enemies had decided to taunt him.

Tierre lay in the bathtub, resting her head on the rim as she hummed a little tune.

Walker sagged against the doorframe. He was awake, he knew it, but there was Tierre, alive and well and in his tub.

She looked up, saw him and sent him her beautiful, slightly crooked smile. "Hello, Walker. I didn't mean to wake you."

Walker remained frozen at the door. "Who are you?" He could barely speak. "Are you a replica? How many copies are there?"

His head suddenly spun with a vision of a dozen Tierres licking him all over, and his mutinous cock started to dance.

She looked surprised. "No copies. There was only one of me. That's another perk of the Practically Perfect model. But I'm not an android, Walker." She reached a hand toward him. "I'm real."

What insane joke was this, and who would be this cruel?

"You can't be. I saw you die." He cleared his throat. "I went to the bottom of the station to look for you, and all this mystic gave me was the chain you wore on your waist."

"Oh, you have it? I like that chain, especially because you liked to play with it." She sent him her sexy smile, but Walker couldn't make himself move.

"Explain."

"The mystic put me back together. Then he made me real."

"How can that be?" Walker grated. "No one can do that."

"The mystics can." Her smile widened as she floated across the tub toward him. "Their race has perfected genetic engineering. PP androids have a tiny bit of genetic material in them, and that's all he needed. But I'm not an android—I'm a real human being. He tried to explain the process to me, but I only understood one word in ten." She laughed.

Walker thought of the small, hunched men with their wrinkled faces and knowing smiles. Brilliant scientists? Probably. He'd learned this trip not to judge a person by what they looked like.

"Are you really Tierre?"

"Yes," she said softly. "And you're really Walker. You like ribs with what you call *barbecue sauce*, and you like to lick it off your fingers." She gave a near-perfect demonstration of his sauce-licking technique.

"Son of a bitch." He powered down his gun and placed it aside, then rubbed his hands through his hair as he always did when flummoxed. "Damn, damn, damn."

"And you like to swear."

Tierre stood up in the bath, her body shining with water. Her nipples stood out dark against her pale skin, the triangle of hair between her legs springing into damp curls.

Walker got his clothes off in record time. He flung them to the floor, not caring if they got wet, and plunged into the bath beside her. He didn't understand any of this and he didn't care. He only wanted her against him—now.

Tierre flung her arms around him and he scooped her to him, loving how slippery her body was. He kissed her hard and she kissed him back just as brutally, her mouth hungry for his. Not content with that, she slid her fingers down his torso and grabbed his inflated cock.

"You believe me," she crooned against his mouth.

"I don't care," Walker said savagely. "I don't care if you're human or android or hybrid or what. I want to be with *you*." He stopped and drew a breath. "I love you."

She kissed his mouth, her lips tasting of bathwater, then she drew back and gave him a worried look. "Wait a minute—you didn't think last night was real."

"Not at the time. I do now."

"So when you said I could go with you when you left the station…"

"I meant it." Walker's rational brain started to protest, but his instincts kicked in and told his rational brain to shut up. "I want you with me. I'll get some job that doesn't involve tracking down dangerous assholes and we'll be together. Let someone else police the galaxy for a while. I've had enough."

"But you love to travel. Please don't stop doing what you love for me—I don't want you to grow to hate me for it."

"I can travel without hunting killers." He started to laugh. "Hell, I can be a tour guide."

She smiled with him and kissed the side of his neck, her lips warm and wet. "I have lots of experience with that."

"I know where I'd like you to guide me right now," he said.

"Where?"

Walker grabbed all the towels in range and flung them to the floor. These were Level 20,000 towels, luxuriously soft and plush. He boosted Tierre out of the bath onto them.

"Hands and knees, love," he said. "I need you in the worst way."

She looked puzzled but lowered herself to the towels. "Like this?"

Her butt was in the air, her breasts skimming the towels. Was she driving him crazy on purpose? He got behind her, his cock so hard it hurt. She was oh-so wet, the bathwater quickly being replaced by her own slickness.

"Just like that," Walker said. "You're perfect."

He nudged her opening with his tip and slid home.

Tierre nearly came off the towels when he slammed inside her. She screamed as Walker buried himself deep, but a scream of pure joy. He was so big, hard, good, beautiful — the adjectives tumbled through her thoughts and she couldn't fix on just one.

"It's *fucking* good!" she cried.

His laughter rumbled, the warm, rolling sound she'd come to love. His voice was always deep and rough, yet it could drop to the gentlest purr.

Walker's laughter died into a groan of pleasure, which then became hoarse gasps as he drove into her again and again. He pounded her hard, his hips slapping against her ass, and she loved every second of it.

He reached around in front of her and began to massage her clit, adding the tingling friction to the beauty of his thrusts. She shoved back toward him, wanting more and more as she spiraled toward ecstasy.

She bunched the towels in her hands, her fingers aching as he kept riding her. She felt her climax come, like she had the night before, a roaring wave that swept her up into wildness.

She screamed and moaned and screamed again, unable to believe what was happening to her. She was coming, even harder and faster than she had last night, and still he fucked her, taking her down one wave of feeling and pulling her up another.

Just when she'd caught her breath she came again, and then again. Three times she came as he pumped into her, the last one whimpering moans as her strength gave out.

"*Fuck*," Walker groaned as his seed burst into her, and then both of them were falling to the towels, gasping for breath and laughing.

They cuddled on the bed for a while. Walker tenderly touched Tierre while she lay in the circle of his arms and wondered at her happiness.

"You can feel my heart pounding," she said, guiding his hand between her breasts.

He smiled, his sensual mouth slanting. "I can."

He looked so good, with his sun-streaked hair mussed from lovemaking, his body stretched out naked for her.

"I'm real, Walker, all of me."

"I know. I believe you." His smile deserted him and he rolled on top of her, looking down at her with his sexy blue eyes. "I'm sorry, Tierre. I didn't understand what you felt for me until you pushed me out of the way of the bullet. I didn't believe you *could* feel it."

"You would have died. I couldn't let that happen."

His gaze grew severe, and he pointed at her. "Don't you ever, *ever* do that again. When I saw you go over that rail, I died inside."

She lightly bit his fingertip. "It was worth it. He would have killed you."

"No, Tierre. Never again."

"I can't promise not to try to save you. I don't want to lose you, either. But I will be careful. If you will."

He smiled but his hands were shaking. "I'll do my best. I have something to live for now."

She arched her brows. "You mean ribs?"

He gave her an incredulous look then broke up laughing. "Oh babe, you're going to pay for that."

"Am I?"

Walker leaned across her to check the handheld on his nightstand. "You will for the next two hours. Then you and I are out of here."

Excitement tingled through her. She'd never been off the station before and the longing for the stars drew her. Funny, when she'd been an android, she'd been content to simply be a Guide to those from far away. She listened to their stories, but now she wanted to live stories of her own.

She slanted a smile at Walker, loving the warm weight of him on top of her. "And how did you plan to make me pay?"

His smile was sinful. "Mmm, I'll show you."

Walker rolled her over, put his hand on her backside and then spanked her, lightly and playfully, until she was squealing with laughter.

She'd never thought such a thing could turn her on, but by the time he finished, she was begging him to fuck her.

He did, for the next two hours.

Walker easily caught Lane—who'd had *no* idea he was being tracked—slapped the man into stasis and stowed him aboard his craft.

Tierre gave the outside of Walker's ship much praise, but he knew she was being polite. The thing looked like a pile of junk, but inside, the craft was state-of-the-art. Walker had learned not to draw too much attention to himself with a beautiful hull. Too tempting for thieves.

The concierge tried to protest that Tierre still belonged to the station and Walker had to purchase her as promised, but Walker brought one of the mystics up to attest that Tierre was now a living human being. Humans couldn't be enslaved, and Tierre could go where she damn well pleased.

Tierre gave the mystic a cheery wave as she left with Walker.

Walker cranked up his engines. Tierre was netted into the copilot's seat, her face flushed, eyes sparkling.

"I love you, Walker."

He traced her cheek with his gloved hand then lifted the little craft off the ground. "I love you too, babe. Are you ready for the stars?"

"Definitely."

Walker shot the craft forward, and Tierre whooped. He reached for her hand and held on tight.

THIRD COURSE
Alexa & Patrick Silver

∞

Dedication

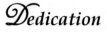

*To Barry, Lee and Ashley. To the folks at TDB — they
know why. To Anna, Di, Zab and A.B. for helping to
keep the creative juices flowing. And to Gordon Ramsay
for absolutely riveting television.*

Chapter One
Amuse Bouche — a small bite

ɷ

Lesley's day wasn't complete until she had a cup of coffee—a very special cup of coffee. It was eight-fifty, an outrageous sum of money for a little cup of the brew, but the atmosphere and the company were absolutely sublime. Wright's was *the* place to dine, but there was no way her husband would spring for the highly regarded and very expensive meals.

So Lesley visited the restaurant every day, drinking the most expensive coffee of her life at the modern bar before going home to the comfort of her mundane life. For these brief cherished moments, she could pretend to be someone special, someone worthy of the dark wood and plush, expensive interior.

And then there was Larkin.

The handsome bartender was a complete rogue who made her feel special, in an utterly forbidden way. Larkin, all naughty English accent and outrageous flirting, brought forth fantasies that had to remain as such. *She* knew she'd never cheat on Brad, but the thought that this man found little old her, complete with extra padding and mussed hair, flirt-worthy was exhilarating.

"Hello, lovie. Cappuccino today?" Larkin offered a smile that was pure sin.

"Please." Lesley settled into her favorite bar chair, sighing as the sumptuous leather cradled her.

Larkin placed the steaming beverage before her, leaning on the bar. "How are you today, dear lady?"

She stifled another sigh. This was her special time and she wasn't going to mar it with self-pity. "Just a little frustrated today, Lark. My birthday is Monday and I'm in such a rut. Another year has passed and my life has never been more boring."

As he often did, he focused his entire attention on her, those hooded sapphire eyes locking on her. It wasn't as if the bar area was busy this time of day, but she knew he had to have a lot of duties beyond chatting with a boring woman every day.

"Mid-thirties rut? You need some excitement. Tell that rogue of a husband to bring you here for a dinner."

Les snorted. "As if he'd spring for a place this nice! And Larkin, I'm a few days away from the big four-oh. I'm such a cliché—boring marriage, thirty extra pounds, I flirt shamelessly with a younger man with a gorgeous accent... And I want more..."

Oh God, had she actually said that? She waved a hand in front of her face, refusing to meet his eyes or let loose the tears of utter embarrassment and humiliation.

"You have everything wrong there, darling. You're no cliché."

His hand cupped her chin and she was forced to meet his eyes. Intensity burned within his gaze and her chest heaved, her nipples hardening to tight points.

"Never, and I mean *never*, talk down about yourself. You're a beautiful woman. I just want to see a sparkle in your eyes. What can I do to get it there?"

She could not—*would not*—risk her marriage but at this moment in time she was so weak. His mouth was close, their breath mingling. He was halfway over the bar, resting an elbow on the edge, his forearm tantalizingly close to her chest. She was so tempted to brush her mouth over his, to take a quick taste, a sip of his essence. It would sustain her much more than her mechanical encounters with her husband had lately.

But she would not disrespect Brad.

"Larkin, I...I have to go. For the sake of my sanity, I have got to get out of here."

She reached for her bag, intending to pay her usual ten dollars, but her hands were shaking too violently and the bag fell to the ground. She followed it, scrambling to the ground and gathering her belongings, eyes downcast. If she looked at him, she'd be lost.

"It's on the house, Les. Go home to your lucky guy."

Larkin watched her go, barely containing the growl of frustration that threatened to boil over. He knew she didn't see what he saw in her, the brilliant, witty and wonderful woman who brightened his days.

He stalked away from the bar, all pretense of being a bartender gone. As he moved to the office just behind the kitchen area, the prep staff all began to move more quickly. What a joke. He and his managers knew how kitchens worked and no amount of furtive glances and nervous, jerky motions would make him think the staff hadn't been slacking.

He glanced around, taking in the kitchen prep. With their prime dinner time beginning soon, everything had to be in order. Despite the staff's guilt, they seemed to have everything well in hand.

He stepped into the office and settled behind his mahogany desk, a family heirloom and an indulgence he'd shipped from the UK. For some reason, he created best at *this* desk. Fingering the letter Lesley had written to the restaurant praising "Larkin's" bartending skills, he glanced at the home telephone number and address on the letterhead. Someone had to treat that woman to an evening she wouldn't forget and he knew just the thing to bring the spark back into her marriage.

In a few minutes, he had organized his thoughts and made an all-important call. "Bradley? Bradley Hollins? This is Colin Wright, of Wright's, a restaurant near where Lesley works. I know you don't know me, but Lesley stops here for coffee often. I understand this is a bit forward of me—actually a *lot* forward of me—but I noticed that she seems a bit down lately. I'd like to cheer her up. I know her birthday is coming up and I wanted to do something special for her... Could you come by my restaurant and discuss this with me?"

Chapter Two
Pre-dinner drink

so

Lesley was exhausted. Her workmates had treated her to a birthday lunch at a trendy place near the office. They had wanted to go to Wright's but it was only open for dinner. Someday she'd get there. She only hoped Larkin wouldn't let on that they were acquainted.

Brad had telephoned her and asked her to come home right after work, so she'd miss out on seeing Larkin and her customary drink at Wright's. She had planned to go in and apologize to the bartender but she supposed that could wait until tomorrow. Lesley hadn't quite worked out what to say anyway.

As she made her way to the commuter rail, she couldn't help but look inside the establishment. The smoked glass windows of the restaurant hid the features of the few people behind the bar, but none had the regal bearing of Larkin, who seemed destined for much more than bartending. He had an air of command and self-assurance about him that seemed directly in contrast to his occupation. Maybe he was one of those men who wrote award-winning plays or sculpted masterful works in his off time. Or maybe he was a humanitarian who volunteered at a children's hospital or a homeless shelter.

I can't keep thinking about him! She'd been racked with guilt the entire weekend, not for the actions she'd almost undertaken, but for the feelings Larkin had roused. Brad was unusually cuddly and attentive lately, which just served to make her feel more guilty. There was nothing wrong with her husband at all. In fact, he was a wonderful guy, a great provider. The spark had just faded from their marriage and they'd both have to work harder to get it back. Together. Lesley was just in a rut.

Brad clearly had something planned for this evening. Her husband had never been someone who could keep a secret totally quiet. His gestures, his smirks, always gave away that he was hiding something. Lesley tried not to torment herself with the possibilities. While her husband was a solid and loving man, he'd never been particularly romantic, and all of her unreasonable expectations led to disappointment in the end.

Lost in thought for the entire train ride home, Lesley almost missed her stop. Her home was at the end of the block, only a minute's walk from the commuter station. When she reached her door, she was surprised to see a silver-colored envelope tacked to it. Stroking the luxurious envelope, Lesley opened it slowly.

"Go directly upstairs. There is a bath waiting for you. Dress in just the clothes I've laid out on our bed. No more. No less. Then come into the dining room. We will be dining at home tonight." She read the note out loud, perplexed, a frisson of excitement dashing up her spine.

A small tingle started between her legs, her clit making its presence known. This was so unlike Brad and yet it was so alluring!

Long evening shadows framed the foyer stairway, softening the sharp edges. She could have turned on a light, but leaving all the details up to her husband was far more preferable. The lack of control was delicious, the darkness adding mystery.

The scent of ginger permeated her senses and Lesley's exhaustion fell away when she moved into the master suite. Brad must have bought out the candle store! Even more candles stood on the marble bathroom counter and ringed the tub. Soft music—her favorite modern jazz artist—played from their audio system. Brad had thought of everything!

Lesley stripped out of her business suit, carefully folding her clothes before placing them well away from the candles. Hearing a whisper of sound, she cocked her head.

"Brad, is that you?"

His masculine chuckle sounded extra sexy. He faded away and only then she realized he had closed the bathroom door. The warm water and the bubbles from her soaking tub stirred the sharp-sweet ginger scent around her, banishing her worries, pampering her, yet keeping her aware of her sensuality.

She reached for a small bottle that sat on the rim of the tub and put a few drops into the water. A blend of ginger and musk wound around the scent from the candles, merging in a sensual feast that she wanted to be a part of.

Lesley eased her body into the water and rested her head against the padded back of the tub. Her eyes fluttered shut and she gave in to the lure of relaxation, pushing her curiosity away. Whatever her husband had in store for her could wait until she had fully surrendered herself to a bath.

Gooseflesh came up on her neck. Had the door opened? "Brad?"

"Right here, darling." The comfort of his voice at her ear, his strong, almost rough hands massaging the knotted muscles of her neck, almost did her in. He slipped a satiny blindfold over her eyes and secured it. All vision was blocked and Lesley found her body sensitizing, readying itself for any touches he would offer.

"Lean forward, darling."

His voice seemed farther away, but before she could puzzle about that fact, he began the most effective massage of her life. He worked her shoulders like a master, flexing and relaxing muscle groups in a way he hadn't in years.

"Feels so good…"

"I know."

Was his voice across the room? She frowned, shaking her head. Of course it wasn't. This was just some silly effect of the bathroom acoustics. But even though she knew that, something niggled at her.

"Brad, where are you?"

A slight rustle, his hands tightening on her shoulders before he ran one long, graceful finger down her spine, stroking outward in long caresses. "Right here, Les."

"Oh…" There was something else bothering her, but the massage was so good, so distracting. Her pleasure centers were on overload and rational thought wasn't possible. Not when those hands were delivering such masterful strokes, such confident caresses. She was putty in his hands.

Just then, he stepped away and another gush of cooler air met her shoulders and face. "Be ready soon, love. Dinner won't wait."

Lesley leaned back in the bathwater, her body shaking and quaking from the stimulus of the massage. Her nipples had hardened to aching points and the caress of the water against her inner thighs brought forth a moan. If she stayed in the tub, she'd climax just from the tantalizing brush of the liquid against her body.

She wanted to see what her husband had in store for her and she didn't want to climax by her own hand. The excitement and anticipation of this experience deserved to be strung out and savored.

Slipping the blindfold from her face, Les breathed deeply. If she could just center herself, she wouldn't be such a ball of desire. She tried to clear her mind as she dried her body and smoothed a delicately scented lotion onto her legs, stomach and breasts. A bottle of expensive perfume sat on the counter and she gasped. *Desire* had been on her wish list for years, but at a hundred dollars an ounce it was a far too expensive indulgence. Yet here the perfume sat in the bathroom as if it had always been there.

Les uncorked the stopper and breathed the potent elixir in. *Desire* was considered to be *the* ultimate indulgence and she knew why. Top notes of chocolate, bergamot, vanilla and musk teased her senses, ratcheting her desire up to another level. The new gush of juices between her legs should have embarrassed her, instead a slow, secret smile crept over her face. For just tonight, she could forget her love handles and soft body and revel in being a sensual creature. She decided then and there that she would return some of this precious gift to their marriage…she would give of herself to her husband as much as he had given her.

Lesley crossed into the bedroom, glancing at the dress spread out on the bed. The gorgeous midnight blue silk slid through her fingers, luxurious and sublime. It was pure elegance in its simplicity, spaghetti straps, a low-cut fitted bodice, the length looking as if it would hit just below her knee. A scrap of lace, a jeweled hair clip and silver heels were the only other items on the bed.

Bending down, Lesley looked under the bed. There certainly had to be a bra. She was far too large up top to go braless!

But there wasn't one set out anywhere. The instructions had been very clear and Les knew that Brad wouldn't be happy if she covered up with a bra. And yet conservative Brad hardly seemed the type to encourage her to go braless. He always shook his head and looked disapprovingly at women who were scantily clad. Once, a long time ago, Lesley had been just as conservative, but with the passage of years she had become much more open-minded, in thought if not deed. She had shared a few of her more scintillating fantasies with Brad, but he had never commented on them.

Lesley shook her head, annoyed at herself for musing for so long. The only way she'd learn what her husband had in store for the evening would be to dress and go downstairs. So far she was very impressed. Brad had never let on that he entertained the notion of blindfolding her before—it was *her* fantasy.

She stroked the scrap of lace, holding it out and examining it. A lace thong? She'd never worn a thong, didn't even know they came in her size! The nude color perfectly blended with her skin tone. Her clit poked against the lace, causing tremors to rack her body from the stimulation of delicate fabric and needy flesh.

Thankful that nobody else would see her in this state, Lesley slithered into the dress. The bodice was close fitting, though her nipples poked out outrageously. She tried not to stare at her chest as she arranged her hair, twisting it and securing it with the clip and applying a light coat of makeup. As Lesley pulled the shoes on, her body hummed with decidedly sexual anticipation. More than the food, more than any celebration, she wanted the magic back in her marriage and her husband had gone a long way toward making that a reality.

She studied herself in the mirror, sucking in a deep breath as she realized how prominent her nipples were. The silk didn't hide or conceal them, but instead of being embarrassed, a secret thrill ran through her. She was ready for whatever surprises her husband had in store.

Chapter Three

Appetizer

ঙ

Lesley felt not only empowered but graceful as she descended the staircase and made her way into the living room. Brad stood there, dressed in a classy, tasteful suit, and handed her a glass of wine.

"You look spectacular, darling. Happy birthday." His hand cupped her cheek, the barest of caresses designed to keep her makeup intact. The gentle touch warmed her heart.

She ducked her head before giving him a small smile, sipping her glass of wine. "Thank you, Brad. This is incredible."

"And the night has only just begun."

He hadn't looked at her with such hunger in his eyes since…forever. His gaze burned into hers, his eyes alight with an intensity that was startling, rooting her in place.

"I have arranged a private dinner, cooked by someone I think you know. This will be the birthday of your dreams. Just relax, Les, and enjoy."

Her husband took the barely touched glass from her hand and placed it on the coffee table. She stood still, absorbing the surprise. She was completely in the dark, but with her husband by her side, that was just fine with her. Brad's gentle breath teased the small hairs at her nape and she swallowed down the sound of need welling up inside her.

His hands found the muscles at the sides of her neck and he rubbed them gently, his touch seeming different from the way it had been in the bathtub. Had she imagined the differences? He had seemed quite a distance away too…

Rational thought fled as her husband awakened an erogenous zone Lesley had never known she had. Oh God, she was already wet...again, her nipples straining against the caress of her dress! As his hands stroked along her neck, Lesley threw her head back, giving in to the desire welling inside her.

A whispered sound caressed her ears, but before she could reason what it was, a hot, wet mouth encircled her nipple and began working the aching bud. Mouth? If her husband was behind her, whose mouth was it?

Lesley started to pull away from Brad, but he wrapped a hand around her waist, fingers splaying close to her drenched cunt. Her eyes flew up, a moan tearing from her throat.

She knew that head! The sandy brown hair, the aristocratic nose—Larkin! Somehow, Brad had brought Larkin here to...

"Oh my God!"

Before she could form a more complete thought, Brad tapped her clit through the silk and lace, soft and slightly rough textures bringing her desire higher.

"Stop! Give me a second, please." She had to have answers, to know more before she could continue this...whatever it was.

Larkin gave one last suckle that almost brought Lesley to her knees before stepping back, and she wiggled out of Brad's embrace to look from one to the other, her chest heaving, her mind racing, her body aquiver. She wanted so much more but she couldn't just take this gift with no questions asked. And it *was* a gift.

"What...what is this? Brad?"

Her husband's eyes narrowed. "It is a special night, just for you, Les. Colin told me that you both had found a connection and offered—"

"Who is Colin?" It was the first question that spilled from her lips.

"Me." The British accent filled the room. "Lesley, I haven't been quite honest with you. Larkin is my middle name. My first is Colin. I'm Colin Wright."

Lesley stared at him blankly, trying to absorb this remarkable news. At least he had the good grace to look embarrassed. "Let me understand here. I've been flirting all the while not with a bartender but with the chef of the most exclusive restaurant in the state? Why didn't you ever tell me the truth?"

He looked away, his jaw tightening. "Lesley, love, I enjoyed our flirting too much. You treated me like a friend, not someone who needed to be fawned over. I got to be a normal bloke with you. It's why I tend the bar afternoons in the first place. And along the way…"

"Along the way what?"

"I bloody got to care about you, a lot. I looked forward to our time together. I ordered my staff to leave me alone then and, Lesley, I learned to desire you so much."

She blinked a few times. Desire? This gorgeous man desired her, thirty extra pounds, crow's feet and all? "I…why? Look at me."

"I am." His throaty growl was liquid sex. "And I want you so much. In addition to cooking you dinner, Brad and I came up with a special dessert—me."

She gaped at her husband. "Him? As in…" Lesley couldn't say the words.

Brad nodded, meeting and holding her gaze. "As in dessert. Us and Colin, unless you object. But you won't, will you? I know you've had ménage fantasies throughout the years and I know you and he have a connection."

This was all so overwhelming. Les grabbed her glass of wine and downed it in a single motion.

"I'll…check on the food." With that, Larkin—Colin Wright, no less—disappeared.

Brad watched his wife sink down onto the couch. She looked as shocked as he had imagined and Brad hoped selfishly that she'd relax and give herself over to this amazing night. He knew deep inside that this was a turning point for them. The rut they'd been in had consumed their marriage, killing all the life out of it. For so long they had been going through the motions, doing what was expected, sharing affection and love. Passion had been lost along the way, and if this was the way to recover it, Brad was all for it.

Though he'd never discussed it with Lesley, his parents had an open marriage, occasionally taking lovers that evolved into long-term relationships. His father had settled down with one of these lovers after his mother had been killed in a car accident when Brad was a teen.

Having been brought up comfortable with unconventional love relationships, when Colin had contacted Brad with his proposal, Brad had been more open to the possibility than most men. When they had met and discussed all the parameters of such a meeting, Brad had immediately relaxed. Colin Wright, hotshot reputation and all, had impressed Brad as being sincere and had assured Brad that he wouldn't make a play for Lesley, that everything considered would be wholly consensual.

The voyeur in Brad was stronger than the alpha male. He wanted to see his wife deriving pleasure from this other guy, as long as *he* would be a part of things as well. And Colin didn't seem to mind that at all, as long as the two men didn't have any contact with each other.

"Lesley, are you okay? Is this something you don't want?"

She shook her head rapidly. What did that mean? Before he could ask, she spoke, her voice quavering. "As long as you are sure of this yourself. If it won't hurt our marriage, Brad, I'd love this. Is this something you want as well, or are you giving this to me as a gift and sacrificing your feelings?"

He grasped her hand, pulling it under his suit jacket. "Feel me, Les. Feel how hard I am. Watching him suck on your nipple drove me crazy. I want more, but only if it is what you want as well."

She laughed, the melodic sound setting his nerve endings on fire. "Oh, I want. I just don't want it badly enough to ruin our marriage." Her hand curved around his length, measuring his hardness, a fingertip stroking underneath his cock head. The caress was tantalizing, especially through the fabric of his underwear and dress pants. He wanted to unzip himself and thrust into her hand, despite the rules that all three had to be in the same room. He wanted to drive his cock between those sweet lips and feed her his cum. And it wasn't yet dessert. He hadn't even had a proper appetizer yet.

"No more, love. Not yet. Anticipation will make this all the more sweet." His beautiful wife worried her lip between her teeth and her eyes softened. He knew that deep in thought look.

"Brad? In the bathroom. Were both of you there?"

He nodded. "Colin was massaging you and I...was watching. You looked so beautiful laid out in the tub." They had both wanted her so badly, their harsh breaths overlapping. Brad had been certain that Les would know that there were two of them watching her, but she had remained unaware, to their great relief.

"What was that like for you? Did you get hard watching? Did you like having another man's hands on my body? I was so turned-on."

He had known it. The scents of the bath oils and what he imagined had to be her own arousal had been a heady mix. He had sucked it in, knowing that Lesley was spicing the very air. "I was so hard, sweetheart. I was fighting my instincts. I wanted to stroke my cock and come all over you and I would have, except the surprise wasn't quite ready yet." He pressed the heel of his hand against his hardness, trying to calm himself down.

His wife swallowed hard, the upper swells of her breasts and collarbone flushing dark pink. And those sweet nipples beaded firmly against the silk. She was as turned-on as he was, as Colin no doubt was.

"I would have swallowed every drop, Brad. I'd like you both to paint me in your cum."

"Later." The strangled sound came from the dining room. Colin was suffering as much as they were. And they had the entire dinner to get through! *What doesn't kill you only makes you stronger* was never more apropos.

"Brad? Les? Dinner is served."

Chapter Four

Soup, salad, sensuality

ഔ

The air was charged with desire. Colin could smell Lesley's arousal, could see the barely leashed stress in the set of Brad's shoulders. This was going to be the longest damn dinner service of his life. He wanted to take Lesley here, wanted more than a sample of her nipples, wanted to drown in her liquid essence. But before he could devour her, he had to feed them. And the menu was a sensual feast all its own.

Stiff legged and stiff cocked, Colin disappeared into the kitchen. When he returned, Brad and Lesley were seated beside each other, just the way they had arranged. Brad had removed his suit jacket and rolled up his sleeves. Good. Lesley's dress was still damp from where his mouth had been on her, her nipple still puckered and pulled up tight. Colin swallowed his groan, thankful for the one mercy of loose trousers. He'd been hard since seeing her in the bath and his cock wasn't interested in softening. By the end of dinner, he might have the worst case of blue balls ever known to man.

"First course is oysters. My special recipe. To get the most out of these little wonders, you must feed them to each other."

His hand shook as he brought the platter near.

"What about you? Aren't you hungry?" Lesley looked up at him. Bloody hell, her mouth was almost level with his hard cock. It would be the work of a moment to clasp her head and thrust into her mouth, ending his torture.

"Are you offering to feed me, love?"

She blinked a few times before nodding. "I— Of course. You shouldn't go hungry."

Good God, she was going to be the death of him! Brushing his hard cock over the silky skin of her arm, he lowered himself to one knee, offering her the plate. "Be my guest, Lesley."

Her delicate fingers plucked a shell, the oyster within quivering at the motion. When her free hand brushed his jaw, he almost forgot how to breathe. But ever the gentleman, he responded to her touch by opening his mouth slightly.

"More." The awkward woman had turned seductress. Something in her eyes had changed, her tentative nature gone in favor of this goddess.

He obligingly opened up wider and she tipped the delicacy into his mouth. Worcestershire and tomato sauces burst in his mouth and the subtle smoke and crunch of bacon melded with the more complex musk of the mollusk. He closed his eyes to concentrate on the complex blend of flavors and chewed carefully, savoring the bite before swallowing. When he opened his eyes again, she was staring at him.

"What?"

She laughed low and Brad joined in. "Colin, it was like watching a sexual experience. You're so passionate about food," Lesley's voice was soft, sexy, promising a night he'd never forget. How could she ever have thought herself dowdy or unattractive? Couldn't she see herself for the goddess she was?

"That isn't the only thing I'm passionate about, sweetheart." He motioned the plate to Brad. "Your turn."

As her husband tipped the treat into Lesley's mouth, Colin began feathering a fingertip along her throat, encouraging her to swallow. Her gasp was arrested when her husband kissed her and Colin stood and backed off, content to watch for the moment, not wanting to disturb the lovers.

Lesley turned to give him a smoldering look before feeding her husband. "We've had enough of these, I think. What comes next?"

"Coffee, tea or me?" Colin managed to choke the words out.

Lesley's lips pursed in an adorable pout. "And what if I'm still hungry?"

"Fine." He rolled his eyes, completely at ease with these two. Brad was taking the back seat for the moment, letting Colin and Lesley explore their flirtation. It took a special man to relax like this and Colin sent out a silent thank you to Brad.

"Well, Chef Wright, feed me. I have...needs." Her gaze zeroed in on his throbbing cock and she licked her lips.

The little temptress knew exactly what she was doing to him. "Soup and salad next, then the main course, then—"

"Can we move right to dessert?"

"That would be the ultimate insult to our esteemed chef, Les." Brad gave Colin an innocent grin, stroking his wife's arm all the while. "Let him stew in his own juices."

"Thanks, mate. Thanks a whole bloody lot." Colin couldn't help but chuckle at the way these two were torturing him.

Brad brought his hands over to cover Lesley's breasts, squeezing gently, drawing the silk over her nipples. She sucked in a breath, eyes widening.

"I'd better get the soup and salad," Colin muttered.

"But we don't like soup, Colin. Or salad. Can we just get to dessert please?" Her look was far from innocent, smug and knowing. She was enjoying this far too much.

"Leees." Brad drew the word out and Colin had a flash of realization. They were playing off each other. It was so easy, the reactions so subtle, that he almost missed it.

Three could play that game. "If you don't eat everything, I can't possibly continue the meal. I'll be absolutely devastated."

"Fine." Lesley's overly dramatic sigh mingled with Colin's and Brad's laughter. Not only were these two a sensual experience he couldn't resist, their sense of humor was infectious.

Colin retreated to get the soup and salad and Brad rested his head against his wife's brow. "This is a fantastic night, don't you think, Les?"

She tilted her head, meeting his eyes. "I'm primed, Brad. I'm so ready for you both." Her expression deepened, the frown lines she hated appearing at the corners of her mouth. "This is really okay with you?"

Brad nodded, pulling in a deep breath. "I've had some time to think about all of this and what I want. Whether it be just for one night or...more. Or even a permanent arrangement. You've had so many longings, so many fantasies. We lost something along the way and this may be the way to not only get our magic back, but to grow and intensify our love."

His wife looked thoughtful. "I don't ever want to disrespect you, Brad. My fantasies can remain that. This doesn't even have to continue. Our marriage means the most to me."

"I know, Les. I know." Brad touched her face in a tender gesture. "What you don't understand is that sharing you with another man, watching him make love to you, this is my fantasy too, Les. I want this. Never doubt that."

She snuggled closer, opening her mouth to continue, when Colin brought a small shot glass of liquid and a plate of greens.

"Roasted red pepper soup, my lady, finished with a little cream swirl. And a pear and gorgonzola salad over mixed lettuce, with an apple-pear vinaigrette. Eat up."

Brad winked at the other man, a prearranged signal that everything was fine. They had been aware of the possibility that Lesley might back out or want to halt the event midstream, so they had devised a few signals.

Colin's tensed shoulders relaxed and he nodded. "Drink the soup as a shot. It is warm but not hot."

Lesley's shit-eating grin always worried Brad. When she nestled the shot in her cleavage, he knew both he and Colin were in trouble. Their sex goddess was turning the tables on them by the minute.

"As our esteemed chef said, drink up, Brad."

The creamy cleavage beckoned him. He lowered his head, nuzzling the soft skin where her breasts began to swell outward. She shivered, her nipples drawing up tightly. He cupped her breasts before lowering his mouth, taking the shot glass between his lips, tossing his head back and swallowing the soup, his Adam's apple working, his fingers rubbing along his wife's nipples. Lesley's head fell back, exposing the graceful length of her throat.

Colin had never been a voyeur, but now, at this moment, all he wanted to do was watch this private moment between husband and wife. It was sexy, it was sensual, it was an honor to watch it.

"Colin? Your turn." Brad's eyes were overbright. His hands continued to work his wife's nipples and she trembled, clearly giving in to the sensations her husband aroused, but a fresh shot glass nestled in the valley between her breasts, the dark orange-red of the soup a delightful splash of color against the creamy flesh of her breasts.

"I want to paint you with this," Colin whispered tenderly, lowering his mouth to taste the warm upper swells. Lesley's moan rent the air, an animalistic sound of need. "God, Lesley, I want you to be the canvas for my food."

"I...Colin, please drink the soup. I can't stay steady any longer."

The rasp of fingers over silk drew his eyes down. Bradley was working his wife's nipples roughly, pinching and twisting. Her scent swirled around them, enhancing the richness of the soup. He wanted to devour more than the soup and one night, one taste of her, would never be enough.

He grasped the shot glass with his hand, scarcely tasting the soup before he buried his head between her breasts, nuzzling, licking, nipping. Lesley gasped for air before stiffening, then letting out a keening cry. Her hand buried itself in his hair, her hips bucking against the very air.

It was the sweetest torture he could imagine. His cock throbbed, an aching length that needed to penetrate her cunt or her mouth. Now! The loose pants he wore hid nothing and he anxiously rubbed his cock head through them.

"If you two don't stop this, we're never going to get to the main course." Brad's voice sounded just as strained and agonized as Colin felt, to his satisfaction. He stepped away, looking into Lesley's face.

"That is the first of many tonight, Lesley." Colin reached for her hand, bringing it tantalizingly close to his hard length. "This is all for you, sweetheart. You're killing me here."

With just one little thrust, he'd be in her hand, but he couldn't. He'd promised Brad that they'd wait until dessert. He just hadn't known that his promise could be the death of him.

"Eat your salad, you two. The sooner we get to the main course, the sooner we get to dessert, and I, for one, can't wait to feast on Lesley."

Chapter Five
Main course

၈၁

Lesley almost forgot how to breathe. Her orgasm had been one of the most intense of her life. Between Colin's mouth on her breasts and her husband's hands on her nipples, she had been lost. She knew the telltale signs of her husband's arousal, but having the new man in the mix was altogether arousing. She reached for a glass of wine sitting before her, sipping it slowly. She had to regain her equilibrium but she was careful not to gulp it. Lesley was not a heavy drinker and she wanted to be clearheaded for whatever the night had in store.

"That was..." Brad didn't seem to have the words to explain the night's events.

"I know." Lesley rested her head against her husband's shoulder, reveling in the strength she found there. She couldn't imagine taking this journey with anyone else at her side. Brad was her champion, her lover, her best friend, and they had frittered away so much time. So many nights had been spent apart, locked in their own little worlds and worries.

"I've missed you, Brad."

Her husband's brows scrunched. "Missed me? I haven't been away in months."

"No, but you haven't been here, either, just like me. We've grown so far apart. Just sitting like this, my head on your shoulder, seems like a luxury."

Her husband tipped her chin up. "Starting tonight, we change all that. Whatever happens, whatever comes, we're a unit, Lesley Hollins. I love you, my beautiful woman."

"I love you too, Brad. And thank you for tonight."

"No thanks needed, gorgeous."

She blushed, looking away. Lesley had never been comfortable with praise, always eager to find the faults in her appearance. But with these two men at her side, at least for tonight she could forget her shortcomings and be the woman they wanted. No, she *was* the woman they wanted. Brad's desire was evident in his dilated pupils and flared nostrils, the heightened color high on his cheeks.

And Colin… She shivered deliciously as she remembered how his pants had tented outward, the waistband pulling away from his body with the force of his erection. She wanted to get to know his cock, what turned him on, what made that gorgeous voice explode with desire.

"All right then. Here we have the main course. I did a few of my signature dishes for you. Roasted chicken served on polenta with a creamy tomato sauce, braised beef with a hint of coffee and seafood risotto, which — "

"Colin, it looks beautiful, but let's eat. Make yourself a plate and join us." Lesley gave him an innocent smile before digging in. Sure, the plate was beautiful, but she wasn't interested in the artistic presentation of their meal or even his culinary skills. She only wanted to use the food as fuel for the night ahead.

Brad, on the other hand, was savoring his first bite, his eyes closed. "Les, why haven't we been to Wright's yet? This is so good!"

"Because the entrees start at thirty-seven dollars, dear. And the complete experience must be closer to two hundred dollars, and you always said that was a frivolous expense."

"Not anymore." Brad ate another forkful of food and made a small satisfied sound.

Colin chuckled, holding a plate of his own. It seemed that he had served himself only the risotto. "You two will never have to worry about dining at Wright's. Dinner is on me, after tonight, when dessert will be on Lesley."

She shivered deliciously, pinned in place by the hope shining in his eyes. "Why only the risotto, Colin?"

"Carbohydrates." He gave her a naughty grin. "I have a feeling I'll need my stamina tonight." He gestured to her untouched plate. "Eat up, and don't rush. That would be the ultimate insult to me."

"You rat," Lesley grumbled, but she took a small forkful of the risotto, surprised when so many complex flavors burst in her mouth. There was citrus, and the buttery cream of the rice itself, but there were more complex, earthy tones that she couldn't quite place. Everything blended so well with the crabmeat, lobster and shrimp morsels. She closed her eyes, savoring the dish.

"You like?"

"Oh yeah, it is incredible, Colin." Even though she wanted to rush, she had to savor every bite, every morsel she had on her plate. The very textures of the food and preparation were so different, yet everything on the plate complemented the other dishes. Though the sexual tension was still high, Lesley thoroughly enjoyed the meal.

To her shock, she was the last to finish. "Dessert now, Colin?"

Everything tonight had been leading up to this moment and she was primed and ready for whatever her two men had to offer.

"Of course, darling. Brad, can you take her upstairs? I'll be up shortly."

Chapter Six
After-dinner drink

ဆ

Lesley trembled as Brad led her upstairs. She knew their house intimately and yet it seemed unfamiliar to her, almost strange in the wake of the newness of the threesome.

Brad passed their bedroom and entered the guestroom, and Lesley gasped. The king-size bed was dusted in rose petals, their scent caressing the air. "You did this for me?" Her unromantic husband had never celebrated a birthday, an anniversary…any event like this!

"Yeah, with Colin's help." He ran a hand through his hair, then reached into his pocket, pulling out a small box. "Happy birthday, Lesley. This gift can be taken multiple ways, so just tell me how you want it to go."

Lesley sat on the edge of the bed and fingered the box. This was another surprise. While Brad was a good solid man and provider, he'd never been one for expensive gifts or jewelry.

She pulled off the wrapping paper and opened the box, staring in surprise at the ring inside. A simple white gold band opened into three gems, a diamond, sapphire and emerald, all three her favorite stones.

"What are the multiple ways it can be taken, Brad?" The diamond was her birthstone, but she didn't understand the rest of it.

Her husband took her right hand and slipped the ring onto her finger. It was a perfect fit, the cut of the ring seeming to elongate her hand. She felt graceful, her stubby fingers giving way to a more elegant hand.

"It depends on how you want to take it, but you know my birthday is next month." Brad touched the emerald. "And Colin's birthday is in September, so in addition to these being your favorite stones, it could mean more, if things work out for the best."

"You mean..." Lesley struggled to find the right words.

"He means that this could be a more permanent arrangement, if that is what we all want," Colin said softly from the doorway. "Consider this a trial run."

He had shed his chef's jacket and stood dressed in a t-shirt and the black pants. "I think we're overdressed," Lesley remarked, looking him up and down.

Colin nodded, plugging something in. "Fondue, chocolate fondue. I've put a bit of amaretto and frangelico in. If I keep it on low heat, it will be ready for us when we're ready for it." He turned to Brad. "May I have the honor?"

Brad nodded, sitting on the edge of the bed. Lesley noticed how much his hands shook when he clenched them into fists and rested them on his knees.

"Come here, Lesley," Colin said, offering her his hand. As if in a dream, she stood, gripping his hand in hers. He tugged her toward him in one slow motion. When she was just a breath away from his chest, he tilted her face up, one hand worming its way into her hair to loosen the clip. "I love your hair down, beautiful." As he brushed a hand through her hair, smoothing it around her shoulders, his face took on a tenderness that almost undid her. "I'm one of those rare guys who won't make love with a woman casually. Know that my heart is involved, Lesley, even if we just have tonight."

As she opened her mouth to reply, his lips descended on hers. He kissed her gently, with restrained passion, his mouth moving gently over hers, tongue only barely dipping inward.

Lesley's body strained. *God, I need to feel more of him!* Colin's hand supported her lower back and she arched into him, breasts brushing the soft fabric of his shirt, belly pressing against his hardness. She hadn't been intimate—hadn't even seriously *wanted* to be intimate—with any other man in many years, but the differences between these two men, and the promise of that ever-so-hard cock held her spellbound.

After drinking in her kisses, Colin pulled back a pace and she felt Brad's body heat behind her. "Will you strip for us? Slowly?"

At Colin's question, Lesley turned to look into her husband's hungry gaze. "Please do it for us, Les." Her husband sank onto the bed and Colin lowered himself to the mattress a bit gingerly, shifting position a few times before letting out a slow breath.

"I...all right." The soft music had been piped in here as well, and Lesley breathed in deep, pulling the scent of chocolate and roses deep. Her husband's dark hair and eyes and Mediterranean complexion contrasted with Colin's more Celtic coloring—light brown hair and piercing blue eyes. While her husband was more lithe, Colin was just a little stocky, his torso more muscled. It helped that they looked different, helped Lesley to compartmentalize them in her mind.

She now knew that the broader hands massaging her in the tub earlier had been Colin's. How had she not seen the difference? Brad had a musician's hands, ever the pianist, while Colin's had the sure strength of a working man.

Lesley drew in a lungful of air, centering herself. The modern jazz instrumental seeped into her soul and she began swaying, the silken folds of her dress moving with her. Those traitorous nipples were still pressing firmly against the bodice of the dress, but she didn't mind so much, not when Brad and Colin were watching her with hunger in their eyes. They both held themselves perfectly still, all their attention on her. It was wanton, it was delicious.

She ran a hand over her stomach, trailing fingertips between her breasts. Colin bit down on his lip and Brad made a tortured sound. Twirling, swaying, becoming one with the music, Les began to move her hips and pelvis, rocking to the gentle rhythm and ebbs and flows of the music. She had never felt more graceful, more in tune with her body. She became the instrument, undulating in flowing movements, holding the men captive.

But temptation undid her. She had to have them — *both* of them. This teasing was all well and good, but it was dessert they all wanted and it would be dessert they'd get.

"Colin, come here and take my dress off."

He stood in a graceful movement all his own and stalked to her, like a predator. She was his meal and that thrilled her. When he bent down, she was momentarily confused until he gathered her dress and pulled it off, making small work of all the fabric and the fitted bodice.

Colin stepped back, his eyes drinking her in. Without thinking too much about it, Lesley cupped her breasts and offered them to him. "Please suck my nipples, my loves."

It was almost comical how her husband jumped off the bed, nearly elbowing the other man in his haste to get a taste of her flesh. Colin ignored him and bent his head, sucking her entire areola into his mouth at the same time Brad lightly bit down on her other crest.

"Oh, God." Lesley's legs trembled mightily. There was no way she could stand on her own through this sensual onslaught. As one, Brad and Colin led her to the bed. As her husband continued to work on her nipple, the other man stepped away, leaving her other nipple tormented.

Colin kicked his shoes off and yanked his t-shirt off, then pulled his pants down in one motion.

"Don't...be...hasty." Brad whispered, his fingers wandering over her other nipple, stealing her ability to think.

But she could still see, and what she saw, she liked. A lot. Colin's chest had only a smattering of light brown hair dusting his pectorals, arrowing down over a defined six-pack to...

My God.

Lesley licked her lips at the sight that greeted her. A thick, hard cock stood stiffly out, a few beads of pre-cum gathering at the head. He was uncut—her first—and the play of veins and ridges fascinated her.

"Bring it here. I want a taste."

He growled—he actually *growled*—giving her a heavy-lidded look that screamed sex. "No. Chef samples the flavors first and that gorgeous little cunt of yours is overflowing."

As he crouched between her legs, burying his face in the lace thong and drenching himself with her essence, her husband pulled away, getting on his knees, slowly and methodically loosening his tie.

"Brad, you're a bastard," Lesley gasped out. Her husband could be so damn cool and collected sometimes. Right now, she wanted his fire to burn higher than ever.

"Shh. Leave a man to his dinner. Knew you'd be bare." The rasp of Colin's stubble abraded her inner thigh. In a motion, her thong had been torn off and he was feasting on her soaked flesh, his tongue coiling around her clit, nose nudging her labia, chin penetrating her lips.

He ate lustily for a few moments before driving his tongue inside, his nose worrying her clit. Les should have been embarrassed by the way she was gushing for him, no doubt soaking the bed, staining the covers, but she couldn't quite bring herself to care. Colin's tongue delved deeply within her and he gusted small breaths over her clit.

She was coming again! She was coming completely undone. Lesley buried her fingers in Colin's hair, holding on for dear life, her legs clenching around his ears, her body riding the waves of orgasm. Liquid lust flowed from her cunt, drenching his face, her fingers digging deeply into his skull.

Then, Brad's hard cock nudged her lips and she came all over again, screaming, sobbing, suckling on her husband's wet cock head. As the shivers abated to a low throb of need, Colin loomed over her, face glistening with her juices, hard cock in his hand. He slid it toward her mouth while Brad backed off.

His musk exploded in her mouth, just as masculine, yet so different from Brad's. Colin's tangy spice burst over her tongue, while Brad's tasted almost fruity. She wanted to devour Colin, but she had more pressing needs. Lesley pulled back, looking up at Colin.

"Are you safe? I'm on the Pill and…"

Colin stroked her hair, a tender expression on his face. "I'm safe. Brad has copies of my test results if you want to see them."

Les shook her head. "No need. But what are you waiting for then? Fuck me, Colin."

He gasped, then gave her a bright grin. "Only if you promise to swallow Brad's cum. I've never wanted to see that so much in my life."

Lesley smiled, nodding. "Brad knows it will be my pleasure."

Chapter Seven
Dessert

ဆာ

Colin slid down Lesley's lush body, kissing her nipples, her navel, laving her clit. She was rounded, curved in all the right places, a goddess of old who was far too much woman for just one man. Did she not know how gorgeous she was?

He turned Lesley to the side and Brad followed, moving at right angles to Lesley's body and angling his cock against Lesley's lips. The scissor position would be best for them all, allowing him deep penetration, as well as being a more comfortable position for Brad. Colin wanted his partner in crime to get the most out of this as well.

All thoughts of Brad fled as Colin brushed his cock head over the nude flesh of Lesley's cunt. Her moisture paved the way for him to glide over her mons and between her lips, sliding into her liquid heat in an endless thrust.

Les cried out around Brad's cock before moaning, a deep lusty sound that fired Colin's nerve endings. He pulled her hips close and began thrusting in and out. Her pussy gripped him tightly, almost to the point of sweet discomfort before he pulled nearly out and then thrust deep again.

She was going to be the death of him. That sweet bare pussy holding him, those intense eyes watching his shaft disappear into her cleft as he moved faster and faster, He was fascinated by her nakedness there and what it revealed.

"Colin...faster," Brad urged. He was fucking Lesley's mouth in short stabs, one hand in her hair, the other frigging his balls.

"Feels good, doesn't she, Brad? God, this cunt is scorching me. And the way she holds on..." He closed his eyes, lost in the sensations, the smell of sex all around them.

"Now, Colin!" Brad pulled almost completely out of Lesley's mouth, his cum seeping out of the corners of her mouth. The vision was so carnal. Lesley's flashing eyes locked on Colin's, her hands reaching for his and Brad's. Lesley guided them to her clit and they began stroking it in quick circles, her hand wrapping around the base of Colin's cock.

It was too much for any man. He threw his head back with a triumphant yell, climaxing inside her just as she clenched around him, milking his seed with ripples that damn near killed him. His heart had to be audibly pounding, the sound of blood rushing in his veins as loud as waves crashing on a beach.

Completely spent, he rolled off Lesley and collapsed beside her. Brad took up position on her other side and they began stroking her hair, cheeks and arms in unison.

"That was..." Lesley's eyes glistened, one tear escaping to work its way down her cheek.

"Don't cry, honey." Brad turned her face to his.

"It's just..." Lesley let out a shuddering breath, ending on a hiccup. "I'm not worthy of this kind of loving."

"Bullshit. You are, Les. Do you have any bloody idea how gorgeous you are?" Colin broke in. "You're a wonderful lass who happens to also be a sex goddess."

She tried to laugh—he knew she gave it a real try—before her face paled. "Look at me. Fat and forty and frumpy and you two are...a woman's fantasy come to life."

Fat? Frumpy? She had no idea what he thought of her. "Lesley, I won't have our woman disrespecting herself. You are beautiful. That hair begs a man to twist it 'round his hand as he's fucking you doggy style. Your eyes are so bloody expressive. Your mouth was made for cocksucking. You have no idea how turned-on I was watching you swallow Brad's dick. Oh love…and your body is curved in all the right places, soft enough to cradle a man. Who wants to fuck a bag of bones when he can have a live flesh and blood woman?"

She looked at him for a long moment, an expression he couldn't quite read in her eyes. Then she turned her attention to her husband. "Do you feel the same way, Brad? You knew me when I was young and thin."

"I love you," her husband replied, and Colin was struck with a pang of longing. What he wouldn't give to have what Brad and Les did. "You mean so much to me. Your body and your mind are beautiful. Your soul and spirit are indescribable. Be mine forever, Les. Be ours."

Ours? Colin gave Brad a long look. What the other man was saying was very premature, but at that moment, hope started to bloom inside Colin. Maybe—just *maybe*—he could be a part of their lives on a permanent level. Forever sounded wonderful in this bed, with these two people.

"Um, boys. I hate to break the moment here—and my answer is yes, by the way. But there is chocolate in this room and I'm in the mood for some!"

After they'd cleaned up, they drizzled chocolate on each other's bodies, only to have to clean up again. Now Lesley crouched on hands and knees, Brad below her. She met his eyes lovingly. Brad had never wanted to take what she was prepared to give Colin now. Her ass. She was going to have her husband's cock in her pussy and her new lover's cock in her ass. She couldn't imagine a better way to end the night, to greet the rest of her life. These two men adored her and Lesley knew it was the beginning of wonderful things.

Brad slid home first, her pussy gloving him. Then Colin placed his well-lubed cock again her rosette and she had to fight to keep still. Brad's hard length throbbed mercilessly inside her, Colin's stiff cock breaching her anus in a slow steady pace that drove her nearly insane with need. When one was fast, the other worked in measured motions that made her want to scream, alternately with frustration and desire.

"Please, Colin. Fuck her, man. I can feel your cock through the wall of her pussy. She's so full."

The hot words got them all going and Lesley exploded again and again around her two men.

"Happy birthday, goddess. I hope it's your best one yet."

Epilogue
Six months later

so

"You two will be the death of me yet." Lesley stretched out in her California king bed, stroking Colin's hair, rubbing Brad's arm. The three had collapsed and stayed in their favorite positions. Brad always curled up beside her, head on the pillow, fingers playing in her hair. Colin usually chose to lie with his head on her stomach. Right before they drifted off to sleep, he'd slide up, kiss her tenderly, ruffle Brad's hair and snuggle against her side.

Lesley still couldn't quite believe that she'd formed a bond with these two special men. After that first night—her fortieth birthday—she had wondered if it would, indeed, be a one-time event. But then a few days later Colin came over with another fondue pot of chocolate, with promises of more romantic escapades to come.

Soon, any self-consciousness she'd had disappeared. Within a month, Colin and Brad were talking about setting up a home together. Within three, they were house hunting.

Both men had been completely accepting of the other and were best friends who happened to share a wife. For all intents and purposes, she was Colin's wife too. The three of them had a commitment ceremony at his British home, had met each other's families and their intimate circle of friends knew the truth of their relationship.

Nobody else deserved or needed to know. They were sublimely happy together and that was what mattered. As Colin's career was very public, discretion had been a must. He'd appeared on two Foodie Channel specials and *Cooking Times* had named him their top chef, as well as the sexiest chef in America *and* Great Britain. Brad was his business partner and, together, they were forming a cooking empire.

Lesley looked back and forth, drinking in her two husbands.

"Colin? Why didn't you want to come in here on our first night together? It always seemed strange that we were in the guestroom, not that I minded. We never did get the chocolate and rose stains out of the bedding in there."

Colin rose up, moving to the top of the bed. "Brad never told you?"

Brad shook his head. "Never did, Col. Thought it was up to you to tell her."

Lesley cocked her head, looking at her lover. "Tell me."

Colin brushed her hair back gently. "This bedroom was your sanctuary, yours and Brad's. I didn't want to intrude unless invited as part of the relationship."

Her heart melted for the thousandth time. Brad and Colin were unfailingly respectful of each other's bond with her. Despite all that could have happened, the three of them had a tight bond, one that grew stronger by the day. Brad and Colin viewed each other as equals and she was never without companionship or a lover. Lesley knew she was the luckiest woman alive. She glanced over at the fondue pot, merrily steaming away in the corner. Was tonight's delicacy the white chocolate with cherry liqueur or the milk with the butterscotch? Or could it be the dark with the orange flavoring? Colin surprised them with a different delicacy every Thursday night. It was their thing. They'd make love passionately, then munch on one of Colin's delights.

Lesley speared a marshmallow and swirled it in the brown confection. Definitely the milk chocolate tonight. She brought the sticky white treat to her nipples, painting them with the chocolate.

"Ready for our third course, boys?"

They didn't disappoint.

Also by M.A. Ellis

ഹ

Hallow's Eve Hunk
Love's Ally
Love's Choice
Seducing the Siren
The Cake Babe
Twisted Steel and Sex Appeal

About the Author

ഹ

M.A. Ellis is a firm believer that everyone should pursue their dreams...no matter how long it takes to achieve them. She wrote her first short story, *What I Want To Be When I Grow Up*, more than a few decades ago. It was read by a total of seven people. (For those who are interested, the answer to that intriguing statement was a toss-up between a veterinarian and a nun.)

Thanks to the encouragement of a creative writing guru at Northern Kentucky University, she stepped out of her neat little writing boundaries and penned an erotic poem, which ultimately led her to the vastly stimulating world of erotic romance. It's a vocation she truly loves — equally as rewarding as furry, four-legged creatures and a heck of a lot more entertaining than Friday nights at the nunnery.

When not devoting her time to crafting tales of hot encounters and steamy romances that always have a happy ending, M.A. concentrates on the delightful task of honing her master baking skills, eagerly focusing on the realms of cheesecake and chocolate which are, in her humble opinion, the only 'c' words that matter.

She lives in northwestern Pennsylvania where temperatures rival those of Ice Station Zebra a good portion of the year—making it the perfect arena for devising stories where one spark can ignite a welcomed inferno.

M.A. Ellis welcomes comments from readers. You can find her website and email address on her author bio page at www.ellorascave.com.

Tell Us What You Think

We appreciate hearing reader opinions about our books. You can email us at Comments@EllorasCave.com.

Also by Tielle St. Clare

ᔓ

Christmas Elf

Close Quarters

Ellora's Cavemen: Dreams of the Oasis III (*anthology*)

Ellora's Cavemen: Legendary Tails II (*anthology*)

Ellora's Cavemen: Tales from the Temple II (*anthology*)

Enter the Dragon (*anthology*)

Fairy Dust

First Moon Rise

Irish Enchantment (*anthology*)

Just One Night

Matching Signs

New Year's Kiss

Shadow of the Dragon 1: Dragon's Kiss

Shadow of the Dragon 2: Dragon's Fire

Shadow of the Dragon 3: Dragon's Rise

Shadow of the Dragon 4: Dragon's Prey

Simon's Bliss

Summer's Caress

Through Shattered Light

Transformations (*anthology*)

About the Author

∞

Tielle (pronounced "teal") St. Clare has had life-long love of romance novels. She began reading romances in the 7th grade when she discovered Victoria Holt novels and began writing romances at the age of sixteen (during Trigonometry, if the truth be told). During her senior year in high school, the class dressed up as what they would be in twenty years— Tielle dressed as a romance writer. When not writing romances, Tielle has worked in public relations and video production for the past twenty years. She moved to Alaska when she was seven years old in 1972 when her father was transferred with the military. Tielle believes romances should be hot and sexy with a great story and fun characters.

Tielle welcomes comments from readers. You can find her website and email address on her author bio page at www.ellorascave.com.

Tell Us What You Think
We appreciate hearing reader opinions about our books. You can email us at Comments@EllorasCave.com.

Also by Dawn Halliday

പ

Devil's Pearl

Sins of the Knight

About the Author

പ

Raised on a boat in the South Pacific and in the quiet rainforests of Hawaii, Dawn Halliday had plenty of time to develop her overzealous imagination. Between exploring deserted atolls, swimming in churning seas, and exploring lava tubes, Dawn started dreaming up stories of love and adventure before she could read them.

When she's not traveling to exotic lands (which she can always justify as "research"), Dawn lives with her True Love and three rambunctious children in Southern California. She writes passionate historical and contemporary romance, and loves every minute of it.

Dawn welcomes comments from readers. You can find her website and email address on her author bio page at www.ellorascave.com.

Tell Us What You Think

We appreciate hearing reader opinions about our books. You can email us at Comments@EllorasCave.com.

Also by N.J. Walters

ဢ

About the Author

ഇയ

N.J. Walters worked at a bookstore for several years and one day had the idea that she would like to quit her job, sell everything she owned, leave her hometown and write romance novels in a place where no one knew her. And she did. Two years later, she went back to the same bookstore and settled in for another seven years.

Although she was still fairly young, that was when the mid-life crisis set in. Happily married to the love of her life, with his encouragement (more like, "For God's sake, quit the job and just write!") she gave notice at her job on a Friday morning. On Sunday afternoon, she received a tentative acceptance for her first erotic romance novel, *Annabelle Lee*, and life would never be the same.

N.J. has always been a voracious reader of romance novels, and now she spends her days writing novels of her own. Vampires, dragons, time-travelers, seductive handymen and next-door neighbors with smoldering good looks all vie for her attention. And she doesn't mind a bit. It's a tough life, but someone's got to live it.

N.J. Walters welcomes comments from readers. You can find her website and email address on her author bio page at www.ellorascave.com.

Tell Us What You Think

We appreciate hearing reader opinions about our books. You can email us at Comments@EllorasCave.com.

Also by Allyson James

ℬ

About the Author

ɛↄ

Allyson James writes romances, mysteries, erotic romance, and mainstream fiction under several pseudonyms. She has made the USA Today bestseller list, has won several Romantic Times Reviewer's Choice awards, and won RWA's RITA award. Her books have earned starred reviews in *Booklist* and Top Pick reviews in *Romantic Times BookReviews* magazine.

Allyson loves to write, read, hike, and build dollhouses. She met her soul mate when she was eighteen, traveled the world with him, and settled down with him and two cats in the desert southwest.

Allyson welcomes comments from readers. You can find her website and email address on her author bio page at www.ellorascave.com.

Tell Us What You Think

We appreciate hearing reader opinions about our books. You can email us at Comments@EllorasCave.com.

Also by Alexa & Patrick Silver

∞

Animal Attraction
Chocolate Destiny

About the Author

∞

Alexa and Patrick are a happily married couple who share their love of reading and happily-ever-afters.

Patrick is the technical geek and he makes sure everything makes sense. This superhero (in Alexa's mind, anyway) can leap tall plot holes in a single bound and defeat logic issues with a slash of his mighty sword.

Alexa is the creative type and she makes sure the romance is high on spice. This love chef mixes Alpha heroes with self-assured heroines, adds a liberal dash of sexual tension and bakes.

Their combined love of books, animal rescue and their family are only a few of the interests they share. While Alexa can often be found at her computer plotting their next project, or reading electronic books, Patrick prefers the challenge of computer games. Their reading tastes are quite different. Patrick loves to read stories from some of the latest and greatest authors in science fiction, while Alexa prefers to curl up with some of her favorite romance authors. They are each other's best friend and maintain that romance, like fine wine, only gets stronger and richer with age.

Alexa & Patrick live in the Northeast with their family.

Alexa & Patrick welcome comments from readers. You can find their website and email address on their author bio page at www.ellorascave.com.

Tell Us What You Think

We appreciate hearing reader opinions about our books. You can email us at Comments@EllorasCave.com.

Why an electronic book?

We live in the Information Age — an exciting time in the history of human civilization, in which technology rules supreme and continues to progress in leaps and bounds every minute of every day. For a multitude of reasons, more and more avid literary fans are opting to purchase e-books instead of paper books. The question from those not yet initiated into the world of electronic reading is simply: *Why?*

1. ***Price.*** An electronic title at Ellora's Cave Publishing and Cerridwen Press runs anywhere from 40% to 75% less than the cover price of the exact same title in paperback format. Why? Basic mathematics and cost. It is less expensive to publish an e-book (no paper and printing, no warehousing and shipping) than it is to publish a paperback, so the savings are passed along to the consumer.

2. ***Space.*** Running out of room in your house for your books? That is one worry you will never have with electronic books. For a low one-time cost, you can purchase a handheld device specifically designed for e-reading. Many e-readers have large, convenient screens for viewing. Better yet, hundreds of titles can be stored within your new library — on a single microchip. There are a variety of e-readers from different manufacturers. You can also read e-books on your PC or laptop computer. (Please note that Ellora's Cave does not endorse any specific brands.

You can check our websites at www.ellorascave.com or www.cerridwenpress.com for information we make available to new consumers.)

3. *Mobility.* Because your new e-library consists of only a microchip within a small, easily transportable e-reader, your entire cache of books can be taken with you wherever you go.

4. *Personal Viewing Preferences.* Are the words you are currently reading too small? Too large? Too... ANNOYING? Paperback books cannot be modified according to personal preferences, but e-books can.

5. *Instant Gratification.* Is it the middle of the night and all the bookstores near you are closed? Are you tired of waiting days, sometimes weeks, for bookstores to ship the novels you bought? Ellora's Cave Publishing sells instantaneous downloads twenty-four hours a day, seven days a week, every day of the year. Our webstore is never closed. Our e-book delivery system is 100% automated, meaning your order is filled as soon as you pay for it.

Those are a few of the top reasons why electronic books are replacing paperbacks for many avid readers.

As always, Ellora's Cave and Cerridwen Press welcome your questions and comments. We invite you to email us at Comments@ellorascave.com or write to us directly at Ellora's Cave Publishing Inc., 1056 Home Avenue, Akron, OH 44310-3502.

erridwen, the Celtic Goddess of wisdom, was the muse who brought inspiration to storytellers and those in the creative arts. Cerridwen Press encompasses the best and most innovative stories in all genres of today's fiction. Visit our site and discover the newest titles by talented authors who still get inspired - much like the ancient storytellers did, once upon a time.

Discover for yourself why readers can't get enough
of the multiple award-winning publisher

Ellora's Cave.

Whether you prefer e-books or paperbacks,

be sure to visit EC on the web at
www.ellorascave.com

for an erotic reading experience that will leave you
breathless.